THE UNBURIED PAST

THE UNBURIED PAST

PAST

Anthea Fraser

Severn House Large Print
London & New York

This first large print edition published 2017
in Great Britain and the USA by
SEVERN HOUSE PUBLISHERS LTD of
19 Cedar Road, Sutton, Surrey, England, SM2 5DA.
First world regular print edition published 2013 by
Severn House Publishers Ltd.

British Library Cataloguing in Publication Data
A CIP catalogue record for this title is available from the British Library.

ISBN-13: 9780727895332

Severn House Publishers support the Forest Stewardship Council™
[FSC™], the leading international forest certification organisation. All
our titles that are printed on FSC certified paper carry the FSC logo.

MIX
Paper from
responsible sources
FSC
www.fsc.org   FSC® C013056

Typeset by Palimpsest Book Production Ltd.,
Falkirk, Stirlingshire, Scotland.
Printed and bound in Great Britain by
T J International, Padstow, Cornwall.

The Families

Harry Carstairs
Lynne Carstairs
Charlotte Carstairs ⎞ their children
Claire Carstairs ⎠

Mark Franklyn, Lynne's brother
Emma Franklyn
Adam Franklyn ⎞ their children
Kirsty Franklyn ⎠
Roy Marriott
Janice Marriott, Emma's sister

Bob and Thelma Franklyn, Mark and Lynne's parents
Clive and Louise Grenville, Emma and Janice's parents

One

Lynne Carstairs glanced up from the list she was making. 'I'm beginning to dread this party,' she remarked. 'It's bound to be emotional – the last time we'll all be together.'

'Oh, come on!' her husband protested. 'No one's going to *die!*'

'Mum's dreading our going; I just hope she doesn't break down in front of everyone.'

'No reason why she should,' Harry said. 'We're not leaving for another six weeks, and with the buyers wanting immediate possession, we'll be with her and your dad for the last four of them. Plenty of time for tears then.'

Lynne put down her pen. 'We *are* doing the right thing, aren't we, Harry?'

'Hey, it's too late for cold feet! Of *course* we're doing the right thing! We've a lovely new home awaiting us, a job with considerably better pay, excellent schools for the kids and a fantastic country! What more could you ask? And there'll still be family on hand – just the other side of it. My folks can't wait to have us there!'

'I'm only just realizing what a wrench it must have been, for you to up stakes and come over here.'

He shook his head. 'Not so – I couldn't wait

1

to do my own thing. And if I hadn't come, I'd never have met you, would I? I've had eight great years in the UK, but now I'd like the kids to get to know Canada and their other grandparents. They're half-Canadian, after all.'

'I know, I know, and I'm looking forward to it really. It's just the thought of all the good-byes . . .'

'Well, as I said, we've six weeks to go so don't let it spoil Claire's party. Mark at least will enjoy himself, recording the event for posterity!'

Lynne smiled. Her brother, an enthusiastic photographer, insisted on preserving every occasion on film. 'He'll be in his element!' she agreed.

Five miles away, Mark Franklyn's mind was, indeed, on photography, though specifically the competition he was about to enter.

His wife glanced over his shoulder at the entry form. 'Have you decided which class to go for?'

'Well, black and white, certainly. And I'd been leaning towards landscape, but Graham mentioned yesterday that's what he's picked.' Graham Yates, who'd been best man at their wedding, was also a keen photographer, and the rivalry between them added an extra dimension to their hobby.

'So what? It'd make for an even keener contest.'

'True,' Mark conceded, 'in which case the timing of the holiday couldn't be better – moun-tains and lakes galore.'

'Uh-oh! If it would mean you waltzing off with your camera leaving me with the kids, you can opt for still life!'

He grinned. 'As if I would!'

2

'Just saying, it's my holiday too. I've been checking what we need to take and they don't provide towels or bedding, which is a pain considering everything else we have to pack into the car.'

'Were you able to arrange cots?'

'Only one, unfortunately. We'll have to push Adam's bed against the wall and put a chair or something on the other side, to stop him falling out.'

'It's not his falling out I'm worried about,' Mark answered grimly, 'it's being woken at some ungodly hour by his jumping on top of me.'

'One of the joys of parenthood! So, this Saturday is Claire's birthday party, and the next we're off to the Lakes.'

'And when we get back, it'll be only a couple of weeks before Lynne and Harry leave.' Mark shook his head despondently. 'It'll be odd, not being able to phone when the mood takes us to suggest going out somewhere. Adam will miss playing with Claire.'

'Once he starts playschool he'll have lots of new friends. It's your parents who'll miss them most.'

'True. I'll take a photo on Saturday and frame it for Mum's Christmas present.'

'It'll produce floods of tears,' Emma warned.

'Par for the course – she cries at everything!'

Emma laughed. 'That's a bit harsh! She'll be losing not only her daughter, but half her complement of grandchildren.'

'Then she'll have to make the most of ours.' He gave her a quick glance. 'Will Janice and Roy be there?'

'I should think so. Charlotte's in Jan's class and they're family, after all.'

Emma's family, not Lynne's or Harry's, Mark thought privately. He always felt ill at ease with his sister-in-law, her colourless face and pale shoulder-length hair, suspecting that a will of iron lay behind that self-effacing exterior. Added to which, with no children of their own, Jan and her husband seemed out of place at a child's party. Still, as Emma had reminded him, she was Charlotte's teacher at primary school, not to mention being his own daughter's godmother. It seemed politic to change the subject. 'What have we got for Claire?' he asked.

Emma gave a short laugh. 'It was a challenge, I can tell you, to think of something they could take on the plane. In the end I went for a fairy outfit: wings, spangles, wand – the lot.'

He nodded absently, turning back to the entry form. 'I'd better fill this in and post it before the expiry date.'

'You're settling on landscapes, then?'

'Yep, and I promise they won't monopolize the holiday!'

Emma patted his shoulder and went to prepare supper.

It was Saturday afternoon and Roy Marriott ran up the stairs two at a time.

'Ready for the gathering of the clans?' he asked, putting his head round the bedroom door. Then, seeing his wife's face, his smile faded. 'Oh, love, not again?'

Janice nodded, her eyes filling with tears.

4

'I was so sure this time. Damn it, I'm five days late, Roy!'

He put a sympathetic arm round her shoulder. 'Never mind, honey, perhaps next month. At least we have fun trying!'

'I can't go to the party,' she said, ignoring his attempt at humour. 'Lynne and Emma will be playing Happy Families and I just couldn't bear it.'

'But we have to go, love,' he said gently. 'It'll be the last time we're all together.'

She turned in the circle of his arm, burying her face in his chest and gripping his shirt with both hands. 'Oh, God, Roy, why can't we have a little girl of our own?'

'Or even a little boy?' he asked, smiling, but she shook her head.

'No, it must be a girl. I see more than enough boys at school.'

'Well, we'll face that when it comes. In the meantime, wash your face like a good girl and put on your glad rags. We owe it to Lynne and Harry to put in an appearance.'

Lynne stood in her kitchen surveying the pink and white birthday cake with its three candles. The children were playing Pass the Parcel, and occasional shrieks of excitement reached her from the sitting room. Once the game was finished she'd call them in for tea.

So far, she reflected thankfully, the party seemed to be going well. Mum, bless her, was putting on a brave face, and it was Janice who looked subdued, God knows why. Since she was always

5

quiet, Lynne mightn't have noticed if Roy hadn't been extra hearty, as if to compensate.

She sighed, wishing she could feel better disposed towards Janice. They'd met at Mark and Emma's engagement party five years ago, and even then Lynne had surprised herself by feeling grateful it was Emma rather than her sister whom her brother was marrying. But it was only when Charlotte started school and was assigned to Janice's class that they met on a regular basis, and the awkwardness between them intensified. Lynne concluded it was the possessiveness in Jan's voice that raised her hackles, the implication that she knew better than herself and Harry what was best for their daughter.

Charlotte, on the other hand, adored her, and had begged for her to be invited to her own birthday party in April, thereby making the invitation to Claire's almost obligatory. Well, this was the last time, Lynne reflected, her stomach lurching at this reminder of their impending departure.

'Need any help?'

She turned as Emma came into the room. 'Don't think so, thanks. How far have they got with the parcel?'

'Depends how small the prize is!'

'It's a set of felt tips. They're water-soluble, so I hope they won't be too unpopular with the parents.' Lynne hesitated. 'Is Janice OK? She seems a bit quiet.'

'She's fine. She came to the rescue a few minutes ago, when someone had to be stopped from opening more than one layer and promptly

6

threw a tantrum. Jan sat on the floor with her and peace was restored.' Emma slipped an arm round her sister-in-law. 'We're going to miss you, you know – having you just on the end of the phone and those spur-of-the-moment picnics.'

'Frankly, I'm trying not to think about it. I know it will be great once we're there, it's the in-between bit I'm dreading – particularly, though it sounds ungrateful, the last four weeks with Mum and Dad. When we've been more or less in each other's pockets, the wrench when we go will be all the harder.'

'We'll do all we can to fill the gap,' Emma promised. 'And I give you fair warning, we'll be out next summer to see you!'

'It's a date,' Lynne said.

The game had ended, the prize was claimed and Janice returned to her chair. A room full of little girls! Her eyes moved fondly over them – crumpled party frocks, flushed faces, bows askew in their hair. Even fifteen-month-old Kirsty was enjoying herself.

As Janice watched, the baby started unsteadily across the floor, intent on a discarded ribbon from one of the presents. But as she bent to claim it one of the children, unaware of her proximity, turned suddenly and knocked against her. For an agonizing moment Kirsty teetered, before falling sideways and banging her head on a chair leg.

Janice jumped from her chair, scooped her up before the first roar and held her close, her face in the dark curls. 'All right, darling, Auntie Jan's got you. It's all right!'

'What happened?' Emma had appeared in the doorway.

'It's nothing,' Janice said quickly. 'She just banged her head.'

Her arms tightened round the child, but Kirsty, hearing her mother's voice and still crying lustily, twisted in her hold, reaching out her arms, and Janice was compelled to surrender her. Bereft, she stood for a moment looking at mother and child before, catching Roy's anxious gaze, she summoned a reassuring smile.

So it was over. Mark had taken a succession of photographs – of the cake, of the little guests, of the entire family, and of the four who were emigrating. Duty done, he, Emma and their children were driving home.

'Pity there wasn't a little boy for Adam to play with,' he commented.

'I doubt he even noticed,' Emma replied. 'And your mother didn't cry, bless her!'

'No, that was a relief. When are they moving in with them?'

'The removal van's booked for a week on Monday. Jan's collecting Claire from the child-minder and taking both girls back to her house for tea. I feel guilty not helping, but of course we'll be away.' She paused. 'Poor Lynne – she's not looking forward to the next few weeks. It's not even as though they'll be in another part of this country; the customs, the climate, the whole way of life will be different over there. She's bound to feel lost at first, even with Harry's parents nearby.'

Emma was right, Mark reflected as he turned into his own gateway. The extended family all lived within a ten-mile radius of the country town of Westbourne, and the departure of Lynne and Harry would leave a noticeable gap. A sudden sense of foreboding washed over him, as though their going signalled the beginning of the end of their comfortable, integrated life, and bigger, more sinister changes lay ahead.

He got out of the car and, still unaccountably uneasy, waited for Emma to liberate the children from their car seats, taking Kirsty from her as she bent to release Adam. Then, as his daughter smeared a chocolatey hand down his shirt, he impatiently dismissed such fancies.

'Bath time with Daddy tonight,' he announced and, with his son trotting at his side, he led his family into the house.

'It's beginning to look like rain,' Roy remarked as they, too, reached home. 'I was hoping to give the lawn a quick once-over; with luck, I'll just make it.'

They went upstairs together, Roy to change into his gardening clothes, Janice into something less formal than the dress she'd worn to the party. Then, as he clattered back down the stairs, she turned on impulse into the little room that, ever since they'd bought the house, she had thought of as the nursery. It was warm and bright in the evening sunshine, though beyond the window the massing clouds that had alerted Roy were piling up.

Her eyes moved over the primrose-painted

9

walls, the white wooden cupboard and neat single bed that had been her own before her marriage. It was ready made up with yellow blankets and a white cotton spread. She'd tried her hardest to persuade Lynne to allow her to keep the children overnight on removal day. 'Your parents' house will be going like a fair – it'll be much quieter and more restful for them here, and I can take Charlotte to school with me the next morning.'

But Lynne, though she'd accepted the offer of tea, had rejected an extension of the visit – unnecessarily sharply, Janice felt. So Charlotte wouldn't be sleeping in that little bed, nor Claire in the inflatable one, and all too soon they'd be leaving for good. Thank God she'd still have Kirsty.

She closed her eyes, reliving the moment she'd held the child close, smelt her baby smell of talc and damp nappy, felt the hot tears against her own face. *Why* had her sister come back at just that moment? Perhaps, she thought, brightening, when Kirsty was a little older Emma would let her spend a weekend with them. But by then, Janice reminded herself, irrepressible hope resurfacing, there might be another occupant in this little room, one who really belonged here.

And as a handful of rain rattled against the window, she closed the door behind her and went downstairs.

'Emma?'

'Hello, Mum. Not at work today?'

Louise Grenville was on the board of two companies and several charities.

'Of course I am – this is my coffee break. In fact,

I'm up to my eyes for the rest of the week, but I wanted to catch you before you go away. So – all packed up?'

'More or less. They can only provide one cot, which is a nuisance. We'll have to hope Adam doesn't visit us too early in the morning!'

Louise laughed. 'I've not heard the forecast, but I hope it keeps fine for you. The weather up in the Lakes can be tricky.'

'Don't worry, we're packing macs and gum boots.'

'Very wise! How did Claire's party go?

'Fine; Lynne's a great organizer.'

'It was good of her to have it, so close to moving out.'

'Yes. Sad to think of all the good times we've had there.'

'I'd like to see them before they go. Perhaps we could arrange a meal when you're back from holiday?'

'That would be great, but you'd better fix it quickly; they're receiving lots of invitations.'

'I'll get straight on to it.' A pause. 'No doubt Jan and Roy were there, rubbing salt into the wound? The longer they try for a baby, the more depressed she gets, and surrounding herself with children can't help. Still, she's only thirty-two; there's plenty of time.'

Emma had a flash of her sister clutching Kirsty and felt a stab of pity. 'Fingers crossed,' she said.

'Indeed. Well, I must get back to work. Have a lovely time, darling, and send us a postcard!'

'Will do. 'Bye, Mum.'

But as Emma ticked off another task on her

11

list, her thoughts were still on her sister. Of the two of them, it had always been Janice who played with dolls and hung over prams, while the more boisterous Emma preferred tree-climbing and kicking balls around with the boys next door. It seemed so unfair, the way things had worked out. But as her mother said, there was still time.

With a sigh, Emma picked up the phone to cancel the newspapers.

Two

Their first sight of Penthwaite came as they crested a hill to see it nestling in the valley below them. From that vantage point it looked larger than they'd expected – a sizeable cluster of slate roofs, a church with a squat Norman tower and, in the centre, a large green space. Some distance beyond it, sunlight shimmered on a gleaming expanse of water.

'Lake Belvedere,' Mark commented. 'I hadn't realized it was so close.'

Emma folded her sunglasses. 'Never mind the view, let's get to the cottage. We've been cooped up in the car for quite long enough.'

It had been a long and tiring journey, not helped by the fact that both children had been fractious. It was typical, she reflected, that just as they'd finally fallen asleep they would soon have to be woken.

As they followed the road downhill and into the village, some of her tiredness fell away and she exclaimed with delight at its winding cobbled streets, the little courtyards and alleyways leading off them, the riot of colour in the cottage gardens. Though the houses were stone-built, the majority had been whitewashed, and in the summer sunshine their brightness was almost blinding.

It had been arranged with the owner of the cottage that the key would be left for them at the post

13

office opposite the green, and Mark accordingly drew up outside it. The upper half of its stable door was open, but little could be seen of the interior from the brightness of the street.

'It seems to double as the village shop,' Mark commented, indicating the window display. 'Shall I stock up while I'm here?'

'What we've brought should see us through the weekend, but a local map would be useful.'

As he pushed his way into the post office, Emma turned to look at the green across the road. On its far side a game of cricket was in progress and an exultant shout reached her as one of the players was caught out. Nearer at hand, family groups sat on the grass, children played, and an ice-cream van was doing a brisk trade.

'It's the first house down a lane at the end of the village,' Mark reported, returning with the key and an Ordnance Survey map, which he tossed on to her lap.

The lane was, indeed, at the end of the village, and beyond it fields bordered both sides of the road. The cottage itself was separated from its nearest neighbour by a field where sheep grazed, and opposite it were several allotments. The gates stood open and Mark drove in and parked on the gravel drive.

Emma glanced over her shoulder at the sleeping children. 'Let's leave them here while we scout out the land.'

The front door opened directly into a large living space furnished with a sofa and easy chairs. There was a bookcase of assorted paperbacks, a shelf containing a pile of board games and what

14

looked like an amateur painting of the village over the fireplace. At the far end, near a door leading, presumably, to the kitchen, stood a dining table and chairs, and in one corner a steep staircase led to the floor above.

'I wish we'd thought to bring the stair gate,' Emma said anxiously.

Mark snorted. 'Along with the kitchen sink? The car's packed to the gunnels as it is.' He looked round. 'No sign of a phone and no TV.'

'All to the good,' Emma replied. 'We can have a holiday from both. Right, let's see how much unloading we can do before the kids regain consciousness.'

They worked quickly and quietly, removing suitcases and a folded buggy from the roof rack and boxes of provisions and household linen from the boot. Emma discovered a pint of milk, a loaf and a pack of butter awaiting them in the fridge. Emergency rations, she thought.

Up the steep stairs they found two bedrooms and a small bathroom. Not exactly palatial, as Mark commented, but enough for their holiday needs. The promised cot had been set up in the smaller room.

'If we make up the beds now,' Emma said, 'they'll be ready for us when we're ready for them.'

They'd just completed their task when the first wail reached them from the car, and they hurried downstairs to release their children.

Lynne stood on the landing of her home and watched it being systematically dismantled. Every room, every corridor was suddenly throbbing

15

with memories – the kitchen, scene of so many family meals, the sitting room where Charlotte had taken her first steps, the extra-bright patches where familiar pictures had hung.

She turned abruptly and went into the bathroom – blessedly unchanged – where she locked the door and allowed herself a few silent tears. If only she could wave a wand and wake up six weeks or even six months from now, when they'd all be happily installed in their Canadian home.

'Mrs Carstairs?' The foreman, Joe, was calling from downstairs. Lynne hastily dabbed at her eyes and went on to the landing.

'What do you want doing with this box? Are we to take it, or is it going with you? There's no label on it.'

'Sorry, it's some of the children's toys – we'll keep it with us. Would you ask my husband to put it straight in the car, so it doesn't get mixed up with anything else?'

Joe wandered off, muttering to himself and, brief respite over, Lynne again took up her job as removal supervisor. She'd never have believed there was so much to be sorted out, to be put in piles for charity shops or the tip. It was a wonder the floor of the loft hadn't collapsed under the weight of all that had been stored in it.

'Lynne?' Harry this time. 'The men want to know what to do with the buggy?'

She closed her eyes against the assault of more memories. 'The charity pile,' she called back, her voice commendably steady. 'Claire's almost grown out of it.'

She glanced at her watch. Four thirty. The children

would be with Janice now. Only another hour before the men knocked off for today, then a welcome break till tomorrow morning, when they'd be back here for the final rites. In the meantime, she needed to check one more time what they'd need for the next four weeks, and make sure she'd not overlooked anything.

Trying to remember where she'd left it, she went in search of the list.

'For pity's sake, darling!' Thelma Franklyn exclaimed. 'What in heaven's name do I do with all this?'

It was three hours later and she was staring aghast at her transformed kitchen. On the floor a stack of bulging freezer bags leaned perilously against a couple of boxes containing the contents of the Carstairs' fridge, while the surface of the table was submerged beneath opened bags of flour, rice and sugar, tins of coconut milk and jars of tahini and green curry paste.

'I don't even know what half of it *is*!' she added plaintively.

Lynne gave her a tired smile. 'Sorry, Mum, but we can't take it with us, and we'll be working our way through a lot of it while we're with you.'

'But in the meantime we need somewhere to put it,' Thelma said distractedly.

'I'll help you clear some space in the larder. It won't look so daunting once it's neatly stacked.'

Bob Franklyn came into the room with his granddaughters, both in pyjamas and dressing gowns. 'Two tired little girls, ready for bed!' he said.

'*I'm* not tired!' Charlotte declared and, indeed, her face was flushed and her eyes bright with excitement. 'Anyway, I don't go to bed at the same time as Claire!'

Lynne brushed back a stray wisp of hair. 'Sweetheart, it's a bit different while we're here. You'll be sharing a room, and—'

'But it's not *fair*!' Charlotte cried. 'I'm twice as old as she is!'

'You won't be able to say that next year, young lady!' Bob teased her.

Harry, returning from locking the car, caught the end of the exchange and picked up his elder daughter.

'Suppose Mummy puts Claire to bed while I read you a story in our room? But you must promise not to wake Claire.'

'Shan't be asleep,' Claire said decidedly.

For a wild moment Lynne wished she'd allowed Janice to keep them overnight, but it would only have postponed the problem.

'Let's do what Daddy suggests for tonight,' she said, 'and we can work out something for tomorrow.'

And before there could be any more arguments, the children were led out of the kitchen. Bob and Thelma exchanged a wary smile.

'OK, love?' he asked.

She nodded. 'I could do with a G and T, though!'

Bob laughed. 'I'll join you!' he said.

In Penthwaite, Mark and Emma's days had fallen into a leisurely and pleasant routine. Each morning they set off with the buggy, sometimes to play with the children on the green and sometimes to explore the village, plunging from sunshine to cool shadow as they followed the twists and turns of the little side streets, while Mark paused on every corner to capture on camera an ancient market cross, a cat in a sunlit courtyard or a wagon wheel against a wall.

When Adam began to flag they'd return home, swap the buggy for the car and, armed with their Ordnance Survey and a picnic lunch, drive off to spend the rest of the day in various beauty spots where Mark could spend an hour or so composing more formal photographs while Emma and the children paddled, or played ball. Lake Belvedere particularly appealed to him and, marvelling at how dramatically its appearance changed under cloud or sunshine, he resolved to take a series of photos at varying times of the day. With luck, one of these shots would become his entry for the competition.

On the west side of the village stood the church of St Oswald, surrounded by its ancient cemetery, and on one of their excursions they wandered among the weathered tombstones, jagged as broken teeth, their inscriptions for the most part illegible. '"And of Louisa, his spouse . . ."' read Emma. 'Promise me you'll never call me your spouse!'

To their surprise, the heavy door was unlocked and they ventured inside, shivering at the change in temperature. The smell of polish and old hymn books filled their nostrils as they read the inscriptions on brass plaques set in the floor to commemorate Penthwaite's long-dead residents.

'I wonder if they allow brass rubbing,' Emma mused. 'Jan and I did a lot of that in our teens.'

In the side aisles, sunbeams shining through stained glass lent colour to the marble cheeks of ancient squires and their ladies lying side by side, hands devoutly folded, and a board on one wall listed the names and dates of previous incumbents, the earliest dating from the sixteen hundreds.

'The tower is the oldest part of the building,' Emma said, reading from the explanatory leaflet on a table by the door. 'Most of the original wooden church was destroyed by fire in the fifteenth century.'

Adam tugged at her skirt. 'Want to go now,' he whined, and his parents, their attention forced back to the present, reluctantly complied.

Most days involved a visit to the shop, where, despite repeated requests not to, Mrs Birchall the postmistress plied the children with sweets.

'Annual fête's on Saturday,' she informed them early in the week. 'Merry-go-round and brass band and all sorts. Folks come from miles around.'

'We saw the posters,' Mark replied. 'It should be fun; let's hope the weather holds.'

Towards the end of that first week they visited the nearby town of Hawkston, finding it odd to be back among traffic, large shops and busy pavements. That evening, when Mark came down from reading Adam's bedtime story, he was surprised to see a bottle of wine on the table. Normally they drank only at weekends, and had not so far bent this rule during the holiday.

'Where did that come from?' he asked.

'I bought it at the supermarket,' Emma said offhandedly.

'Are we celebrating something?'

'Just being on holiday!'

It wasn't until the meal was over and they were relaxing on the sofa that she said suddenly, 'As to the wine, there *was* a reason for it.'

'I thought there might be. Are you going to enlighten me?'

She reached for his hand. 'I bought it because it's the last I'll be able to have for a while.' And, as he looked puzzled, she added with a smile, 'I'm pregnant, Mark!'

He drew in his breath, his hand tightening on hers. '*Really?* Are you sure?'

'I bought a testing kit in the pharmacy while you were getting the sun cream. I tried it before dinner and it's positive.'

'Sweetheart, that's wonderful! What date are we looking at?'

'Oh, it's very early days. Not till the spring.'

'Will you tell the family?'

'I'd have preferred to wait a while, but I'd like Lynne and Harry to know before they leave.'

Mark nodded. 'And hopefully the prospect of another grandchild will help both sets of parents over the gap left by Charlotte and Claire.'

The day of the fête dawned warm and sunny, and their al fresco breakfast was punctuated by bursts of music as the sound system was tested.

'Loud!' Adam complained, covering his ears.

'Almost as loud as Daddy's sweatshirt!' Emma agreed with a laugh.

21

'Hey! Are you criticizing my attire?'

'Red, green and white stripes don't really do it for me, I'm afraid.'

'Nor me, to be honest, but it's the one Harry brought back from Mexico, and since I daren't be seen in it at home, this is the first chance I've had to wear it.'

Emma smiled and patted his hand. 'Then make the most of it, darling! Just be careful not to frighten the horses! Now, we won't need a packed lunch because Mrs Birchall assured me there'll be all kinds of food at the fête and they're sure to cater for children. And today, my love, you can content yourself with taking family photos, such as Adam's first ride on a merry-go-round.'

'And you on the Big Dipper?' Mark asked with a grin.

'In your dreams!' she replied.

As soon as they left their gate they were engulfed in a stream of people making their way to the fête – families for the most part, parents with excited children dancing at their side, but young couples too, hand-in-hand and giggling, and the occasional grey head. Both sides of the road were solid with parked cars, and as they neared the green the volume of music increased to the point where speech became virtually impossible.

The green itself was a seething mass of humanity. Dotted round the perimeter were coconut shies, a tombola and stalls selling bric-à-brac, home-made jams, cakes, potted plants and garden ornaments. There was a face-painting tent where a queue of children had formed, and in a roped-off area three-legged races were being organized.

Their progress was necessarily slow, stopping as they did at stall after stall to buy toffee apples for the children, a ceramic pig for Lynne's collection and a Le Carré paperback Mark hadn't read. There was a penned-off area containing baby animals, where children were admitted in twos and threes, but Adam, though mesmerized by the lambs and chickens, shook his head when offered the chance to go in, and it was Kirsty who struggled to free herself from the pushchair and play with them.

The day passed in a whirl of noise and colour. After a while Adam wilted and demanded the buggy while his parents took turns in carrying Kirsty, but he quickly revived when Mark, trying his luck at hoopla, snared a Donald Duck toy, and vacated the buggy to claim it.

As requested, Mark recorded each event – Adam on the merry-go-round, which he'd refused to brave without Emma; Kirsty stroking a baby rabbit, and another of her with an ice cream in one hand, dragging her teddy by its ear.

'That ear's hanging by a thread,' Mark warned, closing his camera.

'I know; as soon as I can prise it out of her grasp, I'll sew it back on.'

They were passing the dais when an official stepped on to it with a microphone and announced that 'Mr Barry Ferris', who now joined him, was about to present the prizes.

'So will the winners of the egg and spoon races

please come up, and we'll start with the under sixes.'

The crowd surged forward for a better view, pinning them against the steps leading to the dais. On a low table immediately in front of them a selection of prizes was arrayed – jars of sweets, books, a doll, a gaily-coloured beach ball. And as Mark attempted to move back to allow access, Adam freed his hand and, clambering up the steps, reached for the ball.

There was a burst of laughter from the crowd as Mark, red-faced, hurried to retrieve him, and Adam's roar of protest was cut off by the swift presentation of a lollipop. Placated, he allowed himself to be carried down.

The prize-giving lasted about ten minutes as children of varying ages, flushed with triumph, came up to receive their trophies. When the last of them had been reclaimed by their parents, a round of applause was requested for the presenter, after which the brass band struck up again, its amplified music once more drowning out conversation.

'I think we've all had enough,' Emma shouted in Mark's ear. 'Shall we make tracks for home?'

'Agreed,' Mark replied fervently. 'After all this, a cup of tea in the peace of the garden would go down a treat.'

After the uninterrupted sunshine of the previous day, Sunday dawned cool and cloudy. Mark surveyed the grey day from the kitchen window.

'There's a cool breeze today; it won't be much fun wandering around.'

'Let's go back to Hawkston,' Emma suggested. 'There'll be more to do there – something for the children, perhaps. It's on the tourist map – they're bound to provide options for rainy days. Which,' she added, joining him at the window, 'this is now turning into.'

So they drove through the wet countryside where cows stood passively with bent heads and summer foliage drooped under the weight of rain, and once in the town were able, as Emma had hoped, to locate an indoor play area, where the children spent the morning taking turns on the swings, slides and sandpits.

By the time they emerged after lunch the rain had stopped and a shaft of sunlight was pointing a finger at the Norman castle on the hill above the town.

'Let's go up and have a look at it,' Mark suggested. 'It's mentioned in all the guide books.'

'Provided you'll push the buggy up the hill,' Emma stipulated.

It was a steeper climb than they'd anticipated, but from the summit there was a spectacular view not only of the town but of miles of the surrounding hills and countryside. Little remained of the castle itself other than groups of weathered stone arches and walls, jagged against the purple storm clouds.

'We can read up on its history when we get back to the cottage,' Mark said.

The sunshine stayed with them during the drive back, and they reached the cottage just after four.

'Would you mind if I played truant for an hour or so?' Mark asked diffidently. 'I've only about a dozen shots left on this film and I'd like to start out with a new one tomorrow, added to which I haven't any of Lake Belvedere under these weather conditions.'

'You go,' Emma said. 'I'm putting the kids to bed early anyway; they're both exhausted after all that playing, and once they're down I'll take the opportunity to write some postcards; the family will be wondering how we're getting on.'

Halfway through the holiday, Mark reflected, settling down to the fifteen-minute drive; this time next week they'd be back home, and then it would be only a couple of weeks till Lynne and Harry left. And suddenly, unwillingly, he remembered his presentiment after Claire's party, that their departure heralded a more significant ending. He shook his head impatiently, turning on the radio, but his sense of unease persisted, not helped by the lowering sky. There was more rain on the way.

There were only a couple of cars in the usually busy parking place. The uncertain weather must have deterred visitors. So much the better for some atmospheric shots.

Having locked the car Mark paused, considering where to position himself. The lake was surrounded by a semicircle of hills rising quite steeply from its banks. On earlier visits the presence of the children and the buggy had limited them to ground level, but now he had the chance to search out a new angle – one that, from a height, would give an extended view of the lake.

The nearest hill was some two hundred yards from the car park, and he saw that from this side a path offered a more manageable approach to its summit. Not that he'd either the time or inclination to scale it, but he recalled seeing people standing on a wide shelf some third of the way up, which would suit him admirably.

Slipping the strap of the camera round his neck, he picked up his canvas bag and set off across the muddy grass. Soon he was climbing steadily, considering and rejecting possible shots as he went. From the height of the ledge, a series of exposures should give a panorama of the entire lake, putting into perspective the more localized views he'd already taken.

By the time he reached it, out of breath and with aching legs, he was promising himself a brief rest and a drink from his water bottle before starting work. But as he emerged on to the shelf, all thoughts of a rest vanished.

Some distance below him three men were standing at the edge of the lake, and it was clear a heated argument was in progress. A small boat was bobbing at the edge of the water and Mark noticed a fishing line propped against a rock. Curious, he fumbled in his bag for a zoom lens and, supporting the camera, pressed the shutter release. *Figures in a landscape*, he thought.

The man facing him had started waving his arms about, one of his companions was shaking his head, and the third stood passively looking on. Their raised voices reached Mark on the wind but he was unable to distinguish the words. A couple more clicks. *Drama by the lake; every picture tells a story!*

What happened next took him totally, horrifically,

by surprise. The man who'd been gesticulating suddenly lashed out with his fist, catching his opponent on the chin and sending him crashing to the ground. Then, before he could recover himself, the attacker stooped to pick up a rock and brought it down forcefully on the fallen man's head. Aghast, unbelieving, Mark continued to record the scene as more blows rained down until the third man, belatedly galvanized into action, caught the assailant's raised arm and hung on to it. For measured seconds no one moved. Then they both straightened, looking nervously about them and, conscious of his exposed position, Mark ducked out of sight behind a gorse bush.

By the time he cautiously raised his head, the man who'd restrained the attacker had dropped to his knees beside the still figure and was feeling increasingly urgently for a pulse – at the wrist, then at the side of the neck. And as Mark watched, his heart thundering, he raised his head to meet his companion's eyes and slowly shook his head.

For a timeless moment the tableau froze before, simultaneously snapping into action, they lifted the inert form of their comrade between them and, staggering under his weight, tottered over to the boat still bobbing at the water's edge and tipped him into it, causing the small craft to rock violently. One of them scrambled in after him while the other pushed the boat off from the shore before climbing in himself and, manoeuvring a pair of oars into position, started rowing speedily towards the centre of the lake.

A sudden whirring as the film began to rewind recalled Mark to his surroundings and the fact

28

that, disbelievingly enthralled by what he was witnessing, he'd risen from the shelter of the bush and would be in full view should one of the oarsmen happen to glance up. Hastily he ducked down, made his way swiftly off the ledge and began scrambling and stumbling back down the hillside, intent only on reaching the safety of the car. It took several attempts for his trembling fingers to unlock the door, then, having checked no pursuer was in sight, he half-fell inside, started the engine, and with a screech of tyres shot out of the car park and on to the road back to the village.

It was as well that there was no other traffic. Taking corners at breakneck speed, he skidded from one side of the wet road to the other, his heart hammering at the base of his throat, his whole body shaking, and when at last he came to his turning, he swerved round it on two wheels and shot through the open gates of the cottage.

Switching off the engine, he sat for a moment in the sudden silence, head bent, hands still gripping the wheel. Then, grabbing his camera bag, he hurled himself out of the car, stumbled to the front door and flung it open, meeting Emma's startled eyes as she looked up from her sewing.

'Mark!' She came to her feet in alarm. 'For God's sake, what's wrong?'

Mark drew a deep, ragged breath. 'I've just seen someone being murdered!' he said.

Three

Lynne heard the doorbell, but as her mother was downstairs paid no attention. She was making a list – it was all she seemed to do these days – of the tasks to be completed before Charlotte returned from school and Claire from her afternoon play group. It wasn't until Thelma called her, a discordant edge to her voice, that she pushed back her chair and went on to the landing.

'Yes?' she called back.

'Can you come down, please? Now?'

'I'm just—'

'*Now*, Lynne!'

Muttering under her breath, she started down the stairs, stopping short as she caught sight of two uniformed figures in the hall. Immediately alarm bells rang. The children!

She ran down the remaining stairs. 'What's happened? Is it the children? I—'

Her mother interrupted her. 'It's me they want to speak to, but for some reason they'd like someone with me.'

Again, that clutch of fear. Lynne looked quickly about her. 'Where's Dad?'

'He's gone to the bank,' Thelma said distractedly, gesturing the man and woman into the sitting room and pulling Lynne in after them. She turned to face them. 'This is my daughter. Now, please tell me what this is all about?'

The police officers exchanged a glance. They looked very young, Lynne thought incongruously.

'Would you like to sit down, Mrs Franklyn?' the woman suggested tentatively.

'No, I wouldn't! If you've something to tell me, for God's sake get on with it!'

Lynne, however, cold dread settling in her stomach, guided her mother to the sofa and sat down with her, taking hold of her hand. It must be Dad, she thought sickly. A heart attack at the bank? A crash on the way home?

The male officer cleared his throat, but the question that came shocked them by its unexpectedness. 'Could you confirm, please, that you are related to . . .' He glanced at the notebook in his hand. 'Mr Mark Franklyn and Mrs Emma Franklyn?'

Thelma and Lynne stared up at them whitely. 'Yes,' they said in unison.

'Then I'm very sorry to tell you that two bodies believed to be those of Mr and Mrs Franklyn were found in Penthwaite, Cumbria, early this morning.'

There was a moment's total silence, then Thelma said explosively, '*No!*' and, wrenching herself free of her daughter, clapped both hands over her ears. 'No, no, no! There's some mistake!'

Lynne moistened her lips. '*Found?* What . . .?' Her hand went to her mouth. 'Oh, God – the children!'

'They're safe,' the woman officer said quickly. 'They're being cared for.'

'But my brother and his wife? *What's happened to them?*'

Before the officers could reply, Thelma gave a little moan and, slipping sideways, fell across her daughter's knees in a dead faint.

Lying awake in her parents' guest room, Lynne's mind continued to replay the horror of the last two days; horror that, now that the story of the murders had broken, was exacerbated by the persistent and unwelcome attention of the press.

Both sets of parents had immediately flown to Cumbria, the women to reclaim the children, the men to perform the grim tasks of identifying their son and daughter and engaging a firm of undertakers recommended by the police. And it was only on their return that they'd passed on the scant facts they'd been able to establish.

Bob reported that it had been a milkman on his rounds who'd spotted Mark, lying beside his car in the cottage driveway. While trying in vain to revive him, he'd heard a child crying inside the house and, since the door was on the latch, he'd gone in to find Emma lying dead at the foot of the stairs and little Adam bending over her crying, 'Wake up, Mummy!' Kirsty, still imprisoned in her cot, was yelling lustily upstairs. Both children had been examined at a local hospital and, thank God, found to be unharmed. A couple of postcards addressed to the Franklyns and Emma's parents had, together with credit cards found in Mark's wallet, enabled Cumbria police to contact the local forces and confirm next of kin. An inquest would be held to establish identity, then immediately adjourned pending further investigations.

At this early stage the police had refused to divulge any details, saying only that it seemed two perpetrators had been involved and that death in both cases was caused by a blow to the head. The motive for the attacks remained a mystery; Mark's wallet and credit cards were in his pocket and Emma was still wearing her jewellery.

The children had been brought back to the Franklyn home, where it was hoped the presence of Charlotte and Claire might help ease the situation. They were obviously disorientated, but though repeatedly asking for their parents could, to everyone's relief, for the most part be distracted. Bedtime, particularly in Adam's case, proved the most difficult, and Lynne had spent hours reading stories and singing nursery rhymes until he fell asleep. Little Kirsty, though she also cried, could usually be soothed by the presence of her teddy bear.

As Thelma kept saying, it was a blessing they were so young; had they been even a little older, their pain and loss would have been that much greater.

Lynne stirred in the wide bed. 'Harry,' she said into the darkness, 'we *are* going to adopt them, aren't we?'

He stroked her hair. 'Of course, honey. It's the only solution.'

'Bless you for that, though I still think we should postpone Canada. How can we leave Mum and Dad when we still don't know what happened?'

Harry sighed. It was a subject they'd come back to repeatedly over the last couple of days, and one on which, he'd been both surprised and

33

gratified to discover, his parents-in-law agreed with him.

'It's not good for your little ones to stay too long in a house of mourning,' Bob had told them. 'Charlotte is old enough to understand at least part of what's happened. With luck, we'll be bringing Mark and Emma home next week, so the funeral can be held before you leave. For the rest, we'll all have to learn to live with this, and for you to stay on would only prolong the agony.'

'Your parents say we should go,' Harry reminded Lynne now. 'But our main priority is to arrange a family meeting to agree the adoption and get things moving on that front. There shouldn't be any difficulty; Mark named me as the children's guardian in the event of their deaths – which, God knows, we thought at the time was a mere formality.'

Lynne shuddered, and his arms tightened round her. But all she said was, 'Let's try to arrange it for tomorrow.'

Condolence letters were already starting to arrive, and among those the next morning was one from Mark's friend and fellow photographer Graham Yates. *I can't tell you how shocked Sue and I were by this dreadful news*, he wrote. *As you know, Mark and I go back a long way, and in many ways were more like brothers than friends. I shall miss him and Emma more than I can say, and can only imagine the horror you're all going through, not only over their deaths but also the manner of them.*

Wearing another hat, if I may, I'm not sure if

you're aware that Mark asked me to be his exec-
utor? We shall therefore be meeting in due course,
but in the meantime if there's any way at all that
I can be of help, please don't hesitate to ask.

'A nice boy,' Thelma commented flatly. 'I always liked him.'

Since everyone had taken the week off work on compassionate grounds, there'd been no problem in arranging the conference for that afternoon at the Franklyns' home. A friend of Lynne's had offered to take all four children to the park to allow for uninterrupted discussion.

Some of them hadn't seen each other since the tragedy and their meeting was, inevitably, emotional. As they assembled in the sitting room, it struck Lynne for the first time how different the two sets of parents were. Louise Grenville, tall, silver-blonde and immaculately dressed, was rigidly in control, only her shadowed eyes and the tightness of her jaw betraying her inner anguish, while Thelma, smaller and rounder, was openly struggling with her tears. Even the men were opposites, Clive Grenville dark and thin, his intelligent face deeply grooved, and her own father a more cuddly version with his bright blue eyes and sparse greying hair. Janice, clutching Roy's hand, was avoiding eye contact and had barely spoken.

'As it's only two thirty,' Bob began, 'we thought we'd get the discussion out of the way first, then we can relax over tea. So here goes.' He looked round at their tense faces. 'I appreciate that we're all still coming to terms with what's happened,

35

but there are some things that can't be post-poned, one of which is the funeral arrangements. We've been told Mark and Emma are likely to be brought home next week, so we must decide which church to go for – the one where they were married, which, of course, is near Louise and Clive, or the one near where they lived and where the children were christened. Once that's decided, we should book the service as soon as possible, to ensure it's before Lynne and Harry leave.'

Feeling the ball was in their court, Louise and Clive conferred briefly. Then Clive said, 'I think we should go for where the children were chris-tened. Emma took Adam to their Mothers and Toddlers group.'

Bob nodded. 'Then may we leave it to you to contact them?'

'Of course.' Clive made a note in his diary.

'And the other big decision,' Bob continued, 'concerns the children's future. So, Harry, perhaps—'

'Roy and I will adopt Kirsty.'

There was a startled silence as all eyes turned to Janice, ramrod straight in her chair. Then Bob said hoarsely, '*Just* Kirsty?'

'That's right; we've always wanted a little girl, and she's very precious to us – my god-daughter and my beloved sister's child.' Her voice wavered and broke.

Thelma said quickly, 'But the children must be kept together! Poor little souls – they've lost enough, without having to lose each other!'

'They're too young to have bonded properly.'

That was Roy, responding to a nudge from his wife. 'As long as they're loved and cared for, they'll soon adapt to their new life.'

Harry cleared his throat. 'I think I should tell you that Lynne and I were about to suggest our adopting both children. You'll see that Mark appointed me their guardian for as long as they're minors, and—'

'But you're emigrating!' Louise broke in, her voice hard and clear. 'If you take them both, you'd be robbing Clive and me of our only grandchildren!'

Bob held up a hand. 'We're in the same boat, Louise; we'd also be losing all ours, but surely we must consider what's best for them.' He paused. 'Look, I appreciate we're all emotional, and ideally this decision should be shelved for a while. But since Lynne and Harry . . .'

Lynne turned to Janice. 'Surely you must see it's better if we have them?' she said urgently. 'They've known Charlotte and Claire all their lives, and are used to playing with them. It would make things much easier for them.'

Janice leant forward, hands tightly clasped. 'But that's just it! You already have your own children, and despite yourselves you'd always love them just that little bit more; whereas Roy and I have none, and Kirsty would have our undivided love and attention, always.'

'Then why not take them both, darling?' Louise urged. 'A ready-made family for you!'

Janice shook her head decidedly. 'It's Kirsty we want – as I said, she's my goddaughter and I've always taken that very seriously. And surely that's the fairest way, splitting them between us? Lynne and Harry can take Adam, and he'll be with his father's family, and we'll have Kirsty, who'll be with her mother's.'

'Splitting being the operative word,' Harry said grimly.

'But you have a job, Janice,' Lynne argued, 'and she's used to being with her mother the whole time! How can you say you'd give her all your attention, when she'd be in a nursery all day during term time?'

'As are many children of working mothers!' Janice flung back. 'But my school day finishes at three thirty and I have long holidays. I'll spend more time with her than most are able to!'

'They should be kept together,' Bob repeated firmly, albeit aghast at the split widening between them. 'Any adoption agency or social service would insist on that!'

'They might *prefer* it,' Clive said quietly. 'I doubt if they could insist. And it's not as though either of them would be going to strangers. As Jan said, they'd both be with their family, who already love them.'

Harry, seeing Lynne's eyes fill with frustrated tears, cleared his throat. 'Look, I don't want to wield any heavy sticks, but as guardian for both children—'

He broke off as Janice gave a choked gasp, her hands flying to the sides of her head. 'Don't you *understand*?' she cried. 'Do I have to spell it out for you? Very well then – Roy and I have been trying for a baby for three years – *three years!* – and I can't take much more! My sister has been killed in the most brutal way imaginable, and I wake every night thinking about it. But Kirsty is a part of Emma – the next best thing to a daughter of my own! I *must* have her – can't you see that we *deserve* her?' And she burst into a storm of weeping as Roy caught hold of her and held her close, his eyes resting accusingly on Harry.

Bob went for a glass of water while the rest of them sat in silence and Janice's agonized sobs filled the room. Harry reached for Lynne's hand and squeezed it. She turned her head to look at him, tears spilling down her cheeks. For a long moment they held each other's gaze, then he raised his eyebrows questioningly and after a brief pause she nodded and closed her eyes. Janice had won.

At the end of the meeting Janice and Roy left with Kirsty, observing that now her future was decided there was no point in delay, and official procedures could be gone into later.

In the days that followed, Lynne lavished as much time as she could on Adam, and was forced to admit that apart from trotting into various rooms looking for 'Tursy', he didn't seem unduly upset by her absence. It was she who cried for her little niece.

Other difficult meetings lay ahead. On the Monday of the following week, the day before the wills were due to be read, they received word that the bodies had been released. The undertakers would be driving them down in two days' time and delivering them, as instructed, to the funeral parlour near their home. The victims' personal effects, having been examined by the forensic team, had also been cleared and awaited collection, as did Mark's car.

On hearing of this at the will-reading, Graham immediately volunteered to fly up, collect the effects and drive the car home. 'You all have enough to do, and it will let me feel I'm being useful,' he insisted, and both families gratefully accepted his offer.

As to the wills, there were no surprises. Each had left everything to the other, to go in equal shares to their children after their deaths. In the discussion that followed, it was agreed the house should immediately go on the market, and the proceeds from its sale and that of its contents be put in trust funds for the children till they came of age. Any of their toys, clothing and equipment remaining in the house would, however, be released immediately.

The return of the effects necessitated yet another fraught meeting, and since Emma's jewellery came within the terms of the will, it was arranged that this should take place in Mark and Emma's home – neutral though highly charged ground.

Graham had arranged for his wife to pick him up from there and, having handed over the suitcases and other items, tactfully left them to their heartbreaking task. Lynne was reduced to fresh tears on discovering the ceramic pig, which she realized had been intended for her, and Harry's throat tightened at the sight of the sun hat he'd lent Mark for the holiday.

It was as, with relief on both sides, they were

preparing to leave that Roy called for their attention. 'I appreciate that feelings are running high at the moment,' he began, 'but I'd be very grateful if we could talk over a matter that's been concerning Jan and myself.'

They all paused in what they were doing and turned to him.

'Emma and Mark met a violent death,' Roy continued, 'and we've still no idea why. And *because* we've no idea, it's just possible that the children could be in danger. They might, for instance, have actually seen the killers.'

Lynne drew in her breath sharply, but Roy was continuing. 'Fortunately, since they're being adopted, they'll both be changing their surname, and with luck that should deflect any danger. But I think we should reach agreement on what, in due course, we tell them about their parents' death.' He looked round at their tense faces. 'Can you seriously imagine telling Adam that his father and mother were murdered?'

From their expressions he could tell that, as he'd supposed, no one had thought that far ahead. 'Official advice is to volunteer nothing till the children themselves ask about it, which will indicate they're ready to be told. But told what?'

Harry moved uncomfortably. 'What exactly are you proposing?'

'That we agree to say Mark and Emma were killed in a car crash *near their home*, avoiding all mention of the Lake District, which could conceivably link them, even years ahead, to the murders.'

There was a silence as everyone digested this.

Then Bob asked, 'And when do you propose they learn the truth?'

'Not until they're eighteen, at the earliest. But quite frankly the information would be traumatic at any age; there might be a case for never volunteering it.' He looked round at them, raising his shoulders enquiringly. 'After all, what good would it do?'

'Surely they've a right to know at some stage?' Clive protested.

Roy shrugged again. 'Perhaps, but if so, we should try to ensure they're told at the same time, so we'd have to liaise.' His eyes flicked over them again. 'Anyone have any problem with that?'

No one spoke.

'Good. Then I feel we'll have done all we can to protect them.'

Lynne, Harry and the Franklyns had just arrived home when there was a phone call: Graham, asking to speak to Lynne.

She raised her eyebrows. 'It's only a couple of hours since we saw him. I wonder what's come up?'

'One way to find out!' Bob said and she went to take the call.

'Graham, hello.'

'Lynne. I hope you don't mind my asking for you, but I didn't want to raise this at the house in front of everyone, and I felt you were the best person to speak to.'

Her voice sharpened. 'Is something wrong?'

'I'm not sure.' He paused. 'You've finished going through the effects, I presume?'

'Yes?'

'Did anything strike you about them?' And, as she did not reply, he prompted, 'Anything missing?'

'Not that I noticed, why?'

Graham said quietly, 'Where was Mark's camera?'

He heard her draw in her breath. 'Oh my God!'

'I missed it straight away, chiefly because I knew he'd intended taking pictures for a competition we were entering. I immediately queried its absence, and was categorically assured there'd been no camera at the cottage, nor any sign of its carrying bag. So I asked to speak to the officer in charge, who immediately showed interest. He said it was the first positive lead they'd had, and asked me to describe the make of camera and the likely contents of the bag. And Lynne, those contents would have included some very expensive equipment quite apart from the camera – additional lenses, filters, light meters, God knows what – I should estimate over a thousand pounds' worth. It can't all just have vanished into thin air.'

'So you think, after all, it was a burglary that went wrong?'

He didn't reply and a wave of cold washed over her.

'Or,' she went on, feeling her way, 'might something Mark had photographed have led to their deaths?'

'That's what I was wondering. It *could* just have been a burglary; other possible explanations are a) he'd lost it beforehand – in which case he would very definitely have reported it; b) the milkman nicked it, or c) someone in the police did, neither of which seems very plausible. Anyway, I thought I'd better warn you that they'll be in touch about it.'

'I should have missed it myself,' Lynne reproached herself. 'Mark hardly went anywhere without his camera, but being there at the house and with all the trauma about the children, I just wasn't thinking straight.'

In his position as executor, Graham had been made aware of the adoption arrangements. 'Understandable,' he said quietly.

'It probably explains why none of us missed it. We might have done later, but thank God you were straight on to it. Thanks for letting me know, Graham, and again for all you've done – flying up there and everything.'

'Only too glad to help. We'll . . . be at the funeral, of course. Have you settled on a date yet?'

'Yes, next Tuesday, two p.m. at Saint Nick's, Spellsbury, and the church hall afterwards. I suppose that's quite near you?'

'It is, yes.'

'And the week after that we're off to Canada.'

'I meant to ask: were you able to get an extra seat on the plane for Adam?'

'After a bit of wangling, yes. God, Graham, I wish we weren't going, but the parents insist we should.'

'I agree with them,' he said. 'You were here for them during the initial shock of it all, but there's little you can do now, and a new start is just what you all need.'

In her heart, Lynne supposed he was right.

*　*　*

Afterwards, her memory of the funeral was condensed into a series of sounds and barely registered impressions – a ray of sunshine touching the coffins by the chancel steps, someone sobbing quietly behind her, the over-sweet scent of lilies. She moved through the day in a haze, surprising herself by being able to join in the hymns – *till in heaven we take our place* – responding automatically to expressions of sympathy from Mark's work colleagues, dry-eyed and at one remove from everything. She was vaguely aware that Harry, never far from her side, was fielding any awkward comments and queries, and was passively grateful.

In the church hall after the service, Roy approached them a little tentatively, Janice, red-eyed, at his side. 'We probably won't see you again before you leave,' he said. 'We'd just like to wish you all the best.'

Magnanimous in victory, Harry told himself bitterly. 'Thanks,' he said.

'I hope we're parting as friends?'

Poor guy, Harry thought with sudden sympathy; none of this was his doing. 'Of course.'

He glanced at the two women; the fact that each was grieving a sibling should have brought them closer, but what little empathy had been between them had dissolved in the adoption row. There was an awkward pause while both men wondered what to say and neither of the women said anything. Then Roy held out his hand and Harry shook it.

'Bon voyage, then.'

'Thanks.'

45

Later, as they were leaving, Louise and Clive also came to say goodbye, both of them kissing Lynne's unresponsive cheek and shaking Harry's hand.

'Please try not to blame Janice,' Louise said in a low voice as the men made conversation. 'She's been desperate for a baby for years now, and I've been quite worried about her. Rest assured that Kirsty couldn't be more loved.'

Lynne, in her protective cocoon, smiled and nodded, and the Grenvilles moved away.

And now the last people were leaving and they could escape. Emotionally drained both by his own grief and by trying to protect Lynne, what Harry needed most was a good strong whisky, which he knew his father-in-law would supply. Only eight more days, then Canada here they come! God, he could hardly wait!

Four

2012

Charlotte Anderson scooped up her baby son as he crawled determinedly towards the fireplace and replaced him facing in the opposite direction. 'Have you heard from Adam lately?' she asked her mother.

Lynne suppressed a sigh. 'No, but you know what's he like. Not a squeak out of him for months, then he turns up unannounced, expecting the full prodigal son treatment.'

'I've sent emails and left messages on his voice-mail, to no avail. Claire's getting worried that he won't turn up for Jamie's christening, and he *is* the godfather, for heaven's sake.'

'He'll be there,' Lynne said with more confidence than she felt. For Adam was his own person and always had been. Even as a toddler he'd disliked being held, and after those first traumatic days when he'd asked repeatedly for his parents, he'd appeared to dismiss them and his baby sister from both his mind and his memory. At first, Lynne and Harry had been thankful he'd escaped apparently unscathed, but as time went on and they increasingly introduced Emma and Mark into their conversation, he had shown little interest, accepting without comment the story of the car crash and his subsequent adoption.

'He's a boy, honey!' Harry had repeated over the years. 'They're different animals from girls. It's not that he doesn't care, he just thinks it's sissy to show it.'

But Lynne found his detachment hard to accept, especially since, as he grew older, he looked more and more like his father. Sometimes, when he came suddenly into the room, her heart gave a little skip as memory blurred with reality.

Since his mid-teens Adam had been a magnet for girls, all of whom he treated with benign indifference, and Harry had had to deal with several angry fathers along the line. Now, in his late twenties, the amiable but firm distance he maintained between himself and his family meant they'd no idea who his current girlfriend was, if, indeed, he had one.

In one respect, however, they'd had no cause for worry, and that was academically. He'd proved to be an exceptionally bright child, coming top of his class despite invariably being the youngest in it. Since he was fluent in several languages they'd hoped he might join the Diplomatic Service, but he'd surprised them by electing to go into teaching, and now held the position of head of the French department at one of Toronto's most eminent colleges.

Lynne, telling herself she'd a lot to be thankful for and shouldn't quibble, bent to pick up her grandson.

The temperature was steadily rising and it was as well, Adam Carstairs reflected, that the term was almost over. He lay on the bed, an arm

48

beneath his head, watching a fly crawl over the ceiling and feeling the sweat course down his body.

'I really should be going,' Gina said unenthusiastically.

He grunted. Did that, she wondered, mean 'OK' or 'Stay a bit longer'? Resignedly guessing the answer, she swung her feet to the floor and reached for her clothes. They'd come straight from school, and the crumpled dress she retrieved was the one in which, an hour or two earlier, she'd been teaching year four.

The bed dipped as he shifted position. 'Oh, by the way, the sabbatical's confirmed,' he said.

She stiffened. It was months since he'd mentioned the possibility, and she'd been praying he'd changed his mind. 'Where and when?' she asked, keeping her voice level.

'The UK, in September.'

She swung to face him. '*This* September?'

'The very same, though I'll be leaving earlier, to take in a tour of Europe.'

Anger was building inside her. 'And exactly when were you proposing to tell me?'

'I'm telling you now.'

'A bit late in the day, isn't it?'

He raised an eyebrow. 'I don't think so; I've not told the family yet.'

Her eyes widened. 'Your parents don't know you're going abroad for a year?'

'I keep telling you, they're not my parents. But no, they don't; I've been putting it off because sparks will fly when they realize I'll be living amid my estranged family.'

49

It occurred to Gina, not for the first time, how little she knew about this man she'd been sleeping with for the past year. Though he'd occasionally referred to his family, she'd never met them and this was the first she'd heard of any rift.

'Estranged?' she echoed.

'Well, not entirely, but there's always been a coolness between my lot and the couple who adopted my sister.'

Even more bewildered, she struggled to recall the names he'd mentioned. 'Charlotte, or Claire?'

He made a dismissive gesture. 'Neither,' he said impatiently. 'Charlotte and Claire are, and have always been, my cousins. I'm talking of my *real* sister, in the UK. I met her a couple of times when we were visiting my English grandparents, before they moved out here. We didn't hit it off – probably just as well there was an ocean between us!'

'But there won't be, once you're there.'

'Very perceptive, my love.'

She bit her lip. 'So why that particular location, when the world's your oyster?'

'For one thing, Westbourne's arguably the most prestigious school in the south of England.'

'Ah, Westbourne! So this is down to Nick!' A teacher from there had recently spent a sabbatical at their college.

'I liked what he had to say about it, certainly, but I also thought it would be amusing to be the fox in the hen coop. And as it happened, the college were gratifyingly keen to have me.'

Gina stood up, smoothed down her dress and

stepped into her sandals. Then she said quietly, 'What about me?'

He turned his head to look at her, his grey eyes unfathomable. 'What *about* you, my sweet? We've had a good time over the last year, but nothing lasts for ever.'

'I'll miss you,' she said, despising the wobble in her voice.

'Then come and visit. Spend your next vacation in the UK.'

'You will be coming back, though? Next summer?'

'In all probability,' he said.

She switched to what she hoped was a safer topic. 'Shall I see you over the weekend?'

Adam stretched lazily. 'Unlikely. My new nephew, or second-cousin or whatever he is, is being christened on Sunday and I'm expected there in my best bib and tucker. I just hope he doesn't bawl his way through it like Charlotte's brat did.'

'It's supposed to be lucky,' Gina said.

'Not if you've a hangover, it's not.'

She laughed, collected her bag from the chair and turned to the door. 'Have fun!' she said lightly, and left the apartment before the threatened tears could betray her.

James Alexander Hunter behaved impeccably throughout the service, even treating the vicar to a toothless smile as water trickled down his face. Lynne, looking at the circle of her family, felt a wave of happiness. This, surely, was as it should be, all of them here together – Mum and Dad,

51

Harry's parents, her daughters with their husbands and babies, and – making it still more special, as they rarely saw him these days – Adam, looking incredibly handsome in his grey suit. How Mark would have loved to record the occasion, she thought before she could stop herself. For, of course, the family *wasn't* complete, not without him or Emma or Kirsty. How long ago it all seemed.

After the service they returned to Claire and Sandy's home, where a magnificent spread awaited them.

Thelma Franklyn, smilingly accepting a plate piled with delicacies, was, like her daughter, in a reflective mood. It had been a good decision to move out here when Bob retired, she thought with satisfaction. Lynne's departure, following so swiftly after Mark's death, had hit her hard and, as visits to Canada became more and more frequent, it increasingly seemed there was little left for them in the UK. For though she'd tried to keep in touch with Kirsty, the continuing coolness between herself and Janice led to longer and longer gaps as the years went by. Now, sadly, their contact was reduced to emails and the occasional conversation on Skype, though Thelma still cherished hopes her youngest granddaughter would accept her invitation to come and visit.

Another bonus of moving out here was that while they'd never felt close to Emma's parents, Nora and Ed Carstairs immediately made them welcome, and their friendship had deepened as they became joint great-grandparents to the little boys.

Adam joined her on the sofa, balancing a glass of wine on his plate. 'A penny for them, Grandma?'

'Just enjoying the occasion, and wondering when we'll be attending *your* children's christenings!'

He gave a short laugh. 'Don't hold your breath!'

'No one special on the horizon?'

He shook his head. 'Variety's the spice of life – that's my motto.'

'All right when you're nineteen; less so at twenty-nine.'

'Don't rush me, Grandma; but if and when I meet the right one, you'll be the first to know. I can't say fairer than that.'

'Just don't leave it too long,' Thelma advised.

Their conversation was interrupted by Claire's arrival with the christening cake. Glasses of champagne were produced and the baby's health toasted as he lay contentedly in his baby seat. Sandy made a brief speech, the cake was cut and distributed and the occasion began to wind down.

It was then that Adam rose to his feet. 'I hope you'll excuse me butting in with some news of my own,' he began, holding up a hand as laughing speculation broke out. 'I just wanted to let you know that from September I shall be taking a year's sabbatical in the UK.'

More exclamations – of surprise this time, tinged, in Lynne's case, with indignation at the short notice. He raised his voice above them. 'I shall be joining the French department at Westbourne College.'

There was a moment's total silence, ended by Lynne's whispered, '*Westbourne?*'

Adam, scanning their startled faces, caught an exchange of glances between his grandfather and Harry, which, to his annoyance, he was unable to interpret.

'Well?' he challenged. 'It's one of the top public schools, you know. Is no one going to congratulate me?'

'Of course, Adam – well done, fella!' Sandy said heartily and joined Bruce, Charlotte's husband, in slapping him on the back and shaking his hand.

'Why Westbourne?' Harry asked, his voice strained. 'There must be plenty of other choices.'

'One of their guys was over last year, extolling its virtues. And also,' Adam went on deliberately, 'I thought it was time I got to know the other half of my family.' He paused as a sudden idea struck him and promptly acted on it, curious to see its effect. 'Any of you been watching *Who Do You Think You Are?* on TV? So-called celebrities trace their family trees, and often turn up some surprises. It's started quite a trend – there are websites galore for people wanting to trace theirs. I thought it might provide a leisure interest while I'm on the spot, as it were, especially as I know virtually nothing about my family.'

'You've never been interested,' Lynne accused defensively. She'd gone pale, Adam noted, his curiosity aroused. What, exactly, weren't they telling him?

'Well, this will give me the chance to rectify it.'

Quite suddenly he'd had enough of them, of the

54

cloying sweetness of the cake, the champagne, the general air of self-satisfaction which he seemed to have ruffled. To hell with them! He glanced at his watch. 'And now I must be on my way. Sorry to break up the party, but I've a date awaiting me.' He turned to Sandy and Claire. 'Thanks for your hospitality, and blessings on my godson.' And, with a nod encompassing the rest of them, he left the room and, a moment later, the house.

He'd call Gina after all, he decided; if she'd made other arrangements, she could cancel them. She at least appreciated him for what he was, and a spot of enthusiastic sex would restore his balance. His mind churning with half-formed suspicions, he turned the car in the direction of the town.

Back in their own home, Harry and Lynne continued to discuss the bombshell. 'It's ironic that this should have come up now, within days of Mark and Emma's anniversary,' Harry commented, 'but at least even Janice must agree they now have to know the truth.'

Following Adam's departure from Claire and Sandy's, conversation had moved seamlessly to other topics. The surprise expressed by most of those present had been due to his intention to look up the family with whom they were supposedly at odds. Apart from themselves, only Bob and Thelma had appreciated the full impact of his announcement; protecting Adam from the truth had of necessity involved withholding it from their daughters, and they'd been too traumatized on their arrival in Canada to face going through it again with Ed and Nora, who still believed the car-crash story.

'As you know, I've been wanting to come clean for years,' Harry added, 'but she always dug her heels in, and since they had to be told at the same time, our hands were tied. He'll be furious at being kept in the dark, and I can't say I blame him.'

Lynne lifted a hand and let it fall. 'It was never the right time. He's . . . well, we've not been as close to him as we'd hoped, have we, and it wasn't something you could just come out with. It didn't help that he never mentions them. It's as though he's blotted them from his memory.' She turned to Harry impulsively. 'Let's leave it for a while,' she pleaded. 'It's another three weeks before he sets off for Europe, and anything might happen. He could change his mind, the school could – anything. Then all this agonizing would have been for nothing.'

'We've put it off quite long enough,' Harry said firmly. 'Whether he goes or not, it's high time he knew the truth.' He stood up. 'I'm going to email Roy and arrange a time when we can discuss it.'

Roy opened the email the following evening on his return from work and sat staring at it blankly, his mouth dry.

Adam has just announced he's taking a year's sabbatical at Westbourne College from September, Harry had written, after his opening pleasantries. *Also – though I had the impression*

'That's settled, then; we'll tell Adam tomorrow and you let Kirsty know on Sunday. It just remains to say hi to Jan, and . . . the best of luck.'

'You too,' Roy said gruffly, 'and our best to Lynne.'

The die was cast, Harry thought as he switched off the connection. And not before time.

Adam stood with his back to them, staring out of the window. He'd moved there after Harry's opening words, and though he'd now finished speaking, remained where he was.

Lynne exchanged an anxious glance with her husband. 'Well, say *something*, darling!' she prompted.

Slowly he turned, his face hard. 'What the hell do you expect me to say?'

'Just that . . . you understand why we didn't tell you before.'

'When I was a child, yes. But what conceivable right had you to keep it from me all these years? My God, if I hadn't been going to the UK, would you *ever* have told me?'

'But you'd never talk about them!' Lynne burst out in their defence. 'Every time I mentioned them, you just switched off. You never gave us an opening!'

'We were working on a need-to-know basis,' Harry explained in mitigation.

Adam gave a derisory snort. 'And how exactly could you gauge that? *God!*' he added explosively. 'I'm having difficulty getting my head around this!' He returned to his chair and, sitting down,

this was an afterthought – while there he intends to research the family. It seems the time we've been postponing for so long has come at last, and as agreed we need to discuss how and when to proceed. I'm sure you agree this is best done verbally, and the easiest way would be to Skype. Could you let me know your Skype name and add mine, which is Fernbank, to your list of contacts? I suggest we give ourselves a day or two to consider the implications, and I'll call you at 9 p.m. your time, 4 p.m. ours, this coming Thursday, the twenty-first. If by any chance you're not *on Skype, please email me to make other arrangements.*

Roy pushed back his chair and went into the hall. 'Jan!' he called. 'Come here a minute.'

She appeared in the doorway, drying her hands on her apron. 'What?'

'I've just had an email from Harry.'

Her eyes widened and she started towards the open laptop, but Roy forestalled her.

'Adam's coming over on a year's sabbatical, and he wants to research the family. Obviously the time has come to tell them.'

'*Adam?* Oh, God!'

'I suppose one benefit of having left it so long is that it should have less impact.'

'But does she really *have* to know?'

She, not *they*. Clearly Adam's feelings didn't come into it.

'If he's going to embark on family history, he'll be applying for death certificates,' Roy said baldly. 'And when he learns the truth, he's sure to contact Kirsty, if he hasn't already.'

'But why is he coming at all?' Janice broke out. 'Last time we saw him, he hadn't a good word to say for the UK, the arrogant little brat!'

'That *was* about fifteen years ago,' Roy said mildly.

She thought for a moment. 'Well, I doubt if he'll come anywhere near us. The dislike appeared to be mutual.'

'Jan, the sabbatical's at Westbourne College.'

She stared at him aghast. 'He's coming *here*, not just to the UK? And for a *year*?'

Roy nodded.

'Oh, *God*!' she said again, her hand going to her throat.

'We always knew the time would come,' he said gently. 'Just as well to get it over.'

'It's too bad having to upset her, just when her career's really taking off.'

'She'll cope,' Roy said with confidence.

'I hope you're right,' Janice said shakily. 'I'm not sure *I* can go through it all again. And we'll have to warn Mum,' she added, her voice rising. 'It'll bring it all back for her, and she won't have Dad to help her through it.' Clive Grenville had died two years previously.

'It's history now, love. It won't be as bad for any of us this time round.'

'It would at least help if we could say the killers were behind bars. The idea that they're still walking around somewhere, having got off scot-free . . .'

'I know.'

She felt for a handkerchief and blew her nose. 'So you and Harry are going to talk it over?'

Roy nodded. 'Luckily they're on Skype.' He and Janice had installed it as a means of keeping in touch with his mother, who lived in Scotland. 'He suggests this Thursday, at 9 p.m. When are we seeing Kirsty again?'

'Sunday lunch,' Janice said tonelessly. 'And you do remember why we fixed that date?'

Roy stared at her, then understanding dawned. 'God, of course – it's the twenty-fourth! With all this going on it had slipped my mind.' He reached for her hand. 'Don't worry, sweetheart, it'll be all right. I promise.'

The Skype connection was as clear as if they were in adjoining rooms, but neither man had activated the video link, unwilling to face each other. 'I don't suppose you relish this prospect any more than we do,' Harry began. 'I still feel we should have come clean before it was forced on us.'

'You're probably right,' Roy acknowledged heavily. 'At the time I was just anxious that the children, as they then were, shouldn't be remotely traceable should anyone be looking for them. I dare say I went too far.'

'Well, it was done with the best of intentions. Perhaps we should have discussed it again once they were older, but it's too late now to speculate. Quite a coincidence, this Sunday being the twenty-sixth anniversary of the murders, but I suppose that makes this week as good a time as any for explanations.'

'Kirsty was coming over anyway on Sunday; we always go to the cemetery together.'

leant forward with his hands tightly clasped. 'Right, now I want to know *everything*, every last detail. What *exactly* happened to them?'

Harry moistened his lips. 'Well, as I said, you were all on holiday, and—'

'Where, exactly?'

Harry hesitated, but surely the secrecy of the location no longer applied? 'In the Lake District – a village called Penthwaite, near Hawkston.' He paused, but Adam made no comment and after a moment he continued.

'All we really know, even after all this time, is that your father – Mark – was found lying in the drive early one morning, and—'

'Found by whom?' Adam cut in.

'A milkman. He tried unsuccessfully to revive him, then he . . . heard you crying inside the house. The door was on the latch so he went in and found you with Emma, who was lying at the foot of the stairs.'

'Also dead?'

Harry nodded miserably.

'And wouldn't elementary psychology, even then, have dictated that a two-year-old who'd been alone for God knows how long with his dead mother might need some counselling?'

'But after the first day or two you were fine,' Lynne insisted tearfully. 'Added to which we were within a couple of weeks of emigrating and, on top of everything else, trying to rush through arrangements for temporary custody prior to adoption. There was no way you could have seen anyone within that time frame, and once we were settled here you gave no sign of remembering anything about it. It seemed point-less to bring it all up again.'

'How exactly were they killed? Adam asked after a moment.

Lynne shuddered, and it was Harry who replied.

'According to the post mortems, death was caused in each case by a blow to the head with a rock of some kind, fragments of which were embedded . . .'

'In their skulls?' Adam finished brutally.

'Yes. It had been raining that day and there were two sets of shoe prints in the room, neither of which matched Mark's. They . . . wouldn't have had a chance.'

'Was anything taken?' Adam asked after a pause. 'Either from their bodies or the cottage?'

'As far as we know, only your father's camera equipment, which seemed to indicate he'd filmed something suspicious. The police hoped that would narrow the search, but it never came to anything.'

Adam stared at him, his eyes narrowing. 'You mean no one was ever caught?'

Lynne and Harry shook their heads.

'Well,' he continued after a moment, his voice brittle, 'this opens up a whole new area for my family research. Considering all the scientific advances since then, I should have better luck.'

'God, Adam!' Harry stared at him in horror. 'You're not thinking of taking it up yourself?'

'Obviously someone needs to.'

Lynne's voice shook. 'Is this your way of punishing us for not telling you sooner?'

'No, it's a son's natural desire to avenge his

parents, and nothing you say will stop me.' He stood up suddenly. 'Right, I've enough facts to begin my research.'

He started towards the door, then stopped and turned. 'I presume my sister's also been kept in ignorance?'

'Yes.'

'And on learning I'm off to the UK, you panicked and alerted the Marriotts?'

Harry nodded. 'It was agreed you should both be told this week.'

'Well, it will be interesting to hear her reaction,' he said and, turning on his heel, left the room. Minutes later they heard his car start up and drive swiftly through the gates.

Lynne and Harry, who'd also stood up, looked at each other in despair. He put his arms round her, feeling her tremble.

'He's in shock, hon,' he said gently. 'Give him time.'

'He might never speak to us again,' she said.

Five

It was the twenty-fourth of June, a date whose aura of loss and tragedy hadn't lessened over the years, and since it was also a Sunday – and therefore an especially poignant anniversary – Marilyn had been to church after visiting the cemetery, thus providing Dean, a non-churchgoer, with an excuse not to accompany her.

Not that he ever did. Though he'd often promised to come, at the last minute something always prevented him. Possibly he was embarrassed to visit the grave of his predecessor; perhaps jealousy came into it, but whatever the reason she no longer expected it.

Although it was wet he'd gone to golf as usual, and she returned to an empty house. The rain was driving hard against it and she hurried to close the drawing-room window, pausing to gaze at the mountains above the town, now partially shrouded in cloud. *I will lift up mine eyes unto the hills*, they had sung earlier. The cemetery had been particularly bleak this morning, its gravestones dark with rain, its floral tributes drooping with the weight of it.

Twenty-six years, she thought in wonder. Impossible to believe Tony had been dead that long. The date was necessarily approximate, commemorating the day she'd last seen him, though if he'd been alive at the end of it he'd have surely come home. He'd had something to work out, and hoped a day's fishing would help him resolve it. And to compensate for her lonely Sunday he'd promised dinner at the George that evening. Little had she dreamed it would be but the first of many lonely days.

Six agonizing weeks had passed before his body was retrieved from the lake, and by then, battered by rocks and shudderingly mauled by the fish he'd hoped to catch, there'd been no way to establish how he'd died. His boat had been found weeks before, floating some way down the lake, and the consensus was that he'd overbalanced while reeling in a fish. If, in doing so, he'd somehow banged his head, it might explain why, although a strong swimmer, he had apparently drowned.

Dean had been his business colleague, and had proved to be her rock during those first traumatic months. At the time he'd been divorced for two years and, with no family of her own, she'd come to lean on him. Perhaps it wasn't surprising that as the months passed they grew closer and, lonely and vulnerable, she'd accepted his proposal within the year.

Sometimes she wondered if he regretted his precipitous courtship; if, perhaps, it had been motivated by pity. She wasn't clever like his brother's wife, Vivien, who was a chartered accountant and sometimes helped in the family business. She'd never discussed work with Tony and nor did she with Dean, but then it wasn't for her brains that they'd married her; it was, as she well knew, because she was pretty and vivacious and she made them laugh.

This second marriage hadn't been a love-match but it was happy enough, despite the non-arrival of children. Dean himself had two sons, and during the early years the visits of the little boys had been a highlight in Marilyn's life, as if Fate, relenting, were allowing her motherhood at one remove. Though they were now partners in the family firm, the closeness had thankfully endured.

She turned from the window with a sigh. Dean would be home for lunch soon, and she felt a stab of sympathy, knowing that even though spared the cemetery, he dreaded this day almost as much as she did, in particular dinner at the George, during which Tony's memory would be toasted. But this was a tradition she clung to and had no intention of relinquishing. In some obscure way it seemed an honouring of his last wishes.

'You come first all the rest of the year,' she'd told Dean. 'Don't begrudge Tony his day of remembrance.'

She could only hope he'd abide by that.

Leaving the outskirts of Westbourne behind her, Kirsty Marriott settled down for the half-hour drive home.

The twenty-fourth of June, she thought glumly, the anniversary of her parents' death. She wasn't looking forward to the visit, which would entail a trip to the cemetery where her aunt unfailingly succumbed to floods of tears. Though not unsympathetic, Kirsty would have expected, after all this time, that she'd have come to terms with the loss of her sister. For her part, never having really known her parents, she felt sadness at the short-ening of their lives rather than a sense of personal loss. It was tragic that Emma was only twenty-nine when she died, but sadly such tragedies happened every day, and wasn't time supposed to be a healer? Still, since her aunt's grief was obviously still raw, the least she could do was spend the day with them both, knowing that at the end of it she could escape the gloom and return to the house she shared with Angie.

And that in itself had been a battle, she reflected; Aunt Jan had done her best to persuade her to live at home and commute daily, but fond though Kirsty was of her adoptive parents, Jan's clinging love could be stifling and, having made the break, she firmly resisted the plea to return each week for Sunday lunch.

'Don't worry,' she'd assured them, 'I'll be popping back all the time, but let's not make any hard and fast rules.'

Thankfully, her uncle had backed her and Jan, used, as head of the local primary, to her wishes being obeyed, had been forced to give way.

Thank God for Angie! Kirsty thought now. They'd met five years ago on a Cordon Bleu course and, finding they had similar ambitions, decided to go into partnership supplying hand-made cakes to patisseries and coffee shops around Westbourne. They'd invested in a house near the main shopping area and converted the ground floor to business premises – office, packing room and a kitchen conforming to Environmental Health standards – and made their home on the floors above, thereby avoiding overheads. Though they'd become fairly well known and received enquiries from around the country, they were determined to remain a local company, restricting their customer base to a ten-mile radius and keeping their output to a manageable level for the two of them.

Before she'd set off that morning, Angie had asked if she was curious about the parents she couldn't remember. 'Not really,' she'd replied. 'There are photos all over the house, and with Mum being Aunt Jan's sister and Dad the brother of my aunt in Canada, I feel I know them quite well.'

Angie, with a large and close family of her own, hadn't seemed convinced. Nor could she understand how Kirsty could have no feelings for her brother, adopted by the other side of the family and immediately whisked off to Canada. Kirsty had met him a couple of times when the family came over to visit her grandparents, and had thought him obnoxious.

And now she was approaching Spellsbury, the market town where she'd grown up. Her hands tightened on the steering wheel and she spared a quick glance to check that the flowers hadn't slipped to the floor and the cake box remained upright. Oh, God, she thought, I wish it was this evening!

Arranging a suitably sombre smile on her face, she turned into her relatives' driveway.

It was immediately apparent that her aunt was even more tense than usual. Her welcoming hug was more prolonged, her smile tighter, and Kirsty felt a flicker of alarm. Hoping to ease the problem, she handed her the cake box. 'Your favourite,' she said with a smile. 'Chocolate and orange, with pieces of pineapple.'

'Lovely, darling, thank you.' But she sounded preoccupied, and Kirsty's worst fears seemed confirmed when, instead of immediately setting off for the cemetery as usual, her uncle took her arm and led her into the sitting room.

'Come and sit down, sweetie,' he said quietly. 'We need to speak to you.'

'Is something wrong?' she asked anxiously.

He didn't answer, simply motioning for her to sit down and seating himself next to his wife on the sofa. They exchanged a look, and Janice gave a minute nod.

'Although we've always spent this anniversary together,' Roy began, 'there's something we've never told you, and that is how your parents died.'

Kirsty frowned. 'But surely, the car crash . . .?' Her voice tailed off as he shook his head.

He leant forward, clasping his hands between his knees. 'Please believe me, sweetheart, we thought we were acting for the best in keeping this from you. In the early days, of course, we were, but—'

'Uncle!' Kirsty broke in and he nodded, lifting a hand in acknowledgement of her impatience.

'The truth is that you were all on a self-catering holiday in the Lakes, and at the beginning of the second week we received the most terrible news.'

Bracing herself, she waited as he swallowed nervously.

'Early that Monday, a milkman on his rounds noticed Mark lying in the driveway of the cottage. He hurried to his assistance, but to his horror found that he was dead.'

Kirsty gasped, her hands involuntarily clenching. 'But—'

'He could hear a child crying inside,' Roy continued doggedly, 'so he pushed the door open and went in to find Emma lying dead at the foot of the stairs with Adam bending over her, and you yelling your head off in your cot upstairs.'

Kirsty forced herself to speak, though the words came out as a croak. 'What . . . had happened to them?'

Janice gave a strangled sob. 'They'd been murdered, darling! Hit over the head with a rock of some sort, and to this day we don't know why!'

Kirsty felt blindly for the arms of the chair, trying to anchor herself in the familiar. 'But who . . .?'

'We don't know that, either.'

'*You don't know?*' she echoed unbelievingly. 'After all this time . . .?'

'Officially the case is still open,' Roy said, 'but since despite intensive enquiries at the time the police got precisely nowhere, there seems little chance now of finding the culprits.'

'Culprits? There was more than one?'

'It seems so; there were two sets of muddy footprints at the scene.'

Kirsty's mind whirled, trying to find some explanation. 'Could the milkman . . .?'

Roy shook his head. 'He was thoroughly investigated, of course, but the timing was all wrong. He was just being a Good Samaritan.'

'Each year when we visit the graves,' Janice whispered, 'I make a promise that their killers will be caught. And each year we have to let them down.'

Which, Kirsty realized, accounted for the tears. Her eyes raked their strained faces. 'Why are you telling me now?'

Roy said flatly, 'Adam's coming to the UK on a year's sabbatical.'

She looked from one to the other. 'I . . . don't see the connection.'

'While he's here, he's intending to research the family, which will involve obtaining death certificates and so on.'

'You mean he doesn't know the truth either?'

'He didn't, until Friday. It was agreed at the outset that you should be told at the same time, so when Lynne and Harry knew he was coming over they contacted us and we discussed it on Skype. It was decided that we would tell you both straight away.'

'I'm having difficulty taking all this in,' Kirsty said slowly. 'My parents were murdered and my brother, whom I've not seen for fifteen years, is going to spend a whole year in the UK.'

'Not only in the UK,' Janice said grimly. 'He's coming to Westbourne College, no less.'

Kirsty's eyes widened. 'Why here? He doesn't even like us!'

'The college is highly rated,' Roy replied. 'It will look good on his CV. Harry thinks the family research idea was an afterthought. He could never have imagined what alarm bells it would set off.'

But Kirsty, following her own train of thought, had stopped listening. 'There must have been *some* clue as to motive. Were they robbed, for instance? And why was my father outside and my mother in the house?'

'We don't know,' Roy said, 'and as regards robbery, the only thing missing was Mark's camera and its case.'

'His *camera*?'

'He was a keen photographer – we told you that – and according to his friend, Graham Yates, he was about to enter a competition.' He paused. 'All we could think was that someone didn't like being photographed, and took the bag with the camera containing the last film.'

'It's a bit extreme to *kill* him!' Kirsty objected. 'And why Mum?'

'Perhaps she saw something too.'

After a moment's reflective silence, Kirsty mused, 'I wonder what Adam's reaction will be to all this.' She stood up and, walking to the piano, picked up her parents' wedding photograph, studying it more closely than she had in years. And as her eyes lingered on her mother's face, young and radiant, she experienced for the first time an agonizing sense of loss.

Behind her, Roy said quietly, 'Ready for the cemetery?'

Kirsty traced a gentle finger over the happy young faces. 'I suppose so,' she said.

It was an emotionally draining day; knowing what she now did, she had felt genuine grief when laying her flowers on the grave, and her heart ached for her aunt's anguished tears. The lunch that followed was subdued, with Kirsty repeatedly asking questions as they occurred to her, though few of them could be answered. Though ashamed of the fact, she was counting the minutes until she could leave.

'Has Lance been in touch?' Jan enquired at one point, attempting to steer their thoughts away from the tragedy.

'No, and he won't be. It's over, Auntie.'

Kirsty had recently broken off a two-year relationship, but the question called to mind the mysterious email she'd received the day before. It had been sent to her business address – kirsty@gateauxtodiefor.co.uk – and read simply, *Have you any idea how lovely you are?* Unsigned, the sender's name was given as xyz@hotmail. com – not much help. Briefly, she'd wondered if Lance had sent it – though surely he'd have used her private address and anonymous emails were hardly his style, especially, in his present mood, flattering ones. She'd concluded it was spam, but though she'd deleted it from her screen, it still lingered in her head.

Tea was served, the chocolate orange cake in pride of place. But no one had any appetite and when, soon after it was cleared away, Kirsty said she should be going, neither of them tried to detain her.

'I know it's been a difficult day, sweetie, and I'm sorry,' Roy said, 'but at least Adam won't be here for a couple of months, so you'll have time to get used to the idea. Harry says he's taking the opportunity to tour Europe before term starts.'

73

He hesitated. 'As to the rest, you do forgive us, don't you? For keeping the secret so long?'

She smiled wryly. 'I just wish you could have kept it a bit longer,' she said.

She had driven only a few yards down the road when her mobile shrilled and, glad of the diversion, she pulled in to the kerb. The number on the screen was unfamiliar, as was the man's voice that greeted her.

'Kirsty?'

'Yes?'

'It's Nick. Nick Shepherd. We met at Johnnie and Lois's wedding a couple of weeks ago.'

'Oh, yes.' Vaguely she recalled a tall, attractive man in his thirties with whom she'd chatted at the reception.

'If you remember, we had an interesting discussion on the pros and cons of Shakespeare in modern dress. I see *Hamlet*'s coming to the Criterion next week and I wondered if you'd care to see it?'

Kirsty raised an eyebrow at herself in the rearview mirror. Her first date since the break-up! Well, as far as she remembered he was personable and good company, so why not? A spot of light relief would be more than welcome.

'It's in modern dress,' he added, when she didn't immediately reply.

'That sounds very interesting. Thank you, I should like to.'

'Great. It starts quite early – about seven, I think – so I suggest we have a meal afterwards to round off the evening, if that's agreeable?'

'Sounds lovely,' she said a little cautiously.

'Right; I'll be in touch when I've sorted things out, and we can arrange a time to meet. Speak to you soon.' And he rang off.

She restarted the car, almost immediately regretting having accepted the invitation. The call had caught her off-balance while her mind was churning with the ramifications of the day's disclosures, but on reflection she knew she wasn't ready to start a new relationship, if that was Nick Shepherd's intention. The break-up with Lance had been bruising, but there was a certain freedom in being 'single' again. Added to which, she realized belatedly, she knew nothing of this man she'd committed herself to spending an evening with. He could even – a disturbing thought – be the sender of that email.

She frowned, thinking back to their meeting, sure she'd not given him her mobile number. Why hadn't she at least prevaricated, told him she'd have to check her diary? That way she could have thought more clearly about the implications, while any attempt to back down now would be an all too obvious excuse.

Oh, God, as if she'd not enough on her mind without having to worry about this new complication! At least Angie would be home by the time she got back. It would be a relief to talk over the enormity of what she'd learned with someone not personally involved.

Thirty minutes later Kirsty turned into the driveway of the tall Edwardian house and drew up alongside Angie's car, grateful as always for the off-street parking that was at such a premium in central Westbourne.

Closing the front door behind her, she dropped her keys on the hall table and bent over it briefly, her hands resting on its surface as a wave of exhaustion, aftermath of the shock and traumas of the day, swept over her.

'Kirsty?' Angie had appeared at the top of the stairs. 'Are you OK?'

Kirsty raised her head. 'Not really,' she said.

'Oh, poor love. Was it awful?'

'Worse than you can imagine.'

'Come on up and I'll open a bottle of wine.' She disappeared in the direction of their domestic kitchen and slowly, almost painfully, Kirsty went upstairs and into the sitting room, making her way, as she always did on returning home, to the bay windows and their spectacular view.

The town of Westbourne was attractive, historic and, in the view of some, inconvenient, since those approaching it from the north were forced to negotiate roads leading steeply downhill that put a strain on brakes and were especially treacherous in icy weather.

There were, however, compensations, one of which was that houses on this side of town, Kirsty's and Angie's among them, were afforded a bird's-eye view over the roofs of those on a lower level to the large park that lay in the centre of town, the twin crescents that encircled it and, beyond, the towers and turrets of Westbourne College. This evening the familiar view assumed a new significance and the college had never seemed so close. Soon, Kirsty thought incredulously, Adam would be working there.

Behind her she heard Angie come in and set down a bottle and two glasses on the coffee table.

'Come and tell me about it,' she invited.

Kirsty turned, and at the sight of her face Angie gave an exclamation. 'Even worse than usual?' she asked sympathetically.

'Much,' Kirsty acknowledged shakily. 'It seems my parents didn't die in a car crash, as I'd always been told.' She paused and drew a tremulous breath. 'They were murdered, Angie. Both of them. While we were on holiday in the Lake District.'

'It changes everything,' she said. It was two hours later and they were still sitting on the sofa, the bottle of wine two-thirds empty. 'Before today, it had just seemed a tragic accident which could – and does – happen to anyone. But to hear they were killed *deliberately*, as far as we know through no fault of their own, and on top of that, that their killers might still be alive out there, happily living their own lives . . .' Her voice trailed off and she reached for her glass.

'It's – grotesque,' Angie agreed. She paused. 'And your brother's coming over?' Kirsty nodded.

'At least this might bring you closer.'

'It'll have come as a shock to him, too,' Kirsty conceded. 'We've only been told now because while he's here he wants to research the family – a kind of *Who Do You Think You Are?* project – and would have found out anyhow.'

77

'Do you think he'll go ahead with it, in the circumstances?'

'I'm damn sure he will, if only because the family will oppose it.'

Angie smiled wryly. 'You've not much of an opinion of him, have you?'

Kirsty toyed with her glass, her thoughts moving on. 'There's something else.' She looked up, meeting her friend's questioning glance. 'Do you remember someone called Nick Shepherd at Lois and Johnnie's wedding?'

'Can't say I do. Why?'

'He phoned, just as I was about to drive home, to invite me to the theatre next week, and like a fool I agreed.'

'Like a fool?'

'Angie, I don't know the man, and I'm not sure I want to. I certainly don't want to get involved.'

'Hey, slow down! He's not asked you to marry him, has he?'

Kirsty smiled. 'No, but – I don't know, I feel a bit uneasy about him. For instance, how did he get my mobile number? I'm pretty sure I didn't give it to him.'

'If he was interested, he could have asked around. Any of our friends could have supplied it.'

'Suppose it was he who sent that email?'

'Why would he do that, if he was intending to phone you?'

She shrugged.

Angie laid a hand on her arm. 'Look, love, you're overreacting – understandable, after the day you've had. But it's no big deal, is it? Think of it as a night out which at least will take your mind off things, and if you don't like him you need never see him again. OK?'

'OK,' Kirsty agreed gratefully. 'Thanks for putting it in perspective. I just wish we could do the same with the rest of it.'

Six

The knowledge of how her parents met their deaths lodged like a heavy stone at the back of Kirsty's mind, forcing itself to the front any time she wasn't actively engaged.

Janice phoned on the Tuesday, ostensibly to see how she was. 'Come back for lunch on Sunday,' she urged. 'Last week was so difficult, and we missed out on our usual relaxed get-together. You've nothing special on, have you?'

It was true that since her break-up with Lance weekends had been something of a lottery. Angie was invariably with her boyfriend, Simon, and she filled them by going to the tennis club, where she had a crowd of friends, or bringing her correspondence up to date, or, since they'd no garden to speak of, taking a book down to the park where, on summer Sundays, a brass band took up residence on the old bandstand.

But she was not yet ready to face her adoptive parents, and when she woke in the night or in moments of leisure during the day, she pondered her slightly changed attitude towards them. Embarrassment? Resentment at their years of silence? Yet they couldn't be held responsible for that; it had been decreed that she and Adam should be told together and that ancient decree had held good right into their twenties. It was more, she decided, that she knew at their next meeting she'd be under anxious scrutiny, and couldn't face the prospect of a day of play-acting. Not yet.

Adam's pending arrival also featured largely in her thoughts. How would he contact them? Would he still have that arrogant, slightly aloof manner she remembered, or would he have matured differently? And how, exactly, was he reacting to the bombshell that had been dropped on them both?

Nick Shepherd had also phoned, to report that he'd managed to obtain seats at the theatre for the Wednesday. Kirsty, who'd been hoping it would be fully booked, agreed to meet him in the foyer at six forty-five, vetoing his suggestion of coming to the house to collect her. He'd also booked an after-show supper at La Table d'Hôte, the town's newest and most talked about restaurant.

'It should be a great evening,' Angie said encouragingly. 'I'll be interested to hear about the Table. If it's as good as people say I'll get Simon to take me on my birthday.'

Simon Lucas was Angie's long-term boyfriend; they'd been together for the past six years but showed no interest in taking their relationship further. He had his own flat at the other side of town and Angie frequently spent the weekends there. A couple of times Kirsty and Lance had made up a foursome with them, but it had not been a success since Lance, introverted and intense, was noticeably irritated by Simon's laid-back manner. Truth to tell, he hadn't liked socializing with any of her friends, preferring to keep her to himself.

On the Wednesday morning a bouquet was delivered to the house, addressed simply to 'Kirsty'. There was no message and no clue as to the sender. Kirsty phoned the florist for more information, but all they could tell her was that they thought a man had ordered it, but they'd been busy at the time and couldn't be sure, and it was paid for by cash so they'd no record of a name.

'I bet it's Nick Shepherd playing silly games,' she said crossly to Angie, who was admiring the sheaf of flowers.

'Well, whoever it is, just be grateful. They're gorgeous, and if you're not going to put them in a vase, I shall. It always annoys me,' she went on, going to the sink, 'in TV plays when a girl receives flowers from someone she doesn't like, she unfailingly throws them in the bin. As if it was the poor flowers' fault! I always hope someone will rescue them.'

'I didn't say I don't like Nick,' Kirsty defended herself, 'and I wasn't going to throw them away, but it really is rather puerile, all this anonymity routine.'

Angie turned in surprise. 'Routine?'

'This and the email.'

'Oh, for goodness' sake – you're not still on about that? It was spam, or a virus or something. Forget it – it's not worth worrying about.'

But Kirsty did worry, and when she met Nick at the theatre she was unable to relax with him, answering his comments only briefly and not initiating any conversation. She sensed his surprise and disappointment, but was incapable of responding. It wasn't until they were seated in a secluded alcove at La Table d'Hôte that, taking the bull by the horns, she met his eyes across the table and said steadily, 'Thank you for the flowers.'

He looked at her blankly. 'Are you being sarcastic?'

She didn't reply, and his face reddened.

'Is this what the cold shoulder is all about?' he demanded. 'Because I didn't send flowers? Is there some code in this town that specifies bouquets must be submitted in advance of a date?'

She flushed in the face of his anger. 'The point is I *did* receive flowers,' she said. 'Are you telling me they weren't from you?'

'That's exactly what I'm telling you, though if they had been, I fail to see why it should merit this treatment.'

She frowned. 'You really didn't send them, though?'

'No, I bloody didn't. I apologize for the oversight.'

Kirsty drew a deep breath. 'Then it's I who owe you an apology.'

'My thoughts exactly!'

'Look, I'm sorry. I've been on edge all week and I've been taking it out on you. I really do apologize.'

He looked at her sceptically. 'So what's it all about?' he asked more calmly.

He deserved an explanation, and reluctantly she gave it. 'Before you phoned last weekend I received a . . . rather odd email. It wasn't signed. Then you rang out of the blue, and I wondered if there was a connection. And this morning these flowers arrived, addressed to me but with no message or any indication who'd sent them. Since it wasn't you, I apologize again, but these two instances coming immediately after you contacted me – well, what else was I to think?'

'Possibly that I'm not the sort of guy who plays tricks?'

'But I don't know you!' she said helplessly.

He relaxed a little. 'No, you don't, do you? Perhaps we should rectify that, so here goes. Name: Nicholas James Shepherd, born twenty-fifth of September nineteen eighty in Surbiton, Surrey, to parents Pamela and Stephen. Two brothers, one sister. Educated at Kingston Grammar School and Durham University, present occupation head of English at Westbourne College.'

Kirsty caught her breath. 'You're at the college?'

'For my sins. Why?'

But she wasn't ready to go into convoluted explanations, and just shook her head.

'Come on, then, your turn!'

She hesitated, then gave him the truncated version. 'Kirsty Ann Marriott, born twenty-second of March, nineteen eighty-five. One brother. Partner in a company supplying handmade cakes to local coffee shops and patisseries.'

'Really? That sounds interesting.'

'Are you ready to order, sir?' asked a slightly reproving voice.

Nick looked up with a quick smile. 'Sorry – too busy talking. Give us a couple of minutes.'

With their order duly placed, he sat back in his chair. 'Glad we sorted that out,' he commented.

'So, to coin a phrase, apart from that, Miss Marriott, how did you enjoy the play?'

Kirsty looked at him for a moment, then burst out laughing.

'Well!' he said in satisfaction. 'That's so much better! Let's start again, shall we?'

'Actually, I did enjoy the play, very much,' she said. 'I was intrigued by the way they managed to introduce mobile phones and not make them seem out of place.'

They settled down to a detailed analysis of the production and progressed to a range of other topics. As she'd recalled from their previous meeting, Nick Shepherd was an interesting companion, with flashes of wit that made her smile, and the evening that had started so disastrously ended in mutual enjoyment. He walked her home through the warm summer streets to her front door, where she thanked him for the evening and he commented that they must do it again. No firm arrangement and no attempt at intimacy.

Kirsty let herself into the house in a thoughtful mood. As she reached the upper landing the bathroom door opened and Angie looked round it, toothbrush in hand.

'Well? How did it go?'

'Very well, after a shaky start. And he wasn't the sender of either the email or the flowers.'

'What did I tell you?' Angie said with satisfaction.

'I almost wish he had been; it would have – neutralized them. Now I'm back to square one.'

Angie made a dismissive gesture with her

toothbrush. 'To change the subject, Chrissie phoned while you were out to invite us to dinner on Saturday. She apologized for the short notice but Matt's only just suggested it. I said I'd have to check with you, but there's nothing in the diary.'

'"Us" to include Simon, I presume?'

'Yes; she asked tactfully if there's anyone you'd like her to invite, and I said I'd check that too.' She raised a questioning eyebrow.

'Definitely not,' Kirsty told her. 'Nick Shepherd, though a nice enough guy, is a long way from being a significant other.'

'*In*significant's good enough for dinner!'

'Still no. The next move, if there is one, should come from him.'

'Whatever you say,' Angie replied peaceably, and went back to brushing her teeth.

'Adam, what's wrong?' Gina asked quietly.

They'd been sitting in his car in complete silence, and her anxiety for him was mounting. 'Having second thoughts about the sabbatical?' she probed when he did not reply.

That at least provoked a response. 'Most certainly not! I'm even more determined.'

She reached for his hand. 'You've been on edge ever since the weekend,' she said. 'Something's happened, hasn't it?'

He glanced at her and sighed. He disliked confidences, particularly in respect of his own affairs, but he needed to get this off his chest and there was no one else to whom he could unburden himself. Gina would at least be discreet, added to which their remaining time together was limited, so there was no risk of her envisaging a deepening of the bond between them.

He came to a decision. 'You could say that; my aunt and uncle broke their long-standing vow of silence and informed me that my parents had not died in a car crash as I'd always been told, but were in fact brutally murdered.'

Gina gasped, her hand tightening on his. 'God, Adam!' Whatever she'd been anticipating, it was not that. 'How *terrible*! But . . . why didn't they tell you before?'

'Good question, and one I can't answer. They were always talking about them when I was younger, waiting for me to ask questions, but I knew all I needed to know – or thought I did – and as far as I was concerned the past was the past. Yet never in all those years was there the slightest hint that they'd been murdered. It seems that for reasons best known to themselves, my aunt and uncle and the relatives who adopted my sister decreed we should be kept in the dark indefinitely. It was only the prospect of my going over there that forced them to come clean, and now that I *am* showing some interest, they hit the roof and try to warn me off.'

'But what actually *happened* – to your parents, I mean? Or don't you want to talk about it?'

He slammed his free hand on the steering wheel. 'Of *course* I do, Gina! I *need* to talk about it, to try to make sense of it.' He drew a deep breath. 'They were battered over the head while the four of us were on holiday, my father out on the driveway, my mother indoors. By the luck of the gods my sister and I weren't harmed, probably because the killers didn't know we were there.' He turned to face her. 'But I'm having to guess that, because d'you know the best bit? *They never caught them!* Can you believe that? The murdering bastards are still strutting about somewhere, happy as Larry and, as far as I can see, no one seems particularly bothered.'

'But surely it must still be on police files?' she stammered. 'As a cold case?'

'Possibly, but I shall be making it bloody hot again, I can tell you.'

Her eyes widened. 'You're not thinking of doing anything yourself?'

'You bet I am! I'm going to stir it up until they'll be forced to make it top priority. What gets me is that the rest of the family has been sitting meekly back for the last twenty-odd years, waiting for a result. Well, I intend to go out and get one.'

'But surely there won't be anything to go on after all this time?'

'I intend to go right back to the beginning, read up the first account of the murders and follow it as far as it goes, in the local press and elsewhere; check, for instance, if they took DNA samples. It was pretty new back then, and I'm not sure how widely it was used.'

'Suppose the killers find out you're on their trail?' Gina faltered.

'I hope they do,' Adam replied grimly. 'It will make them easier to flush out.'

She looked at him despairingly. 'You will be careful, won't you? Not lay yourself open to any danger?'

'People have been "careful", as you put it, for the last twenty-six years, and it's got them precisely nowhere.'

She was silent, going over what he'd said and fearful of the perils he might bring on himself. 'I suppose,' she said finally, 'there's nothing I can say to make you change your mind?'

'Not a thing.' Then, relenting, he squeezed her hand in his. 'Don't worry, honey; I might be determined but I'm not foolhardy. I shan't take unnecessary risks.'

And with that, she had to be content.

Back in his apartment, Adam was gazing out at the heat haze when his phone interrupted his brooding, and he saw that the caller was Charlotte. He sighed, steeling himself for an argument. 'Hi, Charlotte,' he said resignedly.

'Hi yourself. I'm calling to say you're taking me to lunch tomorrow.'

'That's very decent of me.' He paused but she didn't elucidate. 'Will the brat be with you? Screaming infants are detrimental to my digestion.'

'It would be so nice,' Charlotte said tightly, 'if just *occasionally* you thought of someone other than yourself.'

He dropped into an easy chair, leant back and gazed up at the ceiling. 'This exchange doesn't bode well for our tryst.'

'But since you ask, Ben won't be with me, no. So – is it a date?'

'Your wish is my command. Where am I taking you?'

'The Lysander.'

He sighed. 'I was hoping for a pizzeria.'

'Sorry, we're doing this in style. I've booked a table for twelve thirty.'

'Suppose I'd had a previous engagement?'

'You'd have cancelled it,' she said calmly.

'OK, you win. Twelve thirty tomorrow at the Lysander.'

'See you,' she said, and broke the connection.

The Lysander was a small but prestigious hotel in downtown Toronto, a favourite rendezvous with the glitterati but equally popular with businessmen and women who sealed contracts over its tables.

Though suspicious of Charlotte's motives, it suited Adam to be lunching out. Time had lain heavy on his hands since the end of term, and more than once he'd regretted not having started out earlier on his European tour. It was also increasingly difficult to sidestep the invitations issued weekly by Lynne and Harry, but quite simply he did not want to see them. He presumed Charlotte was acting as their emissary.

'Adam!'

He turned as she approached, offering her cool cheek for his kiss. He obliged, and stood back to study her: crisp linen dress, tanned legs, high-heeled sandals – and brown eyes that met his challengingly.

'You're looking good, cousin,' he said.

'You're not so bad yourself, *cousin*.'

He raised an eyebrow. 'Drink in the bar before we go through?'

'Certainly.'

He settled her at a table and went to order their drinks. 'And a Martini soda for my cousin,' she heard him say.

When he returned with the glasses, she said curiously, 'Tell me, why do you always refer to Claire and me as your cousins?'

He glanced at her in surprise. 'Because that's what you are.'

'But we're also adoptive siblings, a much closer relationship. Calling us cousins is like keeping us at arm's length.'

He gave a wry smile. 'I've never analysed it, but I guess you're right. The fact is, Charlotte, I'm the original lone wolf. I've never been close to anyone.'

He saw that he'd shocked her. 'That's just not true!' she protested. 'You're a member of the family – why won't you accept that?'

'Because the family I *really* belonged to fell apart when I was two. Parents killed, sister taken away. And admit it – part of you always resented my being foisted on you. That's why we fought as kids – and often still do!' he added with a smile.

But she didn't return it. 'If I'm in any way responsible for making you feel that, I'll never forgive myself.'

'Oh, hey, let's not get heavy here! We're meeting for lunch, remember, not analysis!'

'But seriously, Adam, is that why you keep Mom and Pop at bay? It really hurts them, you know, and especially now, when you're about to take off for a whole year and you keep putting off going to see them.'

His face had darkened. 'They know the reason for that.'

She leaned forward impulsively, her small hand on his. 'They told us about your parents – what really happened, I mean. I can't begin to imagine how you feel, specially learning about it at this late date, but it really wasn't their fault, surely you see that?'

He withdrew his hand. 'Frankly, no. What the Marriotts chose to do is their business – they're more than three thousand miles away. But that's no reason for Lynne and Harry not to have told me the truth when I was old enough. I'm not sure I can forgive them.'

'"Lynne and Harry,"' she repeated sadly. 'Mom says that even as a toddler you never called them Mommy and Daddy, and I remember you dropping the "uncle and aunt" when you were about fourteen.' She gave a fleeting smile. 'I asked if I could use their first names too and was given very short shrift.'

'That's the reason you're here, isn't it?' he accused. 'To put in a good word for them, persuade me to see them?'

'It's one reason, yes, but I also wanted time with you before you go. Whatever you might say, I think of you as my brother.'

'Oh, Charlie,' he said softly. He tossed back his drink and put his glass firmly on the table. 'All right, I'll see them, but only for your sake.'

'And you won't be all prickly and difficult?'

He raised his eyebrows. '*Moi?*'

Despite herself, she smiled. 'Promise?'

'I promise. Now, can we change the subject and go and find some lunch?'

'Gladly!' she said.

Seven

On the Friday morning a registered packet arrived at the house addressed to Kirsty. It contained a two-pound box of luxury chocolates and a note reading simply, *Sweets for my Sweet.*

'This isn't remotely amusing any more,' she declared. 'In fact, it's becoming rather sinister, and this time I *am* going to throw them in the bin.'

Angie looked up from a tray of flapjacks. 'In case they're laced with cyanide?'

'I know you think I'm overreacting, but I'm not taking any chances.'

'You could pass them on to me,' Angie suggested. 'I'd be happy to risk death by chocolate!'

But Kirsty shook her head. 'You may be, but I'm not going to be responsible.'

'Oh, come on! I wasn't *serious* about the cyanide!'

'Nevertheless,' Kirsty said enigmatically, and returned to her baking.

The word 'gateaux' in their company name was actually more wide-ranging than it implied, since it also encompassed a variety of less exotic fare such as cupcakes, brownies, meringues and so on. Their customers – coffee shops, patisseries and the odd restaurant – were roughly divided between those who ordered weekly and those requiring only a monthly delivery. However, since all their products were routinely frozen to avoid the need for preservatives, the actual cooking schedule didn't vary much. The two large freezers gradually filled with ready-packed cakes until the requisite delivery day, when orders were loaded into the van and driven round the county by one or other of Angie's three brothers, all of whom worked in their father's wholesale business. Fortunately he had no objection to lending a helping hand to his daughter and her partner. The van itself – an expensive though necessary early purchase – was kept in the small yard behind the house, whose existence had been one of its main selling points. The yard provided access to an alleyway used principally by the dustmen, which meant that the van could be loaded directly from the kitchen and driven out via the alley, confining all business activity to the back of the house.

At lunchtime, when they returned to their living quarters for a half-hour break, Kirsty took the opportunity to swallow a couple of headache pills. 'It's been coming on all morning,' she said in response to Angie's raised eyebrow. Partly due, she admitted privately, to increasing anxiety about the unsolicited gifts coming her way.

Angie was on her wavelength. 'Look, if you're really worried about all this, you should tell the police.'

'What could they do, when I've no idea who's sending them?'

'It's harassment, after all, and they should at least know about it.' She hesitated. 'And without wanting to worry you, whoever it is obviously knows your address.'

Kirsty shivered irrepressibly.

'Look, take the afternoon off,' Angie suggested. 'We're ahead of schedule and I can easily cope with what's left.'

'Would you mind?' Kirsty asked gratefully. 'I'm sure a little fresh air would work wonders.'

'Well, it's dry for once so go and relax in the park for an hour or two – it'll do you good. And on your way home, call in at the police station.'

Accordingly, after lunch Kirsty set off on foot for the park in the town centre, a paperback in her handbag.

Lacy Park, referred to in tourist brochures as 'the green heart of Westbourne', was named after Sir George Lacy, a Regency businessman who had founded the town, and was much appreciated by its residents, containing as it did a bowling green, tennis courts, greenhouses of exotic plants and stretching lawns where, in summer, office workers took their lunchtime sandwiches.

Two crescents of handsome Regency buildings curved round the park on either side, housing such institutions as the town hall, banks, Westbourne's premier hotel and the main library. Very few commercial premises were permitted in this enclave, and those that were – an eminent department store, a high-class delicatessen and a coffee house that had been there from the beginning – were unable, even if they wanted, to alter the frontage of their premises – a decree made by Sir George and reiterated some hundred years later by a diligent town council.

At the southern end of the park, in the gap between the crescents, a road led uphill less steeply than its northern counterpart, and it was here, in a commanding position over the town centre, that the buildings and grounds of Westbourne College were situated.

The office workers had departed by the time Kirsty reached the park and it was given over to young mothers with their children, elderly residents on benches and business people hurrying across it from one crescent to the other. She was making for her favourite place, a secluded spot overlooking a fountain, when she rounded a corner and almost collided with a man hurrying from the opposite direction. They had both started to apologize when they broke off in startled recognition, and Kirsty found herself face-to-face with Lance Pemberton for the first time since they'd split up.

'Kirsty,' he acknowledged briefly, and would have continued on his way had she not moved to block his path.

'Lance, this is silly. We live in the same town; we can't go through life ignoring each other. Can't we at least be civilized?'

He met her eyes unwillingly. 'You're not suggesting we kiss and make up?'

'No, I'm not,' she answered steadily. 'I'm suggesting we behave like a couple of adults.' She paused. He was still hesitating, seemingly anxious to escape. 'How are things? How's your mother?'

'Almost back to normal, thanks.' Mrs Pemberton had suffered a heart attack some six months previously. After a moment he added, 'You're looking tired.'

'Well, thanks!' she said with a half-laugh. 'You know how to make a girl feel good!'

He didn't smile and she added, 'Actually, I'm fighting a headache, and at the moment it's winning.'

'Business booming?'

'It's going well, yes, thanks.' She paused, memories of the flowers and chocolates surfacing again. 'You . . . haven't been trying to get in touch with me, have you?'

His face closed. 'I have not. You made it pretty clear that would be unwelcome.' He frowned, searching her averted face. 'Why do you ask?'

'Nothing, it's just—'

'Kirsty, you must have had a reason. What is it?'

'Just that I've received one or two . . . things . . . lately and I don't know who's been sending them.'

'What kind of things?'

'Well, it started with an email—'

'A threatening one?' he broke in sharply.

'No, no. Quite the reverse, actually, but it was unsigned. Then some flowers and chocolates arrived, again with no indication as to who they were from.'

'And you thought I'd sent them?'

She couldn't tell from his tone if he resented the inference. 'Not really, it was just a process of elimination.'

'Well, let me set your mind at rest. I didn't.'

She gave a small smile. 'Unfortunately that *doesn't* set my mind at rest. If you see what I mean.'

There was a pause, then he said, 'Sorry if this

sounds obvious, but have you tried checking with the post office and the florist?'

'Yes, to no avail.'

'Well, you obviously have a secret admirer. Congratulations.' Again the searching look. 'You're worried about it, aren't you? Why?'

'Just that I don't like mysteries.' And there were enough of them in her life at the moment.

'I shouldn't worry; if he doesn't get any reaction, he'll soon tire of it. But if it continues you should go to the police.'

'That's what Angie said. I might drop in on the way home.'

Lance nodded. 'Good idea.' After a pause he said awkwardly, 'I really should be going; I've an appointment at three and I need to prepare for it.'

'Yes. Sorry to have held you up.'

He shook his head, dismissing her apology. 'Good to see you again,' he said gruffly. 'Take care, and don't let this anonymous bastard get you down.'

And he was gone. Slowly, Kirsty walked on down the path. Not Nick, not Lance, and though she'd never seriously considered either of them, it did leave her with no other candidate. Reaching the bench by the fountain she seated herself and sat for a moment staring at the sparkling water; but its brightness hurt her eyes, and with a sigh she put on her sunglasses and settled down to read.

'Well?' Angie demanded, as Kirsty came slowly up the stairs. 'Did you go to the police?'

'Yes, for all the good it did. They suggested I set up a filter system so the emails go directly to Trash, but that wouldn't stop them coming and I'd rather know what he's saying than worry about it. Nor would it work for the deliveries. They asked if there were any CCTV cameras nearby but of course there aren't, so in the end they just took down details and said they'd keep an eye out, and I should let them know if there are any more "instances".'

'Then we'll have to hope there aren't,' Angie said.

Counting the hosts, there were eight at the dinner party, the guests being Lois and Johnnie, at whose wedding Kirsty had met Nick, Angie and Simon and herself. She'd been apprehensive that a blind date might be have been rustled up for her, and was relieved to find Chrissie's elder sister making up the numbers.

Alicia Penn ('"Al-ic-ia", *not* "Aleesha", please!') was a local GP, a tall, striking woman whose sleek red hair was constrained into a chignon and whose green eyes looked out from behind very large spectacles. Neither Kirsty nor Angie had met her before; Chrissie and Matt themselves were relatively recent friends, having moved into the area two years previously as a newly married couple. They'd all met at the tennis club and became casual rather than close friends, and this was the first time Kirsty had been to their home, a modern bungalow just up the hill from Westbourne College.

After a day of threatening clouds, evening

100

sunshine had broken through and on arrival they were shown into the garden. Kirsty, glass in hand, wandered to its lower end and stood looking down on the handsome college buildings and their grounds stretching down the hill.

Chrissie joined her. 'We were crossing our fingers for the weather to hold so we could have drinks out here. Isn't it a lovely view? It was one of the reasons we bought the bungalow. Mind you, it gets a bit rowdy during school break times – we're just thankful their playing fields are out of town! Oh, and talking of the college, someone asked me for your phone number at the wedding – Nick Shepherd. He teaches there. I hope you didn't mind my giving it?'

One mystery solved. Kirsty shook her head and Chrissie asked curiously, 'Did he contact you?'

'He did, yes,' she acknowledged, and was saved from further disclosures by Alicia's approach.

'I hear you run a cake company,' she remarked. 'It sounds intriguing; tell me more. Lois says you were responsible for their wedding cake?'

'And magnificent it was, too!' confirmed Matt, coming up with a jug to refresh their drinks. 'To taste as well as to look at, which isn't always the case!'

'Thank you, kind sir!' Kirsty smiled at him. She didn't know Matt as well as Chrissie since he seldom played tennis, which was their main point of contact. She gathered he was the author of a couple of well-received novels and was beginning to make a name for himself. At any rate, deadlines and research were frequently given as reasons for his absence from social gatherings.

Now, though, he was the perfect host, charming and attentive to his guests, with a personal word to each in turn.

As he and Chrissie moved on, Alicia returned to the subject of the cake business, seeming genuinely interested in the way they operated and prompting with questions whenever Kirsty, feeling she was dominating the conversation, came to a halt.

'Good for you!' she said at last. 'I'm all for women running their own businesses. I'm only sorry you don't supply the general public – I'd certainly boost your sales, given the opportunity!'

Dinner was served in the conservatory – a perfect summer meal of watercress soup followed by salmon and ending with strawberry Pavlova, and talk continued over coffee as beyond the glass walls the sun went down and the lower end of the garden faded into the shadows. Lois and Johnnie told of their adventures on honeymoon in the Seychelles which included several amusing episodes; Simon kept them laughing as he recounted his experiences with a difficult client, and on a more serious note Alicia spoke of a medical conference she'd attended and a series of talks she'd given to local schools.

'In fact,' she ended, 'I've been asked to collate them into a booklet, so Matthew won't be the only author in the family!'

It was eleven thirty before the party broke up and the guests took their leave. Angie was spending the night with Simon so Kirsty drove home alone, very conscious of her single status.

She was also conscious, as she parked in their drive, of the darkness lying thick in the surrounding shrubbery, and it was with relief that she closed and locked the heavy door behind her. Lance's words about her 'admirer' awaiting her reactions had lodged in her mind. Was he, she wondered with a shiver, actually *watching* her, rather than simply teasing from afar? It was an unnerving thought.

Despite his promise, Adam delayed his visit home until the last minute. He'd arranged the letting of his apartment, had farewell drinks with colleagues from school and spent an emotional night with Gina, who suspected – probably correctly – that his departure signalled the end of their relationship. Now his bags were packed and he was more than ready to go. There was this one farewell still to make, and it was potentially the most difficult.

In the event, it was uncannily like a rerun of the christening party. Little had he realized, then, that news of his sabbatical would give rise to such momentous disclosures. And here they all were again – Lynne and Harry, Charlotte and Bruce, Claire and Sandy, Grandma and Grandpa Franklyn, Ed and Nora Carstairs (who, since they weren't his grandparents, he refused to address as such) – all of them trying to act normally, but surreptitiously treating him with kid gloves as though he were a firework that could explode without warning.

As well he might; excitement was building in him, not only at the prospect of the seven-week trip through Europe visiting places he'd only read about, but the return to the country of his birth and to people who were, incredibly enough, related as closely to him as those present today. And underlying it all was his impatience to start working properly on the mystery of his parents' death.

Today's gathering took the form of a family lunch and, glancing round as they sat at table, Adam recalled as a child searching Lynne's face for any resemblance to his father, familiar from the photographs scattered about the house. He had searched in vain, and it was only when, on a visit to the UK, he first met his Franklyn grandparents that he understood why: Lynne had taken after her father, Mark his mother. It was a source of secret satisfaction as he grew older to recognize in the mirror his own likeness to his father – the narrow-shouldered figure of only average height, the deep-set grey eyes, even the way his hair grew.

'So where are you planning to go in Europe?' his grandmother was asking.

'In a nutshell, I'm flying to Oslo and making my way down to Italy and Spain, seeing as much as I can en route, with some places earmarked for a longer visit. But I've no hard and fast plans and can stay for as long or as short a time as I choose, provided I'm back in the UK a week before term starts on the fifth of September.'

Mention of school and the UK fell with the impact of a lead weight. Harry said with assumed casualness, 'Have you been in touch with Janice and Roy, to let them know when you're arriving?'

'No,' Adam answered steadily, crumbling the roll on his side plate. 'I'm not expecting a reception committee. I'll contact them, of course, once I've settled in.' He paused and added deliberately, 'Principally because I'll be wanting to sound them out on their memories of June, 'eighty-six.'

'It will be very distressing for them,' Lynne murmured.

'And for me,' Adam reminded them smoothly, 'but it's a necessary first step.'

'And Kirsty?' Thelma Franklyn asked after a moment.

He shrugged. 'She won't remember any more than I do.' He glanced at their tense faces. 'I might as well tell you that I'm planning to find out as much as possible about the murders during my first weeks in the UK. Then, at half term, I intend to go up to the Lake District and scout around there.'

There was total silence as everyone digested that. He looked round at them challengingly. 'Did any of you go up there at the time?'

'We flew up straight away with your other grandparents,' Bob Franklyn answered quietly. 'To . . . identify Mark and Emma, and to bring you and Kirsty home.'

'Did you go back later?'

Bob shook his head.

'Then what happened to their things? And they must have had a car up there?'

'Graham Yates kindly saw to all that for us.'

Adam seized on the name. 'Yates? My godfather?'

'That's right. He was a close friend of your father's.'

'Then he'll be a useful contact. I must look him up.'

Harry said gently, 'Don't set your hopes too high, Adam. The police have been working on this, off and on, for a long time and not been able to come up with anything.'

'Then they should welcome a fresh pair of eyes, though I doubt they'd see it that way. Fortunately I don't need police cooperation; in fact, I'm probably better without it.'

Charlotte said, 'You won't do anything rash, will you? I want my brother safely back next summer!' Her slight emphasis on the relationship and the smile that accompanied it was a deliberate reminder of their previous conversation.

'I'll take all reasonable precautions,' Adam said, and the tone of his voice indicated that the subject was closed. Accepting it, conversation resumed on less personal topics and it was only as he was leaving that Lynne, clinging to him as she held back tears, again alluded to possible dangers.

'Darling, take care,' she begged. 'If you do find anything new, pass it to the police and don't attempt to follow it up yourself. Promise me that!'

'I promise I'll be careful,' he said, and she had to leave it at that.

Eight

During the week following the dinner party there were no unwelcome deliveries at the house in Springwell Road, and Kirsty was beginning to hope they'd played themselves out. Those hopes were dashed, however, when, ten days after the chocolates, another bouquet arrived – not, this time, delivered by a florist, but found lying on the front step after the doorbell had alerted them.

'All right, all right,' Angie said quickly, 'I'll see to them. A bit much, leaving them out here,' she added. 'The cars are in the drive – he could tell we were in.'

Kirsty thrust the cellophaned sheaf into her hands. 'Do what you like, as long as you keep them out of my sight.' She'd returned to checking orders for the following day when a sharp cry reached her and, hurrying into the kitchen, she found Angie at the sink sucking her fingers, the flowers scattered on the draining board beside her.

'Something *bit* me!' she said indignantly, turning to her friend.

Kirsty looked bewildered. 'Something in the flowers, you mean?'

'Yes. I'd just cut the twine holding them together when I felt this sharp pain.'

'So rather than cyanide in the chocolates, it was a snake in the flowers?'

Despite her discomfort, Angie laughed. 'It would have to be a pretty small one!'

'You didn't just stab yourself on a thorn?'

'No, I didn't.' She picked up a wooden spoon and began carefully separating the stems with the handle. Suddenly she stopped. 'My God!' she said slowly.

'What?'

'It seems impossible, but . . . surely these are stinging nettles? Among the foliage?'

'*What?*' Kirsty hurried over, stared incredulously at the offending leaves then picked up the discarded wrapping. 'Yes, look!' she exclaimed, holding it out for Angie's inspection. 'The pieces of sticky tape are different widths – which must mean the florist wrapped the bouquet, then whoever bought it slit it open and inserted the nettles before resealing it. That's why it was left on the step. Too bad we *haven't* got CCTV.'

Angie glanced back to the blisters rising on her inflamed fingers. 'Well, it's pretty painful, I can tell you, and not a dock leaf in sight! God, I'd like to get hold of this joker and wring his bloody neck!'

'You and me both,' Kirsty said feelingly. 'I'll get the antihistamines. Hold your hand under the cold tap or squirt lemon juice on it. That might help.'

She ran upstairs to retrieve the pills, closing her mind to all but the need to soothe Angie's pain. But as she handed them over with a glass of water, she had to face the fact that the nuisance value of the so-called 'gifts' had escalated, and for the first time there was open malice behind them.

* * *

As it happened, the doctored bouquet heralded an increasingly disturbing week. As instructed, Kirsty informed her contact number at the police station, but the impersonal voice that took her message proved little comfort when, two days later, another email from 'xyz' appeared on her screen. It read: *It's polite to say thank you when you receive gifts. The latest offering was to teach you better manners.*

Angie, hearing her exclamation, reached out and caught her hand as the cursor hovered over the Reply button. 'Don't answer it!' she cautioned urgently. 'Remember what the police said: he's trying to provoke a response – don't let him succeed!'

'I'm just going to tell him to go to hell – that I don't *want* his blasted gifts, so why should I thank him for them?'

'He already knows that. He's just needling you.'

Kirsty looked up at her despairingly. 'But how much of this do I have to take? If he was using my personal address I could change it, but I can't alter the business one – it would cause all kinds of problems. I'm a sitting duck!'

Angie nodded in sympathy. 'At least the police know about it. They'll catch him if he makes a slip, as he's bound to, but in the meantime, love, you've no option but to sit it out.'

The third incident, however, made the others pale into insignificance, and came in two instalments. Over breakfast the following morning they were shocked to hear on the news that a thirty-five-year-old woman had been attacked and raped in Lacy Park the previous evening.

They stared at each other in disbelief.

'*Lacy Park?*' Kirsty repeated incredulously.

'A bit close to home, isn't it?' Angie agreed with a shudder.

'It's . . . appalling! God, think of all the times we go there! It'll never feel the same again!'

Minutes later, predictably, Janice phoned. 'You've heard the news?' she began and, without waiting for confirmation, rushed on. 'In that park just near you! I can't believe it! Is nowhere safe these days? Darling, promise me you won't go there until they catch this man.'

Kirsty rolled her eyes. 'I can't do that,' she said gently. 'For one thing, it's a useful shortcut. Look, I know what's happened is dreadful, but let's keep a sense of proportion. I shan't go after dark, if that makes you feel better.'

'Not much, it doesn't. You've mentioned going there to read, which means finding a quiet spot. I shudder to think what might happen!'

'He's unlikely to attack in broad daylight, Auntie,' Kirsty pointed out, for her own reassurance as much as her aunt's. 'There are always people about then, and anyway, everyone will be on the lookout for him now. He's not likely to go back there.'

'Don't they revisit the scene of the crime?' Janice asked wildly.

'Only murderers, I think.'

'Don't be so flippant, Kirsty – it might *be* murder next time! At least come for lunch on Sunday so we can discuss it sensibly.'

'Auntie, I can't. Really. But don't worry, I promise not to take any risks.'

'Well, don't say I didn't warn you,' Janice snapped. 'And keep a pepper spray or something in your bag.'

Half an hour later, Lance phoned. 'Don't panic,' he began, 'I'm not trying to restart anything. I just wanted to advise you to avoid the park at the moment. Its hazard rating has just soared.'

'Thanks for the warning, but I really don't think—'

'Especially,' he was continuing, 'in view of those unwanted emails and things. You did go to the police, didn't you?'

Kirsty went cold and her mouth suddenly dried. 'I did, yes,' she said after a pause, 'but you surely don't think it's the same man?'

'Not necessarily, but . . . *two* nutters in the area?'

'Well, thanks,' she said bitterly. 'You've made me feel a whole lot better.'

'I'm trying to make you see sense, Kirsty, that's all. Don't go round thinking you're impregnable. No doubt that's what that poor woman thought.'

'OK,' she said with difficulty. 'I'll be careful. Thanks for phoning.' She switched off, a hand going to her throat. There *wasn't* any connection, was there? Surely there couldn't be?

The sense of unease, both general and personal, stayed with her all day, and during their lunch break she stood for some minutes at the window staring down at the park, green and innocent in the fitful sunshine. Angie came up and put a hand on her shoulder.

'Lance is an idiot,' she said bluntly, 'putting such ideas in your head. 'Of *course* there's no connection between what happened down there and your "admirer".'

111

'"Stalker", Angie,' Kirsty corrected aridly. 'No point in avoiding the word; that's what he's become.'

'Well, the police will be joining the dots, in the unlikely event there are any to be joined.'

Slowly the day passed. When he returned the van after the day's deliveries, Toby, Angie's youngest brother, added his own words of caution.

'Don't go out alone after dark, either of you,' he ordered. 'And don't relax and think it's safe if nothing happens for a while. No one's safe until this man is caught.'

'Even more than usual,' Kirsty remarked as they closed the kitchen door firmly behind them. 'Thank God it's Friday!'

It was as they were going upstairs that Angie said suddenly, 'Dammit, I've just remembered! Chrissie wanted the name of the dressmaker who did those alterations for me, and I never got back to her. I'll give her a call now, before I forget.'

'OK, I'll make a start on dinner.' Kirsty went into the kitchen, turned on the radio to catch the latest news bulletin and took two salmon steaks out of the fridge. She surveyed them for a moment, considering what to do with them, then reached for the pot of coriander on the window sill. She had scrubbed new potatoes, washed and chopped the coriander and poured two glasses of end-of-the-week wine before she heard Angie come into the room behind her. 'We're out of green vegetables,' she said without turning. 'I know you don't like carrots with fish, but that's all we've got.'

Angie didn't reply and Kirsty turned to see her leaning against the door frame, her face white.

'Angie – what is it? What's happened?'

'You're not going to believe this,' Angie said, her voice shaking. 'Kirsty, it was Alicia who was attacked last night.'

'No!'

'I could tell from Chrissie's voice that she was upset, and when I asked what was wrong she broke down and blurted it all out. Then she immediately regretted it and spent ages making me promise not to tell anyone, because the . . . victim's identity mustn't be disclosed.'

'But . . . what actually happened? Did she say?'

'Alicia was on her way home from a meeting at the medical centre at about ten o'clock. It wasn't even properly dark, Chrissie said, but he jumped her from behind.'

'So she didn't see his face?'

'No, he was wearing a balaclava and he never said a word, so she didn't hear his voice either. He just . . . dragged her into some bushes.'

Kirsty sat down slowly at the kitchen table. 'He must have been pretty strong – Alicia's tall, and I bet she put up a fight.'

'I suppose he had the advantage of surprise – it all happened so quickly. And when it was . . . over . . . he just sprinted off into the bushes, leaving her lying there.'

Angie came into the room, picked up a glass of wine and took a sip. 'Remember the attack near Bellington station, a month or so ago? It was the same MO, and Chrissie said the police

113

aren't ruling out the possibility of it being the same man.'

Kirsty thought back. Bellington was the stop before Westbourne on the London line. 'The girl who'd just got off the train?'

'Yes; according to the papers other passengers said she'd spent the whole journey on her mobile, talking loudly about some business contract she was negotiating. They think it's likely her attacker was also on the train and followed her when she got off. You know the houses down that road – they all have long front gardens. He dragged her into one of the driveways.'

Kirsty said shakily, 'Moral: don't talk loudly on your mobile!'

Angie smiled fleetingly. 'I know I don't need to say it, but we must keep quiet about Alicia. She's carrying on as usual, and even went into the surgery today, brave soul. Imagine having to face her patients if this became public.'

The news hung over them for the rest of the evening, and although they talked of other things and watched television, they kept coming back to it.

'She's the last person I'd have thought something like this would happen to,' Angie said at one point. 'I mean, she's a bit intimidating, isn't she? So confident and sure of herself.'

'She's probably not all that confident now, poor thing.'

They went to their rooms soon after ten thirty, but Kirsty couldn't settle. The police would have more on their minds now, she thought, than a few unwanted emails and nettles in a bouquet.

Fragments of talk at the dinner party kept coming back to her – Alicia's quick, decisive voice, her succinctly expressed opinions. God, if it could happen to Alicia Penn . . .

She climbed into bed, settled the pillow at her back and picked up her library book, but she couldn't concentrate. The words swam together and she kept rereading the same paragraph. After a while there was a tap at the door and Angie came in bearing two mugs of hot chocolate.

'I saw your light on, and thought you might be having trouble getting to sleep.'

'Thanks. Stay for a minute – push Bear off the chair.'

Angie smiled, depositing the soft toy on the floor. 'If I were you, I'd have him in bed. You need something to cuddle tonight.'

'He was my equivalent of a comfort blanket,' Kirsty admitted. 'My aunt says when I first went to her I screamed every time he was out of sight, and even in my teens he soaked up my tears when I failed an exam or the boy next door didn't phone.'

'I think it's lovely that you still have him. When we moved house all our toys were recycled to charity shops.'

'Well, there were four of you; the combined collection must have taken up a lot of space.'

'All the same, I cried for a week when I found they were gone.' Angie stared into her mug. 'I hope Alicia has some sort of comfort blanket.'

Kirsty smilingly shook her head. 'I rather doubt it, don't you?'

And Angie had to agree.

* * *

115

Angie had offered to cancel her weekend with Simon to keep her company, and although Kirsty insisted she'd be fine, by the time Saturday morning arrived she wasn't looking forward to two days on her own, and was actually reconsidering Janice's invitation when, out of the blue, Nick phoned.

It was over ten days since their evening together, and as the college had now broken up for the summer, she'd concluded, with mixed feelings, that she wouldn't be hearing from him again.

'I'm just back from a week in Ibiza with the lads,' he began breezily. 'A spur-of-the moment decision at the end of term. And as I'm off to Scotland next week to see the parents, I wondered if by any chance you're free this evening? Sorry for the short notice, but as you'll appreciate, life's pretty hectic at the moment.'

Kirsty hesitated. A second date suggested he might be hoping for a deeper understanding between them and, though attracted to him, she wasn't sure she was ready for that. But it was good of him to contact her again after her previous suspicions, and at least she'd have company for the evening.

'I am free, yes, and thank you, that would be good.' She gave an awkward little laugh. 'As it happens, I could do with cheering up at the moment.'

'Oh?'

'You won't have heard, since you've been away, but a woman was attacked in the park this week.'

'*Lacy* Park?' he asked, unconsciously echoing her own surprise.

'Yes; it's shaken us all up a bit.'

'I bet it has. That's terrible. Is she OK?'

'Not dead, anyway,' Kirsty said grimly.

'My God. Well then, let's go out and enjoy ourselves and take your mind off it. Pick you up about seven?'

'That'll be fine,' she said.

He was tanned after his week in the Mediterranean, and Kirsty was surprised at how pleased she was to see him.

'There's a new chef at the Mulberry Tree who's making a name for himself,' he told her. 'I thought we might drive out and give it a try. Pity it's not a better evening – they've a lovely garden there.' Like most of that month, it had been a day of heavy showers.

'It seems to be clearing now,' she said.

In confirmation, the sun broke out as they drove into the countryside, glistening on wet hedgerows and forming prisms on the surface of the road. The Mulberry Tree was a genuine old pub with a thatched roof and blackened beams. It stood in an ideal location on a small rise overlooking a stream, its gardens sloping down to its banks. This evening, though, in the false sunshine, the iron tables bore pools of water, umbrellas drooped and chairs were tipped to allow the rain to run off them.

With no outdoor option, the interior was crowded and noisy with the chatter of its clientele, and they had to queue for some minutes at the bar.

117

'I booked a table in the restaurant,' Nick said, finally moving away with their two glasses. 'I suggest we take these straight in.'

He led her through the jostling crowds to the low-ceilinged room, rustic with dark oak furniture and horse brasses winking on the walls, and they were shown to their table. The conversation level here was at a lower volume, and Kirsty seated herself with a sigh of pleasure, looking around her.

'So,' she said, 'you have the long summer holidays stretching before you, lucky thing!'

'We've earned it, believe me. The last weeks of term were frantic, what with reports to be written and concerts and leaving ceremonies and sports days. There weren't enough hours in the day. Now we need to regain our strength before the next onslaught starts in September.' He took a sip of his drink. 'Actually, next year should be quite interesting; someone I met in Canada is coming to us for a year's sabbatical.'

Kirsty, who'd been reaching for her glass, froze. 'I didn't know you'd been to Canada?' she said carefully.

'Yes, I took a sabbatical there myself a couple of years ago. This guy mentioned he had relatives in Westbourne, though I gathered they weren't close. Seems I must have sold the college to him, though, since he's following me over. He's an interesting chap – a bit introverted, but very brainy and an excellent teacher. His name's—'

'Adam Carstairs,' Kirsty said numbly.

Nick put down his glass and stared at her. 'Now how the *hell* do you know that?'

118

She took a deep breath, but the time for prevarication was over. 'Because he's my brother,' she said.

'Your *brother*?' Nick shook his head in disbelief. 'But how . . . I mean, you've got different surnames.' A quick suspicion. 'You've not been married, have you?'

'No, I haven't been married.'

He sat back in his chair. 'I think you'd better explain,' he said.

'It's a long story, but basically our parents died in a car crash when we were very young and we were adopted by different sides of the family. Adam's were on the point of emigrating to Canada, and took him with them.'

'I see.' He paused, then said awkwardly, 'I hope I wasn't talking out of turn, saying he wasn't close to his family.'

Kirsty smiled fleetingly. 'Actually, that's putting it pretty mildly.'

'Perhaps he's hoping for a reconciliation?'

'I very much doubt it.' Adam, as she well knew, had a totally different agenda.

'Then why come to this neck of the woods when he has the whole world to choose from?'

'Perhaps you sold it to him. He's also planning to research our family history while he's over, and we originated around here.'

Nick was silent for a moment. Then he said curiously, 'So you knew he was coming. When, exactly, were you planning to tell me of the connection?'

She met his eyes challengingly. 'When and if it became necessary. We might never have

119

met again, in which case there was no point in complicating things.'

He held her gaze for several long seconds, and she guessed he was deciding whether to pursue the subject or to let it drop. To her relief, he chose the latter course. 'A sensible precaution,' he said briskly. 'Now, I think it's time we thought about eating.'

For the rest of the evening they avoided personal topics and Kirsty realized, a little sadly, that the constraints of their first evening were back in place. When he dropped her back at the house he left her with a quick kiss on the cheek, and she doubted if she'd hear from him again.

'Damn!' Nick said softly to himself as he drove away. This was a complication he could do without. Adam would be part of his personal as well as his professional life for the next nine months, as unmarried members of staff tended to live together in Staff House. It was therefore doubly important that nothing should sour their relationship.

As for Kirsty, he was undeniably attracted to her, had found himself often thinking about her, and been looking forward to seeing her again. But it hadn't been plain sailing on either occasion and he couldn't really get a handle on her. She'd begun by suspecting him of anonymously pestering her, and although he'd been able to put that behind him, she'd closed up again this evening when speaking about Adam. Admittedly she hadn't known they'd already met, but he'd told her that first evening that he taught at the college; surely it would have been natural to mention the imminent arrival of her brother, even if they were estranged? The reason she'd given for not doing so didn't entirely ring true, and he had the feeling there was a great deal she wasn't telling him – which, he admitted, was her right. As she'd pointed out, she barely knew him. Nor he, her. And she could undoubtedly be prickly when the mood took her.

All in all, he concluded, drawing into his designated parking place in the college grounds, it might be prudent not to let the relationship develop any further until he saw how the land lay with Adam. A pity, but there it was.

Nine

Kirsty and Angie took their annual holiday each year at the beginning of August. It was a slack time anyway, and a frenzied stint of baking during July ensured that those customers who needed to could stock their freezers.

For the last five or six years – since before the company started – Kirsty and a group of old school friends, now scattered round the UK, had come together in some exotic location to enjoy relaxation and good food. Husbands and boyfriends were firmly excluded, a rule Lance had bitterly resented. At least this year she wouldn't have his sulks to contend with. Nor, she reflected a little ruefully, anyone else's.

There'd been no word from Nick, but she'd not expected one. Admittedly he'd now be in Scotland, but even on his return she doubted if he'd contact her. With hindsight, she could understand his grievance; on hearing his connection with the college, it would have been only natural to have mentioned her brother. He wasn't to know of the sinister background they shared that lay behind her reluctance to speak of him.

Towards the end of July, the weather that had been so dreary for the last couple of months began to brighten and the sunshine, combined with the absence of any further threats or deliveries, lifted Kirsty's spirits, though she still found herself hurrying when she crossed the park and, as she'd promised Janice, she hadn't ventured there after dark. Nor, despite the sunshine, did she take her book, so she was at home one Saturday when Angie returned unexpectedly.

'What are you doing here?' she asked in surprise. 'I thought you'd be enjoying a pub lunch somewhere.'

Angie didn't meet her eyes. 'We've had a row,' she said, dropping her overnight bag in the doorway.

Kirsty raised her eyebrows. 'You and Simon? But you *never* have rows!'

'Not in public, perhaps.'

'You're saying you do? Not serious ones, though? Simon's so laid back; I can't imagine him losing his temper.'

'He doesn't often,' Angie replied, 'but when he does, fireworks fly, believe me.'

'Come and sit down and tell me about it.' She took two glasses from the cupboard and a bottle of Frascati from the fridge, and carried them into the sitting room. Angie followed her in silence, settled on the sofa and tucked her feet beneath her.

'It was about where to go on holiday, of all things,' she said, accepting the glass Kirsty handed her. 'What with one thing and another, we're late booking it this year.'

Unlike Kirsty and her friends, Angie and Simon, claiming superiority, habitually backpacked wherever the fancy took them.

'We'd been discussing it last weekend,' she continued. 'I suggested Greece – we've never been there – but Simon wanted to go back to Austria. I don't see the point of revisiting when there are so many places we've not been to, and last time we were there we spent a lot of time in bierkellers, which he enjoys but aren't my scene. Anyway, we argued a bit but didn't reach any decision. Then, this morning, he calmly announced he'd booked our flight to Innsbruck. I was . . . thunderstruck. I said I'd *told* him I didn't want to go to Austria, and he suddenly let fly, accused me of never considering anyone but myself and being too independent for my own good.'

'Wow!'

Angie sipped her wine pensively. 'I think a bit of jealousy comes into it; he knows our business is going well and at the moment he's struggling. People are thinking twice about spending money on home improvements in the present climate. Anyway, he made some acid comment about women bosses and I accused him of being sexist, and then we both said things we'll probably regret.'

'Oh, Angie, I'm so sorry,' Kirsty said quietly. 'It'll work out, though, won't it? It always has before?'

'Only if I climb down, and this time I'm not going to – I'm quite determined on that. It ended with him saying he'd go by himself, and me saying I didn't envy him the company.'

'You'd be welcome to join us in Barbados,' Kirsty said after a minute. 'I'm sure you could get a late booking.'

'That's sweet of you, but no. You all know each other from way back – I'd be the odd one out.'

124

'Then what will you do? Stay here and brave Olympics fever?'

'Mum and Dad are going to the caravan in Cornwall. I'll probably join them. At least the weather's improving.'

'I still can't get over Simon having a temper,' Kirsty said wonderingly. 'It seems so unlike him.'

Angie pulled a face. 'It's the quiet ones you have to watch,' she said.

That night, as Kirsty was settling to sleep, the conversation came back to her, and with it her surprise that Simon, outwardly so laid back, seemed to resent women bosses and had accused Angie of being too independent. It struck an unwelcome chord with their earlier discussion about the girl on the train, who'd bragged about a contract she was negotiating. No doubt he'd have resented her, too.

Kirsty turned suddenly, grabbed a handful of pillow and pulled it under her chin. *Don't even go there!* she ordered herself and, closing her eyes, willed sleep to come.

It was two days later that, discovering her library book was overdue, Kirsty slipped out in her lunch break to return it, to be met by notices advertising a talk by 'well-known local author, Matthew Armstrong'.

'Has Chrissie been on to you?' enquired a voice behind her, and she turned to see Lois clasping one of his books. 'She practically press-ganged Johnnie and me into going.'

'I haven't heard from her, no. Actually, I've

not read any of his, and live in fear of being found out! What are they like?'

'A bit noir for me, though Johnnie quite enjoys them. He says at least they're well written. This is to coincide with publication of his latest, and there's wine and nibbles laid on. Do come and keep us company.'

Kirsty glanced back at the notice. 'Thursday evening; I'll check the diary and see if we can make it.'

'Odd that Chrissie didn't phone us,' she commented, having reported back to Angie.

'She's probably avoiding us because she let slip about Alicia.'

'Well, what do you think? Shall we go?'

'I suppose we should do the decent thing, but I've not read his books either.'

'No doubt there'll be a pile for sale, even in the library!' Kirsty rejoined.

When they arrived there was a daunting number of chairs set out and only about a dozen occupied, though admittedly it was still fifteen minutes before the talk was due to start. As Kirsty had prophesied, a pile of new books lay on a side table and Matt himself was engaged in conversation with the librarian.

Chrissie caught sight of them, hesitated a moment, then came over. 'Thanks for coming,' she said. 'I hope to goodness more people turn up.'

'They're sure to,' Angie said soothingly.

Alicia's shadow lay heavily between them and, after checking they couldn't be overheard,

Chrissie said quickly, 'Thanks for being so understanding about . . . everything.'

'How is she?' Angie asked in an equally low tone.

'Pretending it never happened.'

'No nearer finding whoever was responsible?'

She shook her head and the conversation ended with the arrival of Lois and Johnnie. Several more people drifted in, and by the time the librarian stepped forward to begin proceedings about half the chairs had been filled, quite a few by personal friends.

Matt, however, gave no sign of disappointment and launched with practised ease into a witty and erudite talk that delighted his admittedly small audience. It was followed by some interested questions, a vote of thanks and a discreet reminder that he would be delighted to sign copies of his latest book.

'We're a captive audience,' Lois whispered in tones of mock doom. 'There's no escape!'

Accordingly they joined the short queue and Matt inscribed personal messages in each copy. Library staff were circulating with trays of canapés and glasses of wine, and when the queue for books dried up, Matt mingled with various groups of his friends.

'Well done, mate!' Johnnie said, clapping him on the shoulder as he reached their circle. 'That was first rate. I always wondered how writers set pen to paper – or should I say finger to computer?'

'We all have different methods,' Matt said with a smile. 'I can only describe how I go about it.'

'Must be great to be creative,' Johnnie continued. 'You with your writing and Kirsty and Angie with their cakes!'

Angie smiled. 'Our "creations" are much more ephemeral, though. Here today, gone down someone's throat tomorrow!'

'But, we hope, giving pleasure on the way down!' Kirsty added with a laugh.

'Unlike my books?' Matt asked with raised eyebrow.

'That's not what I meant at all!' she protested.

He laughed, laying a light hand on her arm. 'Relax, Kirsty, I was teasing. Anyway, I don't expect my books to give pleasure *per se*. Excitement and trepidation are what I'm aiming for.'

'And that's what they deliver,' Johnnie confirmed on cue.

Matt glanced at the copies under everyone's arms. 'Well, enjoy them, whatever emotion they arouse,' he said smoothly and, as Chrissie called his name, moved away.

On the Saturday, since the stand-off between Angie and Simon was holding, she and Kirsty spent most of the day watching the Olympics on television. But when the coverage ended at ten o'clock and the news came on, their precarious world was again shaken.

The body of a policewoman had been discovered in an alleyway in Bellington, and there were indications it was an attempted rape gone wrong. Police were considering the possibility that it was the same perpetrator who was behind the recent attacks in Bellington and Westbourne. A photograph of the victim, PC Megan Taylor, appeared on the screen – a smiling girl in her mid-twenties, and distressed family and friends spoke of her generosity and readiness to help people.

'At least that will step up enquiries,' Angie remarked as their initial shock subsided. 'When one of their own is harmed the police really swing into action.'

'That settles it, though,' Kirsty said. 'With a murderer on the loose, there's no question of your staying here alone while I'm away.' She flicked her friend a glance. 'You'd be much safer, you know, with a strong man around.'

'I have three brothers,' Angie pointed out.

'But not here.'

Angie smiled. 'If that's your way of suggesting I get in touch with Simon, the answer is no way.'

As it happened, though, Simon himself made the first move, arriving at the house the next morning as they were finishing a lazy Sunday breakfast.

It was Kirsty who answered the door and she stared at him in surprise, unsure how to greet him.

He met her eyes steadily. 'I'd like to speak to Angie, please. If she'll see me.'

Kirsty stood to one side. 'Come and wait in the office while I go and check.'

She opened the door on the right and showed him in, closing it behind him before returning upstairs.

'If that was the paper boy wanting his money,' Angie said, licking marmalade off her fingers, 'I left it on the hall shelf. Did you find it?'

129

'It's Simon,' Kirsty said baldly. 'He's in the office, waiting to hear whether or not you'll see him.'

Angie's head reared up. 'Simon's *here*?'

'Yep.'

'I'm not giving in about Austria.'

'Then go and tell him.'

She rose slowly to her feet and left the room. Kirsty began to clear the table and load the dishwasher, hoping they'd manage to make up without either of them losing face. Despite learning of Simon's temper outbursts, she was fond of him and he and Angie were so much a pair in her mind that she had difficulty separating them.

It was twenty minutes before Angie returned, and a glance at her face showed Kirsty all had gone well.

'He apologized,' she said, 'and so did I. I just came to tell you I'll be out for the rest of the day. He's waiting for me downstairs.'

'Fine. And where are you going on holiday?'

A smile spread over Angie's face. 'Greece,' she said.

They were both due to leave the following Saturday and, during that week, with all the extra baking and freezing done and deliveries made, the workload diminished and they were able to spend time making last-minute preparations. Kirsty emailed the five friends she'd rendezvous with at Heathrow and went for dinner with Janice and Roy, who were now even more concerned for her safety.

'Thank goodness you'll be away from it all for the next two weeks,' Janice exclaimed. 'Perhaps

130

by the time you come back they'll have caught him.'

'And also by the time you come back,' Roy added, 'Adam's arrival will be imminent. It'll be interesting to see how long it takes him to make the first move.'

'We'll have to invite him for a meal,' Janice said. 'Your grandmother's anxious to see him so she can talk some sense into him.'

Kirsty looked surprised. 'What kind of sense?'

Janice bit her lip. 'We weren't going to tell you, but Harry says he intends to look into your parents' deaths, for God's sake!'

Kirsty stared at her. 'But . . . how?'

Janice shuddered. 'God knows.'

'How do you feel about that?' Roy asked quietly.

Kirsty considered. 'I'm not sure; I have to admit I'd like to get to the bottom of it.'

'It's a shame we had to tell you the truth,' Janice declared. 'You were much better off believing it was an accident.'

'But it can't be put back into the bottle, Auntie,' Kirsty said gently. 'We know now, and I suppose,' she added apologetically, 'we have to make our own decisions.'

'You're not saying you'll help him?' Janice demanded incredulously.

'I'm not saying anything. Let's just wait and see what happens.'

On the drive home she reflected on the conversation, and how Adam's arrival might impinge on any future relationship between herself and Nick. As Janice had said, it was good that she

131

was getting right away from all the doubts and troubles of the last month or so; ever since she'd learned the truth about her parents things had started to go wrong: strange emails, unwanted deliveries, and on a less personal front, thank God, rape and murder. The break couldn't come soon enough.

It was after eleven when she reached home, and Angie had gone to bed. Kirsty poured herself a glass of water and, since she'd been out for some time, checked her emails for any urgent messages.

There was only one. It read: *Watch your step, my lovely. Gateaux aren't the only things to die for.*

Ten

Adam looked out of the plane window as the fields and woods of England slipped past beneath him; it was still, despite industrialization, a green and pleasant land. It had been a momentous year for this country of his birth – the Queen's Diamond Jubilee, the London Olympics, and the wettest summer on record. He'd missed it all and now the end of August had belatedly settled into a series of warm, golden days to welcome him home.

Home, he thought, trying out the word. For though he'd lived in Canada for over twenty years, his roots were undeniably here, and it was here, somewhere, that the mystery of his parents' deaths lay buried. As they began the descent to Heathrow, he vowed that by the time he crossed the Atlantic again, it would be a mystery no more.

Two hours later, having collected the hire car he'd booked in advance, he was on the M3 bound for Hampshire and Westbourne College, excitement mounting in him. The last seven weeks touring Europe had been exhilarating, exhausting and packed with interest. Now, however, tired of his own company, he was looking forward to meeting the people who would figure in his life for the next year or so, and to renewing his friendship with Nick Shepherd.

He'd also be expected to contact the family in the near future, as Charlotte had stressed in her latest text. Indeed, until he met them he'd be unable to decide on his first steps in tracking down the events of that long-ago summer. And Kirsty: what of that prim, stand-offish girl he'd last seen fifteen years ago? Where was she now? And would she be any help in his investigations, or side firmly with the family in trying to dissuade him from them?

He reached Westbourne in the late afternoon, down the vertiginously steep hill that led to the town centre and, having traversed it, up the gentler gradient where the side entrance to the college was located.

The iron gates, he saw, were electronically controlled. Adam leaned out of the car window and pressed the button set into the intercom on the adjacent wall, stating his name and business to the disembodied voice that responded. The gates swung ponderously open and he drove through to be confronted with a signpost, one arm pointing to the staff car park, the other that for visitors. Alongside them a notice board reinforced the verbal request he'd received to report to the porter's lodge on arrival.

Turning left as directed, Adam wound his way behind some buildings to the appropriate car park, where a space had been reserved for him. Then, having extracted his bag from the boot, he retraced his steps and went to register his arrival.

'Mr Carstairs, yes, sir.' The porter ticked him off on his list and handed over a set of keys. 'This one's for the college building, sir, in case you need to be there after hours. The other two are the outer door to Staff House and your own room. You're in number twenty-six, on the first floor. Now, sir, if you'll come outside with me, I'll point you in the right direction.'

He emerged from behind his counter and together they walked a short distance to the corner of a building, round which a vista opened up before them. Immediately ahead lay a large expanse of grass and trees criss-crossed by a series of paths. To the right, at the lower end of the enclave, sprawled the college itself, and encircling the grounds on the remaining three sides were the boarding houses, making the layout a perhaps conscious replica of the town itself.

The porter indicated one of the buildings in the semicircle ahead of them.

'That's Staff House, sir, the middle one. You mightn't find anyone at home, though. Several gentlemen haven't arrived yet, and those that came earlier went out again.'

'No matter,' Adam replied, 'it'll give me a chance to settle in. Has my trunk arrived?' It had been sent direct from Toronto, all he had with him being what he'd needed in Europe.

'In your room, sir,' he was assured. 'Once you've unpacked, just ring and someone will come and remove it for you.' The sound of a buzzer signalled another arrival awaiting admittance and, excusing himself, the porter hurried back on duty while Adam paused a moment longer to take stock of his surroundings.

Admittedly the college itself faced outwards and he was presented with its rear aspect, but in this Georgian town it was a disappointingly ungainly building, to which, he'd read in the brochure, the rapidly growing school had moved at the end of the nineteenth century. The boarding houses, on the other hand, though presumably not Georgian, were at least in the Georgian style and more in keeping with their location. In the late-August sunshine an air of tranquillity lay over the scene; no doubt the following week when the boys returned it would be decidedly less peaceful.

Adam picked up his bag and followed one of the pathways to Staff House, pleased to find his room was at the front of the building overlooking the grass expanse. As promised, his trunk stood in one corner and on the table was a bottle of wine with a scrawled note.

Welcome to the UK! Suggest we have dinner à deux so we can catch up on news. Will be in touch. Nick.

By the time Nick knocked on his door a couple of hours later, Adam had emptied the trunk and had it removed to storage until needed. Already the room was personalized, with familiar objects about him and his books on the shelves.

'Good to see you, Nick!' he exclaimed. 'And many thanks for the wine. Shall I open it?'

'No, save it for later. I thought we'd go down to the Regency to eat; it's one of the better pubs and they do good food.'

'Sounds great. It seems a long time since my plastic lunch on the plane.'

'Then let's go. There's a dining hall here, of

136

course,' he added as they went downstairs, 'but we're not all back yet, and it doesn't really kick in till term gets under way. In any case, I thought I could fill you in with what you need to know and answer any questions before you meet the rest of the guys.'

'All guys?' Adam asked with a smile.

Nick laughed. 'Afraid so; there aren't many females on the staff, and those who are, are married. This is singleton territory, and we're all male. As, of course, are the pupils; we've not succumbed to admitting girls yet.'

They walked across the grass, through a side gate operated by a keypad and down the hill to the town centre. The Regency pub was situated at the end of the road and boasted a paved area at the back where, on this summer evening, its customers were enjoying a drink or a meal.

'How was Europe?' Nick asked as they settled at their table.

'Brilliant; I can't imagine why I've left it so long. After all, I've been around quite a bit – Australia, South America, the Far East and so on, but this was a serious omission. Still, I've made a start now, and I'm intending to go back as often as I can while I'm over here.'

'Excellent.' Nick leaned back with his glass of beer. 'So what have you been up to since we last met?' Despite their best intentions, their contact had lapsed until Adam wrote of his impending arrival.

'Nothing spectacular,' Adam replied. 'And before I forget, several people sent their salaams, including Paul and Steve.'

137

'I must email them,' Nick said. He grinned. 'So you're not married yet?'

'I am not.'

'What about that girl who was always hanging around? Gina, was it?'

'Still hanging,' Adam replied.

Nick laughed. 'Hard-hearted bastard! How does she feel about you being away for a year?'

'Not best pleased but there are no commitments, and to be frank I'm hoping it will die a natural death while I'm away.' He drank some beer. 'How about you? Any wedding bells on the horizon?'

Nick unaccountably sobered, meeting Adam's questioning glance. 'No, nothing like that, but there *is* something I should tell you.'

'Well? Get on with it, then!'

'I've . . . been seeing your sister,' he said.

Adam put down his glass. 'You've *what*?'

'Kirsty. I'd no idea you were connected – how could I have? Different surnames and so on, but—'

'When you say *seeing* her . . .?'

'We've been out a couple of times, that's all.'

'She lives locally, then?'

'Yes, just minutes away. Up one of the roads at the far end of the park.'

Just minutes away. Adam had a long drink, his thoughts whirling. 'Well,' he said steadily, 'as far as I'm aware, it's not a capital offence.'

'It's embarrassing, nonetheless, considering the two of you aren't exactly on the best of terms.'

'She told you that?'

'She hinted at it, but you told me in Toronto that your branch of the family are estranged from

138

the English side. I don't remember any mention of a sister, though.'

'What's she like?' Adam asked curiously. 'I've not seen her for fifteen years.'

Nick hesitated. 'Attractive, clever, *complicated.*'

'Complicated?'

'Charming one minute, prickly the next.'

'Ah! Perhaps we've something in common, after all!'

Nick smiled briefly. 'I'm not sure I'll be seeing her again.'

'Don't stop on my account. I'll be seeing her myself soon.'

'So you *are* going to make contact?'

'Of course. It's not a daggers-drawn vendetta, you know.'

'Actually, Adam, I *don't* know. Neither of you has been forthcoming on that point.' He smiled crookedly. 'I did suggest you might be hoping for a reconciliation, but she seemed to think that unlikely.'

Adam raised an eyebrow. 'What else did she say?'

'That you were intending to research the family.'

'Did she happen to explain why the Atlantic Ocean lies between us?'

'Your parents died when you were young. You were adopted by different sides of the family, and yours emigrated to Canada.'

'That's all?'

Nick frowned. 'Yes. Why, is there more?'

'Oh, a whole heap more, but it'll keep.' He paused. 'You like her, though? Kirsty? Even though she can be prickly?'

'Yes, I like her, but I've not been in touch since I learned you're her brother. Not only for that reason,' he added as Adam started to protest. 'I've been in Scotland for the last month or so, first with my parents, then walking in the Highlands with an old school pal.'

'Nonetheless, it's something else she can blame me for,' Adam said resignedly.

'I doubt if she cares.'

'Like me to find out?'

'No, I should not!'

Adam held up a palm. 'OK, OK, I only asked! Anyway, enough navel-gazing. Tell me more about the rules and regs of Westbourne College.'

And as their plates were set before them, Nick thankfully complied.

Adam waited a couple of days before phoning the Marriotts, setting himself out to be charming – the best way, he reckoned, to get the information he required.

'Oh, Adam.' It was Janice who answered, her voice slightly strained. 'We were wondering when we'd hear from you. When did you arrive?'

'Wednesday afternoon. I've been acclimatizing myself with the town, which, of course, I don't remember at all.'

'Did you enjoy your trip to Europe?' She was walking on eggshells, Adam thought.

'Very much, thanks. Ridiculous to have reached this age without ever setting foot there, but I made up for lost time.'

'I'm sure you did.' A pause. 'And when are we going to see you?'

140

He took a deep breath. 'Well, I was wondering if you and your husband would have dinner with me? I hear there are some good restaurants in Westbourne.'

'That's kind, but it would be much better if you came to us. For one thing, my mother is very anxious to see you, and of course Kirsty will be here.'

Bingo! 'I don't want to put you to any trouble.'

'It will be a pleasure. How about this weekend? Sunday lunch?'

The traditional family get-together, he thought sourly. 'Thank you, I'd enjoy that.'

'Shall I get Roy to email you directions?'

'Don't worry – the car has sat nav and I know your post code. I'll find you all right.'

'Till Sunday, then.'

'Till Sunday,' he repeated. *Fait accompli*. It would be interesting to see what developed.

He had dressed with care for the occasion, opting for a cream shirt, cream linen jacket and light blue trousers and tie. The pale colours accentuated his dark hair and the tan acquired on his travels, and he hoped they'd give a good first impression.

As he drew up at the gate he saw that two other cars were already parked there. Belonging to neighbours, or members of his family? The gathering of the clans, he thought, and most probably all arrayed against him.

Janice opened the front door as he reached it and for a moment hesitated, as though unsure how to greet him. He stepped forward quickly to kiss her cheek and she gave him a nervous smile.

'Adam – how good to see you after all this time! Do come in.'

And he was suddenly in the midst of them – Grandma Louise, as thin and chic as he remembered, though there was more silver than blonde in her hair; Roy, blustering in his initial embarrassment, and Kirsty: Kirsty, who was the biggest surprise of all, though Nick's description should have prepared him. His own height, she had stood back as the others hurried to greet him, her grey eyes guarded, but as he moved forward to kiss her, the spicy tang of her scent tickling his nostrils, he admitted to himself with grim irony that she was exactly the kind of girl who most appealed to him.

'God, you're like Mark!' Roy exclaimed involuntarily, then flushed. No doubt he'd been primed not to mention his parents. Louise, however, smoothed over the gaffe.

'Roy, get this young man a drink while I quiz him about Florence.' Her ice-blue eyes met Adam's. 'You did get to Florence, I trust? It was where your grandfather and I spent our honeymoon.'

'Certainly, it was on my list of places not to be missed.'

The initial awkwardness overcome, everyone relaxed, though Adam noted that Kirsty remained at the far side of the room. Complicated, Nick had called her; he could believe that.

Talk settled into an easy rhythm – questions on the European holiday, enquiries after the family in Canada and a reprise of the successful

Olympic Games. More immediately, he learned of Kirsty's home-made cake company, that Roy had had a hip replacement, and – to his considerable surprise – that there'd been a series of attacks in the area, one of which took place in Lacy Park just opposite the college. It seemed that Westbourne wasn't the placid and elegant place he'd supposed. At one point he intercepted a 'so far, so good' look passing between Janice and Roy, and smiled to himself. They needn't think they'd escape so easily.

Lunch was roast chicken with all the trimmings followed by apple pie and cream, and it was as they were sitting over coffee that Adam said casually, 'By the way, I'd be grateful if you could give me Graham Yates's address; there are some points I think he could help me with.'

There was instant silence while everyone avoided each other's eyes. 'He's my godfather,' Adam added blandly. 'He sent cheques on my birthday till I was eighteen, but I've since lost his address and forgot to ask Lynne before I left.'

Roy cleared his throat. 'Yes, of course. I'm sure we must have it somewhere. I'll find it for you.'

'You're not in touch with him, then?'

'No; he was your father's friend rather than ours.'

'Which, of course, is why I want to see him.'

Louise laid down her coffee cup with a little click. 'Adam, I know you must have a lot of questions, but I do hope you're not going ahead with this foolish idea of looking into your parents' deaths.'

Here we go. 'Sorry, Grandma, but I'm afraid I am. It seems no one else has.'

143

Janice said on a high note, 'That's not fair! The police did all they could, and opening it all up again would be . . . quite unbearable.'

Out of the corner of his eye, Adam saw Kirsty lay a quick hand over her aunt's. Closing ranks, he thought.

'There's no need for any of you to get involved,' he said quietly, 'though of course I was hoping for a little cooperation.'

'Nothing you do will bring them back,' Janice said unsteadily. 'If you want to research the family history, by all means go ahead. You might find something interesting. But please, please let your parents rest in peace.'

Despite himself, Adam felt his anger rising. 'You really think they can, when their killers are still at large?'

'They probably died long since,' Roy said.

Louise leaned across the table. 'Adam, you and Kirsty were too young to be much affected by the trauma. I have always thanked God for that. But for the rest of us life was a living hell from which it took a long time to emerge. Please don't plunge us back into it.'

There was another silence, measured in heartbeats. Then Adam said evenly, 'Very well. I shan't abuse your hospitality by mentioning it again, but for my own part, I must be free to proceed as I think fit.' He looked at Kirsty, who was watching him intently. 'As must Kirsty,' he added.

Everyone instinctively turned to her, but she simply looked down, shaking her head. Not much help there, seemingly.

Somehow the conversation teetered back to

normal, but Adam felt he'd outstayed his welcome. Soon afterwards he made his excuses and, having issued an invitation for everyone to join him soon for a meal in Westbourne, he took his leave, imagining the collective sigh of relief as the front door closed behind him.

That evening, having obtained her mobile number from Nick, Adam phoned Kirsty, hearing her intake of breath as he identified himself.

'Have I been blacklisted?' he asked with grim humour.

'Of course not.'

'I meant what I said, you know.'

'I don't doubt it.'

'I have to know, Kirsty. Are you with me in this, or not?'

She hesitated. 'It's different for me, Adam; in a sense I've been closer to it than you have. I can't just . . . turn against them.'

'God forbid! That's the last thing I'd ask you to do!'

'But going along with you and your enquiries . . . I don't know . . .'

'We didn't get much chance to talk, did we? I rather think you saw to that. I know we didn't like each other as kids, but can't we move on, especially in view of what we've just learnt? We can't just ignore this . . . elephant in the room. At the very least we need to talk it through and see where we both stand.' He paused. 'Do you know where Graham Yates lives?'

'I'm afraid not. I don't think I've ever met him.'

'I've probably burned my bridges as far as Roy's concerned.'

'No,' she contradicted, 'if he said he'd get it for you, he will.'

'In the meantime, will you meet me for a drink? No one need ever know,' he added sardonically.

That stung her. 'You might not think it, Adam, but I am my own person and I make my own decisions.'

'Sorry,' he said meekly. 'So . . . will you?'

A brief hesitation, then, 'All right.'

'I'm not well up in local rendezvous; can you suggest somewhere?'

'There's the Orange Grove, about ten minutes out of town on the Bellington road.'

'I'll find it. Tomorrow, about seven thirty?'

'I'll be there,' she said, and rang off.

Adam drew a deep breath. The game, he thought whimsically, is afoot.

Eleven

It was a cloudy, humid evening as Adam drove out on the Bellington road. It was not a route he knew – but then, as he reminded himself, he didn't know any of the neighbourhoods surrounding Westbourne. He'd have to acquaint himself with them, though, because high on his list of priorities was a drive out to the house where he was born and the district that'd been familiar to his parents – though on reflection it would probably have changed beyond recognition in the intervening years. Come to that, his old home might not even still exist. The possibility of its demolition disturbed him, as though some vital piece of the jigsaw might be missing.

Meantime, the meeting ahead of him was, he knew, crucially important. The success of his investigations might be determined by whether or not he and Kirsty could establish some sort of alliance, and he'd spent the day veering between being impatient to meet her and half-dreading the prospect. Would they even like each other? They hadn't in the past. Would she continue to resist him? If so, how could he win her round?

The sign for the Orange Grove came up ahead of him, and he turned into its car park and switched off the engine. The garden behind the building was full of people sitting at small tables, but he couldn't see his sister. He made his way into the pub and looked about him. Still no sign, but he was five minutes early.

He ordered himself a beer and went to sit at a vacant table near the window. It was marginally cooler in here, and he hoped she'd agree to remain inside. Then, suddenly, she was there, cool-looking in a lemon dress. He stood as she came towards him but made no move to kiss her, sensing the gesture would be uncomfortable for both of them.

'Are you happy to stay inside or would you prefer the garden?' he asked, pausing before pulling out her chair.

'In here, I think. It's very humid out there.'

'What can I get you, then?'

'A spritzer, please.'

He had to queue at the bar, mentally rehearsing how best to bring up the subject that had brought them here. Then he was being served and time had run out. On his way back to the table an odd fact struck him: this was the first time he'd deliberately set out to win someone round – make them like him. Previously he'd not cared one way or the other; the realization that this time he did came as a slight shock.

They lifted their glasses to each other, uncertain what they were toasting, and Adam sat back, taking stock of the sleek dark hair, the steady grey eyes, the challenging lift to her chin. This sister of his would not be a walkover.

'So,' he began. 'It might sound like a cliché, but how has life treated you? Would you say you've been happy?'

Her mouth twitched. 'You get straight to the point, don't you?'

'Had we been a normal family, I wouldn't need to ask; as we're not, I'm interested to know. Have you? Or were you always aware something was missing?'

Kirsty took a sip of her drink, her eyes on the bubbles in her glass. 'I've never analysed it, but yes, I've been happy – there's no reason why I shouldn't have been. I never knew Mum and Dad, so I couldn't grieve for them. I do remember, at primary school, feeling badly done by that I couldn't produce parents on Sports Day like everyone else, and had to make do with an uncle and aunt. But that was only in passing. How about you?'

He was silent for a moment. Then he said simply, 'I've never felt I belonged anywhere.'

'Oh, Adam!' The exclamation seemed startled out of her. 'Surely the family—'

'Did all they could? Of course they did. They couldn't have shown me more love and support, but I was incapable of responding. Despite all their efforts, I always felt an outsider.'

'That's sad,' she said quietly.

'I suppose it is, but I've always been self-sufficient. I didn't mind being a loner.'

'So if I'd asked you the same question, you'd have said you've been happy?'

'Contented would be nearer the mark. I was bright, and that was my escape route; I could spend evenings alone in my room under the pretext of studying. Sometimes I was, sometimes I wasn't.'

'But you must have had friends outside the family? At school, for instance?'

'There were guys I hung around with, sure, but if I'd never seen any of them again it wouldn't have bothered me.'

'And you think it's all down to what happened when you were two years old?'

'Who knows? It could be, or it could be that I was just born what our American cousins call ornery.'

'You didn't make much effort to be liked, did you?' she asked, unconsciously echoing his own reflection. 'I have to say that when you came over I thought you were a total waste of space!'

'And I thought you were a stuck-up little prig!'

They held each other's eyes for a minute, then both laughed.

'You've improved with keeping, though,' he added.

'Oh my God, was that a compliment?'

'The closest you're likely to get from me.' He paused. 'I hear you know Nick Shepherd.'

'Ah!'

'Which translates as what?'

'That I know him, yes. As he has clearly told you.'

'I asked him what you were like, and he said you were attractive, clever and complicated.'

'Did he now? He could be right about complicated, at least.'

'OK, there are no doubt issues between you and I'm not going into them, even if you'd allow me to. What concerns me now is how you feel about the task I've set myself. You were ambivalent on the phone.'

150

'I still am. If I helped you reopen the case, I'd be causing my aunt considerable distress.'

'But she must want to know who was responsible?'

Kirsty said slowly, 'She's never got over it. Every anniversary we go to the cemetery and it never fails to break her heart. I've always wondered why it was still so raw after all this time – people are killed in car crashes every day, and somehow their relatives come to terms with it. It was only this year, when I learnt the truth, that I understood.' She looked up, finding his eyes intent on her face. 'What exactly are you planning to do?'

'I've already accessed the archives of the weekly paper up there, the *Hawkston Gazette*, and read reports of the case and the inquest and various comments made at the time. For instance, the milkman who found them, one Fred Harris, is quoted as saying "How could that nice young couple, who've only been here a few days, deserve this?" It brings it home, doesn't it?'

She nodded soberly.

'In fact,' he continued, 'I went through all the editions from April to August of that year, making a note of everything that happened locally. Most of it was routine stuff – silver weddings and school prize-givings, a firm in financial difficulties, a drowning accident and so on. There might be some buried clue that's been overlooked, but there's no way of spotting it without speaking to the actual people concerned wherever possible. Which is why . . .' He paused, gauging her reaction to what he was about to say. 'I intend to go up to Penthwaite

151

at half term and scout around myself. How do you feel about coming with me?'

Her eyes widened. 'Me? What good would that do?'

'Nick said you're clever, remember, and two pairs of ears and eyes are better than one. Well?'

'For heaven's sake, Adam, I can't give you an immediate answer! I'll have to think about it.'

'Fair enough, though I'd like to feel you're with me on this. Kirsty, we're the only people who can do it. Even if they wanted to, the others are too emotionally involved to be objective. And let's face it, we were the two most affected, even if we weren't aware of it.' He drained his beer. 'Did you tell them we were meeting?'

'I haven't done, no.'

'Will you?'

'Of course, next time I speak to them. I'm not going to make an issue of it.'

He nodded. 'Incidentally, have you ever been back to the house we lived in?'

She shook her head. 'I asked to see it once, when I was six or seven, but my uncle said it would hurt Auntie Jan, and that the house we lived in now was my home.'

'Graham Yates lives in the same area,' Adam mused. 'You were right about Roy, by the way; he called this morning with his contact details. I might do a detour on my way to visit him – always supposing he's around and can see me. I've never met him, but he did his godfatherly duty until I turned eighteen.' Adam paused. 'He was the one that went up afterwards, collected their personal effects and drove their car home.'

'God, I didn't know that.'

He stood up abruptly. 'I'm going for another beer; can I get you anything?'

'No, thanks, this is fine.'

She watched him cross to the bar, a slight figure in his open-neck shirt. This was the first time she'd been alone with him, and she needed time to consider if and how much her opinion of him had changed. They weren't kindred spirits, that was clear, but she was surprised to sense vulnerability beneath the self-confident, offhand manner.

'I presume we were told the same thing,' Adam said without preamble as he rejoined her. 'They were bashed over the head for no reason, discovered by the milkman, camera missing?'

'Put a little more sensitively, but yes.'

'Nothing else that might be relevant?'

'I don't think so. Our grandparents flew up to . . . identify the bodies and bring us back.'

'They didn't speak to anyone else up there, apart from officials?'

'Who, for instance?'

'*I* don't know!' he said impatiently. 'Anyone from the village? I don't think they even *went* there. Everything seemed to have been handled in the town.'

'They'd have been too distressed to linger, and concentrating on getting us home as soon as possible.'

Adam was silent, swirling the beer in his glass. 'I might put a notice in the *Gazette*'s personal column, to pave the way for us.'

'Us?' she queried with a wry smile.

'I always think positively. Something on the lines of *Information sought concerning the murders of Mark and Emma Franklyn in Penthwaite, June 1986. Confidentiality guaranteed.* And a box number.'

'You'd probably need to offer a reward, and you'd get all sorts of crank replies.' She was, she felt, an unwilling expert on cranks.

'I could sort the wheat from the chaff. It would be a starting point, at least – I'll give it some thought.' He straightened his shoulders. 'Still, we've talked it into the ground for now, so let's change the subject. Tell me about this business you run.'

So they talked on less serious matters for another half hour before she glanced at her watch and said she must go.

'I should have suggested driving out together,' Adam apologized. 'It never occurred to me; proof of my innate selfishness.'

They walked out to the car park, the air still heavy and oppressive. 'Let me know how you get on with Graham,' Kirsty said.

'Ah, so you *are* interested!'

'Of course I'm *interested*, dammit. I'm just not sure what could be gained by stirring things up.'

'Well, I'd be glad to have you on board, but with or without you, I'm going ahead. And the first thing will be to call him as soon as I get back. I've three more days before school starts, and I intend to make the most of them.'

'Graham Yates?'
'Speaking.'

'This is Adam Carstairs.' There was an uncertain pause, and he added, 'Franklyn, that was.'

'My God, *Adam*! This is a surprise! Where are you?'

'In Westbourne. My aunt didn't tell you I was coming over?'

'No, we only exchange Christmas cards. But . . . are you on holiday?'

'No, I'm taking a year's sabbatical at the college.'

'I heard you'd gone into teaching, but here in Westbourne? Well, well!'

'I was wondering if we could meet.'

'Of course! I'd be delighted, and so would my wife.'

'I should warn you that I'll be looking into my parents' deaths while I'm over, and would welcome anything you can tell me.'

A pause, then: 'I see. Are you sure that's wise?'

'Wise or not, I intend to do it.'

'Then of course I'll help you all I can,' Graham said slowly. 'How about coming out and having a meal with us? I'll be most interested to hear how you're getting on.'

'Thank you. That would be great.'

'Just a moment, I'll check with Sue.' A hand was put over the phone, muffling the conversation taking place, then he came back on the line. 'Sue reminds me I've a PCC meeting tomorrow evening. How would Wednesday suit you?'

Which meant kicking his heels for an extra day, but there was no help for it. 'Thank you, that would be fine.'

'About seven thirty, then? You know where we are?'

155

'I have sat nav, thanks.'

'Good. See you then.'

Whether he'd expected any flicker of recognition when he saw his old home, Adam could not be sure, but he didn't experience one. His main feeling was relief that it was still where it had always been and appeared to be occupied by a family, since there was a child's trike in the garden and a man washing his car in the driveway.

Had his father stood on the same spot to wash *his*, before setting off on his ill-fated holiday? He looked up at the frontage. There were three windows on the first floor, two presumably being the main bedrooms, and a little room over the porch. Perhaps that had been his. For several minutes he concentrated on trying to remember, but to no avail. This pleasant semi-detached house gave no hint of its tragic history, and that was as it should be.

The car-washer turned to look at him enquiringly, and with an apologetic wave Adam drove on.

Graham and Sue Yates lived just ten minutes away, in a similar style of house. It had, however, been modernized with double-glazed picture windows and sun panels on the roof, which in Adam's view did nothing to improve its appearance.

As he was locking the car Graham came striding down the path, his hand outstretched. He was a tall man with a high-domed forehead surrounded by curling black hair; his eyes were large and brown and, Adam thought inconsequentially, cow-like in their liquidity.

156

'Adam! How very good it is to see you! Come inside!'

His hand was clasped in a strong grip, Graham's spare arm going round his shoulders. Sue was waiting in the hall to welcome him, a small woman with short fair hair and glasses, whose face lit up as she smiled, reaching to kiss his cheek.

'My goodness, you're like your father! I suppose you get tired of people telling you that!'

'Really, darling,' Graham reproved gently, 'next you'll be telling him that he's grown!'

Sue laughed good-naturedly. 'Now, I know you two want a chat, so off you go to the sitting room. Dinner won't be ready till eight, so you've plenty of time.'

They moved obediently through the indicated doorway and Graham waved towards an easy chair. 'Beer? Wine? Whisky?'

'Beer will be fine, thanks.'

Graham absented himself, returning with two glass tankards, and handed one to Adam. 'Now, you've some questions, you said. Fire away, and I'll do my best to answer them.'

'I'd like you to tell me everything you can about my father,' Adam said.

'He was my closest friend. We met at uni, were each other's best man, and then he and Emma asked me to be your godfather. Unfortunately we were never in a position to return the honour.' He had a drink of beer. 'I've been a pretty mediocre one, I'm afraid. I'd have liked to do a lot more, for Mark's sake, but you were so far away and I didn't want to tread on Harry's toes.'

'The cheques were much appreciated.'

Graham shrugged dismissively. 'What else can I tell you? We shared the same hobby – photography – and used to vie with each other in competitions. In fact, we were about to enter one when . . . he was killed.'

'And his camera went missing?'

'Yes, the entire bag.'

'What would have been in it?'

'Well, the camera itself, of course. Otherwise, mainly filters and lenses – wide-angle, zoom and so on. Expensive equipment, all told.'

'You think that was the reason for the theft?'

'Quite frankly, Adam, I don't know what to think. I do know he'd been intending to take a selection of photos while he was away, with the competition in mind, and it's odd there was no evidence of this – no used cassettes or anything in the cottage, though possibly they were in the bag too.'

'I know you went up to collect their stuff; did you go to the village? Penthwaite?'

'No, everything had been taken to the police station in Hawkston.'

'I find it strange that none of the family went.'

'Surely it would have been too painful, and not served any useful purpose.'

'Well, I'm going up myself at half term, to have a dig around.'

Graham looked startled. 'You said you wanted to look into it, but I didn't realize you meant to be quite so hands-on.'

'I read the local archives on what happened in and around Penthwaite that summer. There

are one or two things that could do with following up.'

'You do realize that if the killers are still
around, you could be making yourself a target?'

'Fine, if that means flushing them out of the
woodwork.'

Graham was silent for a while, staring down
at the clasped hands between his knees. Then,
reaching a decision, he looked up. 'In that case,
I have something to show you. I'd decided
against it, on the grounds that it doesn't take
things much further and might be distressing,
but if you're really set on this path and nothing
I can say will dissuade you, it's only right you
should see it.'

He stood up, walked over to a cabinet and took
out a video cassette. 'A few years ago there was a
series of programmes on TV examining what
are known as cold cases – you probably have
something similar over there.'

Adam had stiffened, his eyes fixed on Graham.

'The Lakeland Murders, as they were called,
were featured in one of the programmes.' Graham
glanced at him briefly. 'It might be worth saying
that the journalist carrying out this research had
considerably better facilities than you're likely
to have, yet he didn't get anywhere. I doubt if
you'll have better luck.' He gave Adam a crooked
smile. 'After all of which, I presume you'd like
to see it?'

'Most definitely,' Adam said inadequately.
Graham switched on the player under the TV
and inserted the cassette.

For the next half hour Adam sat mesmerized

as places whose existence he'd only learned of in the past few months materialized before him – the village of Penthwaite with its winding main street, the cottage where they'd all been staying – now with a garage that, they were told, wasn't there in the eighties, the village green across the road from the post office. He was even more interested in the interviews with the villagers, many of whom had been there at the time – the milkman, whose comment he had quoted to Kirsty, the woman who had kept the village shop; and he caught his breath at the inclusion of a clip from an old *Crimewatch*, broadcast only weeks after the murders, in which actors played the parts of his parents walking through the village pushing a buggy, with a child masquerading as himself trotting alongside.

Lost in the past, it took him a minute to readjust when the programme came to an end and Sue put her head round the door to announce that dinner was ready.

'That was . . . mind-blowing,' he said. 'May I borrow it, to show Kirsty?'

Graham brightened. 'You're in touch with her? I'd hoped to see more of her while she was growing up, but I'd the feeling her relatives wouldn't welcome it. Janice in particular was very posses-sive of her.'

'I've seen her twice,' Adam said. 'Once at a family lunch, and once over a drink to discuss my plans.'

'And is she in favour?'

'Not really, but I'm sure I can win her round.'

'Well, take the video by all means. In fact, keep

160

it. It might help to jog memories while you're up there.'

'That's very kind of you – thanks.'

The subject dropped as they went through for dinner, and Adam resigned himself to answering all their questions about his life in Canada. They asked kindly after the family – 'Such pretty little girls!' Sue said – and whether Lynne's parents had settled happily out there.

'It was the best thing for them,' Graham commented, 'with both Mark and Lynne gone.'

But though Adam kept the conversation going, he was on autopilot, longing to be alone to weigh up what he'd learned and to sift through it for anything concrete that might help him. And now, damn it, with term starting tomorrow and weekends not giving sufficient time, he must control his impatience until the end of October – an aeon away. It would not be an easy task.

Twelve

Flashback: June, 1986

Tony Vine was tired and frustrated as he drove home from work in the Cumbrian town of Hawkston.

When he'd joined Ferris Engineering six years ago, the sky had seemed the limit. He was bursting with ideas which, in his position as Development Manager, he was anxious to put into effect, certain he could boost production by a significant amount. But from the first day he'd been thwarted; the Ferris brothers, having inherited the firm on their father's death, were determined to follow rigidly in his footsteps and resented any implication that things could be done better.

Tony had watched with dismay as business slowed, profits diminished, and more go-ahead rivals overtook them. Several times he had broached suggestions that would improve turnover, only to be ignored. But he'd continued to turn his ideas over in his mind until they coalesced in the form of a machine that he knew without doubt was the answer to their production problems.

Eager and excited, he'd approached his bosses; but on hearing it would require a capital outlay of several thousand, Barry, the elder brother, had refused even to discuss it.

'With business in the state it is, we can't afford to invest a substantial sum in a contraption that mightn't even work,' he'd said. 'Sorry, Tony – in happier times we might have given it a go, but not in the present climate.'

'It's because it can *change* the present climate that now is exactly the right time!' Tony had argued, but Barry had shaken his head.

'And I don't want you wasting any time on it during working hours, either,' he added. 'We have to keep our heads down and concentrate on doing what we do best, and eventually the tide will turn.'

Well, Tony thought now, he *hadn't* 'wasted' as much as a minute of the firm's time. Instead he'd worked long hours in the evenings and weekends, jiggling and tweaking at his invention until it evolved into exactly what he'd envisaged. And now that he had his prototype, the idea that had been forming almost below the level of consciousness had swum to the surface. It was time to make a break and set up on his own.

All he had to do now was write out the specification of his invention for submission to the Patent Office. And when it was accepted – as he was confident it would be – he and Marilyn would move south and he'd start his own business. An elderly aunt had died the previous year, leaving him her modest savings and her house in Surrey, which would make an admirable base for the new venture. All that remained, in due course, would be to hand in his notice and, of course, break the news to his wife.

He hadn't confided in her earlier because, bless

163

her heart, she was totally incapable of keeping a secret and he didn't want his plans known before he was ready. In any case, she'd told him often enough that she'd follow him to the ends of the earth, as long as there was somewhere she could go shopping.

Tony smiled, remembering. He loved her dearly, but he'd known from the first that she'd little interest in the work that paid for their comfortable lifestyle. On the rare occasions he *had* tried to discuss it, she'd laughed and said, 'Sweetie, you know I haven't a head for business!' and promptly change the subject. Very different from Vivien Ferris, whose sharp mind and astute brain were such a help to Barry.

Still, Tony thought, his heart lifting as he turned into his drive, he wouldn't swap his pretty, dippy wife for a hundred Viviens. And, switching off the engine, he went in to greet her.

Vivien Ferris turned into the gateway of the unimposing little semi on the edge of a housing estate and switched off the ignition. For several minutes she sat unmoving, her hands in her lap, too dispirited to go in.

She *hated* it, she thought passionately; hated its smug complacency, its metal-framed windows and nineteen-thirties pebbledash, the small, sad square of grass that comprised its front garden. And that was just the outside!

The last year had been a nightmare as things at the family firm spiralled steadily downhill. They'd exhausted their overdraft with the bank, and although Barry had kept it from her, Vivien

164

knew that other loans applied for had also been turned down. Thank God her job at least was holding up, but her salary alone couldn't finance their lifestyle and they'd been forced not only to sell their home but to remove their daughter from her private school. She still burned with the humiliation of it.

Yet far more important was the effect it was having on Barry. Night after night she'd hear him slip out of bed to go to sit at the kitchen table, endlessly going over figures and specifications, a glass of whisky beside him. Living on his nerves and drinking too much, his personality was noticeably changing as he became more irritable and more aggressive, flying into a rage for no reason. It broke her heart to see Daphne cowering away from him, though he'd never touched her in anger and, she was certain, never would.

Apart from the overriding worry of finances, there was the awkwardness with Tony Vine, the Development Manager. Vivien liked Tony and his empty-headed little wife, and more than once had suggested he be made a partner, but Barry and Dean clung stubbornly to their father's maxim: that all partners in the firm should be Ferrises.

Some months previously, Tony had come up with an idea that he insisted would revolutionize production. The drawback was that it would require a capital outlay, on the grounds of which Barry had refused even to consider it. She'd tried to persuade him at least to listen to the proposition but he'd become even more adamant, possibly because he feared Tony was brighter than either himself or Dean, and resented the fact. And so what might have been a viable and much-needed solution had fallen by the wayside, leaving them to sink still lower.

'Mummy!' twelve-year-old Daphne called from the front door. 'Are you going to sit out there all night?'

Recalled to the present, Vivien picked up her briefcase and, with a sigh, went to join her.

It had become a tradition for staff members to meet in the pub after work on Fridays. Numbers attending varied from two or three to a dozen or more depending on circumstances, but the Ferris brothers made a point of being there – mainly, Tony suspected, to demonstrate their accessibility to their workers. He'd been about to set off for home when Dean hijacked him into joining them, and as it happened they were the only three that week.

'Sorry we couldn't run with that idea of yours, Tony,' Dean said unexpectedly, as they settled at a corner table, 'but I'm sure you appreciate we have to keep our eye on the ball and can't go chasing after every fanciful notion someone gets into their head.'

It was a red rag just when he least needed it, and before he could stop himself he retorted, 'Except that *my* "fanciful notion" actually works!'

Dean smiled dismissively. 'Sadly, without testing it we'll never know.'

He should have left it there – of course he should – but that damn pride of his reared up before he could stop it. 'Ah, but you see, it *has* been tested!' he told them and, seeing he had their attention, recklessly continued. 'When you wouldn't consider it I cashed in my savings and I've been slaving every night and weekend for the past six months. And when it was finally finished and I ran it, it worked like a dream. It'll literally halve production time – and this is just the prototype.'

Too late, he'd realized what he'd done. *God*, he could have bitten his tongue out! He'd blown it, when he'd only had to keep quiet for another week or two, and all would have progressed as planned.

They were both staring at him, unsure whether or not to believe him. 'Well,' Barry said at last, 'that's great, Tony.'

Crunch time, then. No point now in beating about the bush. 'The specification's ready for the Patent Office, and once it's been accepted—'

'We can put it to use?' Dean's voice rose in sudden hope.

Tony shook his head. 'Sorry, boys. I hadn't meant to come out with it now, but I'll be handing in my notice. I'm planning to move to Surrey to avoid conflict of interest, and start my own business there.'

A long silence, during which he'd measured his heartbeats. Then Barry said slowly, 'Aren't you forgetting something? Since you developed the process while working for Ferrises, any patent will by law belong to us, with you named as inventor.'

'Actually, no, I've checked. That would apply only if the invention had been made during what are referred to as "specifically assigned employment duties". And, of course, you expressly forbade that. Not a second of the time I spent on the machine was during working hours.'

Barry took a long, slow drink of beer, his eyes never leaving Tony's face. Then he wiped his mouth on the back of his hand. 'Look, there's no need to be hasty, I'm sure we can talk this through.'

But he didn't trust himself to stay any longer. 'Sorry,' he told them pleasantly, 'it's too late for that. Now if you'll excuse me, I must be going. Marilyn will be waiting.'

And he made his escape.

The Ferris brothers watched Tony Vine shoulder his way through the crowded pub towards the door.

'Do you believe him?' Dean asked anxiously.

Barry's hand was shaking as he lifted his tankard. 'I wish to God I didn't, but I rather think I do.'

'So what now?'

'Well, if he really *has* invented this miracle machine, and it really does work, it could completely turn the tide for us.'

'Except that we won't have it.'

'We *have* to have it!' Barry said savagely. 'Do you think I'm going to let him waltz off and make his fortune elsewhere, while we continue to stew in our own juices?'

'I don't see how we can stop him. Anyway, as we said all along, we haven't the funds—'

'If this machine is even half as good as he says

– and knowing Tony, I'm willing to bet it is – the banks will be falling over themselves to lend us the wherewithal, knowing we'll soon be rolling in the stuff. God, Dean, we have to talk him round. Offer him a rise, a partnership, anything he bloody wants!'

'We should have listened to him before,' Dean said miserably.

'Hindsight is a great thing. Look, get some more beer; we've some urgent planning to do.'

When Dean returned with two brimming glasses, Barry put his elbows on the table and leaned forward. 'Point one: *we have to talk him out of leaving!* Whatever it takes! I accept he's pissed off that we wouldn't let him fly with this, but basically he's a reasonable chap. He's always been conscientious and I'm sure he has the good of the firm at heart.'

'We should have given him his due long since,' Dean said.

'Well, we can make up for it now, but we have to act quickly. He's about to send off his application.'

'What difference does that make?'

'Ideally we want the name on it changing, but if he won't buy that, we need at least some reference to our right in it.'

'But we haven't any,' Dean said baldly.

Barry swept that aside. 'What would be the best approach? It'll have to be over the weekend; time is of the essence, and it's better discussed away from the office. I reckon we should drop in unannounced, though; don't want to give him time to think up excuses.'

'Suppose he's not home?'

'We'll ring first to check, hang up if he answers. What have you got on tomorrow?'

'Same as you,' Dean returned, lifting his glass. 'A command performance at the Penthwaite fête.'

'Bloody hell, I'd forgotten that. Can't we get out of it?'

Dean shook his head. 'Not a chance. Les Phillips is the organizer and I don't need to remind you he's one of our biggest customers. What's more, he thinks he's doing us an honour, getting me to open and close the show, and you to present the prizes. In case you haven't seen them, the posters refer to us as "local dignitaries".'

'It'll have to be Sunday then, but there's no way we can get out of golf. As far as Ted and Larry are concerned the weekly game's written in stone. We'll just have to pray Tony doesn't post the thing tomorrow.' He paused. 'In the meantime, the fewer people who know about this the better, so don't go pouring it all out to Pauline. I'm not even going to tell Viv. She's been on at me to give Tony more recognition, and she'd only say "I told you so". Any shop talk at the fête is strictly taboo, OK?'

'OK,' Dean agreed. 'But roll on Sunday. I'm not going to get much sleep till this is settled one way or the other.'

'There's only one way it *can* be settled,' Barry said grimly, 'and that's getting Tony back on board.'

It was too bad this wasn't Dean's weekend to have the boys, Vivien thought, watching a couple

170

of little boys screaming in delight as their faces were painted – though doubtless Pauline, his current girlfriend, wouldn't agree. Vivien had noted her sulky expression whenever the boys were mentioned, and her extra possessiveness in their presence.

Looking at the young woman now, she hoped the relationship wasn't serious. Dean and Cindy had been divorced barely eighteen months and the atmosphere between them was still fraught. The last thing Hal and Josh needed was any tension on the weekends they saw their father.

Come to that, she thought suddenly, perhaps it was as well, even discounting Pauline, that they weren't here, because there was an atmosphere between Dean and Barry that she was having trouble analysing. At first, she assumed they'd had one of their periodic disagreements, usually caused by Dean rebelling against one of Barry's diktats. But it wasn't animosity she detected, more a tightly coiled control, as though each of them was keeping himself on a tight rein. Before they'd left home, Barry had had one of his increasingly frequent outbursts, swearing loudly and sweeping papers off the table simply because a form he'd expected in the post hadn't arrived. Veins had stood out on his forehead, raising her concern for his blood pressure. She really must find some way of calming him down.

'Mummy!' Daphne was tugging at her hand. 'Can I go on the Dodgems? Daddy says he hasn't any change.'

'How wise of him!' Vivien responded, opening her handbag. 'Come straight back here when it's

171

finished.' She watched her daughter skip off, then went to join the others at a rickety metal table in a roped-off area selling refreshments. Pauline, she saw, was looking bored.

'How long do we have to stay?' she asked, twirling a strand of hair round her fingers – a habit Vivien felt she should have long outgrown.

'Till the bitter end, my love,' Dean replied. 'Having opened the show, I have to be here to close it.'

'And when will that be?'

'Five thirty, I think.'

'What time is it now?'

'Ten past three. Almost time for Barry to present the prizes.'

Pauline sighed gustily as Barry returned with a tray bearing cups of tea and a glass of lemonade.

'Where's Daphne?' he asked, setting them out on the table.

'On the Dodgems. I told her to come straight back.'

'Are you watching the time?' Dean enquired. 'Don't forget the prize-giving's at three thirty.'

'God, yes! I'd better get this down quickly; it'll take time to work my way through this mob.'

'We can see the dais from here,' Vivien commented, 'so we might as well stay put and avoid the crush, and you can come back and join us afterwards.'

'Mind your genial smile doesn't slip!' Dean said, and Barry shot him an enigmatic look that Vivien couldn't interpret.

'Every child's favourite uncle, me!' he said.

Daphne, flushed and excited, rejoined them,

172

dropping on to the chair beside her mother and reaching for the lemonade. 'That was great!' she exclaimed. 'I bumped *twelve cars*!'

'Remind me not to go driving with you!' her father said and, finishing his cup of tea, got to his feet. 'See you in a bit.'

Minutes later the music over the loudspeakers ceased and a man appeared on the dais, microphone in hand. 'Ladies and gentlemen, boys and girls,' he began in the sudden hush. 'The time has come for the prize-giving, and we're lucky enough to have Mr Barry Ferris, a well-known local businessman, to present them for us. So will the winners of the egg and spoon races please come up, and we'll start with the under sixes.'

A sudden roar of laughter brought Vivien to her feet in time to see a toddler, who had climbed the steps and was reaching for one of the prizes, being reclaimed by his father as Barry looked on, his indignant yells silenced as the quick-thinking announcer produced an opportune lollipop.

She sat down again, smiling.

'What was that all about?' Dean asked.

'An attempt to snaffle one of the prizes!'

The next fifteen minutes or so saw a succession of children climb the steps to claim their rewards, to accompanying applause from the crowd. Pauline, quickly bored, dragged her chair closer to Dean and laid her head on his shoulder and, after a minute, looking slightly embarrassed, he put an arm round her. Vivien hoped sincerely they weren't about to embark on a kissing spree; she disliked public displays of affection, particularly in front of Daphne.

173

'Anyone like another cup of tea?' she asked brightly.

'All I'd like is to go home!' Pauline muttered.

'Oh, for God's sake!'

To Vivien's amazement, Pauline's shock and Daphne's open-mouthed surprise, the usually placid Dean withdrew him arm and pushed her head off his shoulder.

'All you've done ever since we arrived is moan! If you're so all-fired bored, then *go* home! We'll be better off without you!'

People at the surrounding tables, who had paused at the sound of his raised voice, hurriedly resumed their conversations. Pauline was gazing at him with tear-filled eyes and trembling lips but, his face closed and angry, he studiously avoided looking at her.

After what seemed an age, Vivien said, 'Well, *I'd* like another cup, and I'm sure Barry would, without having to rush this one; he'll probably be back by the time I've queued for it. More lemonade, Daphne?'

Daphne, still staring at her uncle in disbelief, nodded, and Vivien, despising her cowardice but feeling it was best to let them sort it out themselves, made her way to the stall dispensing beverages and joined the end of the queue. What was *wrong* with the men today? She'd never heard Dean snap like that before. She could almost feel sorry for Pauline, even though she wholeheartedly endorsed his sentiments.

What, if anything, had happened in her absence she didn't know, but as she'd predicted, she arrived back at the table at the same time as

Barry. During his account of the prize-giving and comments on some of the recipients the atmosphere gradually teetered back to normal, though Pauline remained subdued for the rest of the afternoon.

As they made their way back to their reserved parking places, the two men fell behind.

'Regarding tomorrow,' Barry said in a low voice, 'we'll aim to be back in the pavilion by one thirty, but there's no saying we'll make it. Even if we do, by the time we've had showers and a bar lunch we'll be lucky to get away by three. It's a bloody nuisance but there's nothing we can do about it.' He glanced sideways at his brother. 'Not arranged to see Pauline, have you?'

Though Pauline had been angling to move in with Dean, he had not so far succumbed.

'Not on your life – I've had enough of her today! She's done nothing but moan.'

'Well, well! Thorns in the bed of roses?'

Dean hunched his shoulders and didn't reply. They had reached their cars by now and the women stood waiting for them.

'I'll pick you up at nine thirty, as usual,' Barry said, taking out his keys and, nodding to Pauline, he opened the car door for Vivien.

'Why was Uncle Dean cross with Pauline?' Daphne asked as they made their way out of the crowded car park.

Barry flicked a glance at Vivien, eyebrow raised.

She ignored it. 'Because she kept grumbling,' she replied.

'But Uncle Dean's never cross.'

175

'Unlike your bad-tempered father?' Barry demanded, only half-joking, and wasn't sure whether to be hurt or relieved when his daughter didn't reply.

On the outskirts of Hawkston, Tony Vine watched the grey light filter through the curtains, his thoughts as heavy and dismal as the day. He'd lain awake most of the night, his mind endlessly circling Friday's conversation in the pub. Why, oh why hadn't he held his tongue, instead of blurting everything out before he was ready?

Unable to lie still any longer, he inched his way to the edge of the bed and swung his feet to the floor, holding down the duvet lest the sudden draught disturb Marilyn. She didn't stir. Her gold hair was spread over the pillow, her face as unlined as a child's. Ten years his junior, he reflected she could as easily have been twenty.

God, if only he could talk things over with her! He didn't want his last weeks at Ferrises to be marred by bad feeling, nor to be perpetually bombarded with questions about his invention, so it was essential to work out his best strategy before going to work tomorrow. And since he'd get no help from his wife, he needed time alone to think things through.

With a sigh he retrieved his dressing gown from the chair and, shrugging into it, tiptoed downstairs for a mug of coffee.

An hour or so later, showered and dressed, he set the breakfast tray down on the dressing table and went to draw back the curtains, noting the purple

176

clouds massing over the hill. Behind him, Marilyn gave a squeak of protest and pulled the duvet over her head.

He turned back into the room. 'Breakfast is served, *modom*,' he said.

She re-emerged, hair ruffled, blinking in the sudden light. 'Oh, sweetie, how lovely!' Struggling into a sitting position, she took the lace shawl he passed her and slipped it round her shoulders.

'Tea, toast and a lightly boiled egg,' he said.

'Perfect.' She looked up at him, suddenly suspicious. 'What brought this on? You're not trying to get round me, are you?'

He laughed, pouring the tea. 'Am I that transparent?'

'Well, are you?'

'Guilty as charged, my love. There's a problem at work that's bothering me and I need to get my head round it. If it's all right with you, I'll take my tackle down to the lake and have a day's fishing.'

'Oh, Tony!' she pouted. 'It's *Sunday* – that's supposed to be a family day.'

'I know, sweetheart, but this is really important, or I wouldn't ask. And when I get back, we'll go the George for dinner.'

'We . . . ell . . .'

He bent forward and kissed her. 'That's my girl!' he said.

Thirteen

The morning after his dinner with the Yates, Adam phoned Kirsty's mobile.

'I've been to see Graham,' he told her, 'and amazingly enough he had a video of a programme featuring the murders.'

'How do you mean, featuring them?'

'It was from a TV series a few years back, covering cold cases. A reporter retraced Mark and Emma's arrival in the village and various places that, according to the residents, they'd visited, in the hope of jogging memories. It also included part of an old *Crimewatch* programme that had been shown just weeks after the murders, with people dressed up to look like them, and two kids supposed to be us. It was . . . weird, seeing it all being acted out.'

Mark and Emma, he'd called them. Perhaps it was easier that way. 'Did he come up with anything new?'

'Not really, but it gave me a few pointers to pursue.' He paused. 'I'm guessing you'd like to see the video?'

'I certainly would.'

'Can you lay your hands on a VCR? There's one here, if you're into DVDs.'

'We still have one, thanks.' She paused fractionally. 'Could you bring the tape round?'

'OK, but it'll have to be the weekend. The boarders come back this afternoon and the next two evenings are tied up with meetings and such.' He paused. 'Do you think your uncle and aunt would like to see it?'

'No, we should wait till we've something definite to tell them. If we ever have.'

'They know we've met again?'

'Yes; Aunt Jan sounded a bit tight-lipped, but she's probably accepted she can't keep us apart for a whole year. I didn't tell her what you're proposing to do, though.'

'Any thoughts yet on whether you'll accompany me?'

'I'll let you know at the weekend.'

'Adam?' Angie enquired, coming into the room as Kirsty switched off the phone.

'Yes; he has a video of a programme looking into our parents' murders.'

'God, where did he find that?'

Kirsty explained. 'He's coming round on Saturday to show it to me.'

Angie perched on the arm of a chair, searching her face. 'So, after two meetings, what do you think of him?'

Kirsty smiled. 'The same as he thinks of me. That he's improved with keeping!'

Nick said, 'A crowd of us are going sailing tomorrow. Like to come along?'

It was late Friday evening and they were in the

179

bar of the Regency, part of a group of staff members whom Adam was gradually beginning to put names to.

'I'd have loved to, but unfortunately I've something else planned.'

It sounded a bald excuse, and after a minute he added, 'Actually, I've arranged to meet Kirsty. I've something to show her.'

'You've established a truce, then?'

'A partial one. Not treading on your toes, am I?'

Nick shook his head. 'She's . . . OK, though, isn't she?'

Adam frowned. 'How do you mean?'

'Well, it's just that . . . part of the misunderstanding between us arose because she'd been receiving odd emails and presents and she thought I might be responsible.'

'Anonymously, you mean?'

Nick nodded. 'No doubt it was all a flash in the pan, but to be honest I've been slightly concerned, in view of the attacks in the area.'

Adam stared at him. 'God, you don't think it's the same guy?'

'No . . . no, of course not.' Nick drained his glass. 'Top up?'

Adam nodded absently. 'She never mentioned anything to me.'

'Then I'm sure it's all blown over,' Nick said and, picking up Adam's glass as well as his own, returned to the bar.

Kirsty, too, had been hoping it had blown over; there'd been nothing untoward since she'd returned from holiday over two weeks ago. Nor,

180

thank God, had any more attacks been reported, and the press had relegated the policewoman's murder, though still unresolved, to the inside pages. Nonetheless, the culprit remained at large, as did her parents' murderers, and her subconscious linking of the crimes caused a superstitious shudder.

As it happened, the respite came to an end just as Adam and Nick were discussing it. Preparing for bed, Kirsty remembered she'd not closed down her laptop, and from force of habit checked her emails before doing so. Her gasp brought Angie to look over her shoulder.

Enjoy the film last night? one read. *You looked so delectable in that blue dress that I almost reached out to touch you! Next time, perhaps.*

Kirsty groaned in despair. 'What can I *do*, Angie? The police haven't been much help, and now they've got their work cut out with their colleague's murder.' She shivered. 'He was *there*, at the cinema! How creepy is that? All the time we were chatting, eating our ice creams and everything, he could have been in the row just behind us!'

'Can I tell Simon about it?' Angie asked worriedly. 'I know you said not to, but this has gone on quite long enough, and if the police aren't helping he might be able to suggest something.'

Kirsty stabbed viciously at the delete key. 'If I confide in anyone, I'd prefer it to be my uncle. Trouble is Auntie Jan would find out, and she'd go ballistic.'

'So? Can I?'

'Not just yet,' Kirsty prevaricated.

'But why not, for God's sake?'

'Pride, I suppose; I hate being made to look
. . . defenceless, a sitting duck waiting for whatever he chooses to throw at me. Damn it, I'm an
independent career woman with my own business, and I bitterly resent being cast in the role
of victim.'

'He seems to have built up a love/hate relationship with you,' Angie said uneasily. 'One minute
he's sending you nettles and telling you to mind
your manners, the next you're so "delectable" he
wants to touch you.'

Kirsty shuddered and slammed down the lid
on her laptop. 'He'll get tired of it eventually,'
she said. But each time she told herself that, it
seemed less convincing.

As arranged, Adam called at the house at two
thirty the next afternoon. Angie had left to meet
Simon and Kirsty was alone.

'Nice pad,' he said approvingly, looking around
him.

'The ground floor's the business-side – kitchen,
office, packing room. We live on the first and
second floors.'

She led the way up and into the sitting room
where, as she usually did herself, he went
straight to the window. 'A bird's-eye view. Very
impressive.'

'Isn't it? We were lucky to find it.' She paused,
and as he continued to gaze at the view, added
encouragingly, 'I'll switch on the VCR, shall I?'

He turned. 'One thing, before we watch it. Nick

182

tells me you've been receiving some unwanted attention.'

She felt a flash of annoyance. 'Nothing I can't handle.'

'It's still continuing then? He hoped it might have blown over.'

'It's really nothing to do with him,' she said shortly.

'Since he came under suspicion, he might think it is. Suppose you tell me about it?' And, as she started to protest, he raised a hand. '*All* of it,' he said.

Perhaps, she thought, this was after all the best solution: not to confide in either her uncle or Simon, but in her big brother who, surprisingly, seemed concerned on her behalf. So she went through the harassment campaign from the beginning – the emails, the flowers, the chocolates, the nettles, the cinema.

When she came to an end he was silent, staring down at the carpet. 'You've reported it?'

'Yes, but to be fair if I can't give a name there's not much anyone can do, and the police have their work cut out on more important matters.'

'You haven't the slightest idea who this could be?'

'Not the slightest.'

'No disgruntled boyfriends in the offing?'

'No; there's only been one in the last two years, and he phoned after the attack in the park to advise me not to go there.'

'Double bluff?'

Kirsty shook her head. 'Not Lance.'

'Emails can be quite random, but as things were

actually delivered to the house, it must be someone who either knows you or knows *of* you.'

'That had crossed my mind,' she said drily.

'Well, I don't like it.'

'I'm not wild about it myself.'

'You *are* taking precautions? Not going out alone, and so on?'

'Not after dark, certainly.'

'You came to the pub. It would have been dark before you reached home.'

'I only had to go from the drive to the front door,' she pointed out. 'Look, I've no intention of becoming neurotic about this, so let's drop it, shall we? I'm being sensible; I'll be fine. Now, can we please look at this tape?'

He was still frowning as it took it out of his pocket, but his attention switched as he slid it into the machine. 'I'll play it through without making any comment, then see what you think of it. I've watched it several times myself, and different things strike me each time.'

They sat together on the sofa as the long-ago events were played out for them on the screen. The story that unfolded was basically as they'd been told, but there were embellishments, personal recollections, anecdotes. Photographs in the press after the murders had elicited memories from people who'd seen the family around the village – Mark constantly taking photographs, Adam climbing on the dais at the fair. A barman in Hawkston remembered them having lunch in their family room; one or two people – holidaymakers like themselves – recalled seeing them several times picnicking at the lakeside. The milkman spoke of his gruesome discovery, the postmistress of giving the children sweets.

'And that wasn't the only tragedy that summer,' she added sadly. 'A gentleman from Hawkston drowned while fishing in Lake Belvedere, and they didn't find his body for six weeks.'

In the *Crimewatch* snippet two adults, the man slight and dark, the woman wearing a pink cotton dress, wheeled a pushchair through the village with a little boy trotting alongside and a baby girl inside. Kirsty's eyes blurred as she watched them. They looked what they had been, a happy family on holiday. How could it possibly have ended in murder?

The reporter went on to mention the missing camera and the belief that it contained incriminating evidence of some kind, but any initially promising leads had soon fizzled out and the case remained stubbornly unsolved.

A click signified the end of the recording. Adam glanced at her enquiringly, and Kirsty said, 'If the murderers took the camera because it contained evidence against them, it stands to reason they'd have destroyed the film straight away. So I don't see there's any way they could be identified, let alone convicted.'

'Anything else strike you?'

'Not immediately. How about you? You said there were pointers.'

'It was that woman mentioning the man who drowned,' Adam said slowly. 'I'd read about it in the *Gazette* archives, but since it was reported in July I didn't pay much attention. But after hearing that comment I checked back and found that his wife last saw him on Sunday the twenty-fourth of June. Ring any bells?'

Kirsty's eyes widened. 'The day of the murders!'

'Exactly. Might be a coincidence, of course, but I think it could be worth investigating, especially since we know Mark and Emma often went to the lake.'

'Wouldn't that coincidence have struck the police?'

'God knows. If it did, it didn't seem to get them anywhere. I read the guy's obit but there was nothing out of the ordinary, just that he'd been a "valued colleague" at the firm where he worked, and had left a wife but apparently no children. Incidentally, I've put an ad in the personal column, asking for information – it'll have gone in this week's edition. We'll see if that opens any cans of worms.'

He stood up and started pacing the room. 'Watching the video again just now, something else struck me, something I'd not registered before. That barman at the pub where we had lunch said I was clutching the Donald Duck toy and Mark told him he'd won it at the fête. You see what that means, Kirsty? *It must have been that last day!* Perhaps we've been on the wrong track, and whatever it was Mark snapped was in *Hawkston*!'

'That *would* widen the field!'

'We need to find out exactly what they did there – who they spoke to, where they went and so on.' He turned to look at her. 'So – are you coming with me up to Penthwaite?'

'Yes,' she replied, 'I rather think I am.'

* * *

186

Adam left soon after, saying he didn't want to take up any more of her weekend, and Kirsty, who had no firm plans, changed into her tennis whites and drove to the club. An energetic game or two would help dispel the restlessness that was plaguing her since seeing the video. Johnnie and Lois were playing doubles with Matt and Chrissie, and Kirsty saw with a sinking heart that Lance was sitting in a deckchair on the pavilion veranda.

'Come and join me,' he invited, patting the chair beside him as she went up the steps. 'I won't bite.'

'I was hoping for a game,' she said.

'OK. I'm your man.'

Kirsty glanced at him in surprise. In the park back in July it had taken him all his time to speak to her. Perhaps the Great Healer had been at work.

'You're on,' she said.

He was a strong player and they finished three hard sets before, flushed and breathless, they returned to the pavilion and joined the other four on the balcony.

'Well, well!' Chrissie murmured, as Lance went to get drinks. 'Do we take it the romance is rekindled?'

Kirsty flushed. 'It was a game of tennis, that's all.'

'If you say so!' Chrissie returned smugly.

'Don't tease, darling,' Matt interposed and adroitly changed the subject. 'Been on holiday, Kirsty?'

'Yes, I had a couple of weeks in Barbados. It was great. How about you?'

'Three weeks in Italy. We got back last weekend.'

'Our holiday this year was all taken up by the honeymoon,' Lois said. 'With luck, we might manage a weekend in Brighton before the winter sets in!'

Lance returned, handing Kirsty an ice-cold glass of lemonade and catching the end of the conversation. 'Now summer's finally arrived, I'm happy to stay put,' he said.

Kirsty leant back in her chair, sipping the icy liquid and letting the conversation wash over her. Here in the sunshine, surrounded by her friends, thoughts of murder and harassment seemed ludicrously unreal. Just for a while, she could fool herself that they were.

'Good heavens!' Marilyn Ferris exclaimed.

Dean, his attention on the match, glanced at her irritably. 'What?'

'Someone's asking for information about that young couple's murder, the summer—' She gave a little gasp as her husband sprang out of his chair and snatched the paper from her hands.

'Where is it?'

'In the personal column,' she faltered. 'I always read it – I like the birthday messages.'

'*Where* in the . . .' His voice trailed off as he located it and read aloud: '*Information sought concerning the murders of Mark and Emma Franklyn in Penthwaite, June 1986. Reward for information leading to conviction of perpetrators. Confidentiality guaranteed. Box number: 650817*'

'Fancy that coming up again, after all these years,' Marilyn ventured, as Dean continued to stare down at the paper in his hands. He'd gone pale, she noticed with a stirring of anxiety. 'Darling? What is it? Are you all right?'

He didn't reply and she came to her feet, taking hold of his arm. 'Dean?'

'Why drag that all up again?' he said in a low voice. 'Wasn't it enough . . .?'

He broke off and Marilyn, suddenly under-standing, reached up to kiss his cheek. 'You're worried it'll stir up memories of Tony's death,' she said, taking it as confirmation when he turned sharply to stare at her. 'I know it happened around the same time, but it's all right, dear, it won't upset me. It's a long time ago now.'

He shook himself free of her and moved away. 'I have to go out for a while.'

'But I thought you were watching the football? You've been looking forward—'

'I've just remembered something I have to do. I . . . shan't be long.'

He hurried from the room, leaving her staring after him, and it wasn't until she heard the front door close that she realized he'd taken the paper with him.

Alone in the car, Dean found he was shaking uncontrollably. God, what had happened? What, after all this time, had brought those terrible deaths back to public attention? His first instinct had been to speak to Barry, and he'd actually started to drive to his house before it struck him, with a crushing sense of helplessness, that he was as alone in this as he'd been twenty-six years ago. Drawing in to the side of the road, he switched off the engine and rested his forehead on the steering wheel.

Barry's recovery had been slow, and Dean had been left to run the company single-handed, buffeted by nightmares of the missing Tony and his patent – nightmares that had intensified when, weeks later, his bloated body was finally recovered. Although Barry's memory of the last hours before the stroke remained obliterated, Dean had considered telling him the truth on several occasions but, in his heart, he acknowledged the uselessness of it. Nevertheless, he bitterly resented the ease with which his brother had left him to deal with his nightmares alone.

He raised his head, smoothed out the crumpled newspaper and read the advertisement again. The urgency that had driven him out of the house had evaporated, but he'd told Marilyn he had something to do, and he must fill in an appropriate amount of time. He'd drive slowly round the block before returning home and trying to pick up the threads of the match he'd abandoned.

With a sigh he switched on the ignition, telling himself that if no suspicion had come their way at the time, none was likely to arise now, and whoever it was who was asking for information would have to accept that none was forthcoming.

Though he'd spoken of it to no one, Barry's memory – or what he took to be his memory – had, over the last year or so, begun to emerge from the shroud that had buried it. Sudden scenes would flash into his mind, disturbing, out of kilter, and like a dream fade before he could grasp them. He started to suffer his own nightmares, waking screaming and drenched with sweat. Vivien had insisted he see the doctor, but none of the prescribed medications had any effect.

Something terrible had happened the day of his stroke – he was sure of it. Dean, of course, held the answer, but Barry dared not question him. His brain had blotted it out, perhaps as a defence mechanism, and God knew what might happen if he attempted to reinstate it. Recalling his state of mind immediately before his illness, it was possible that during that summer of 'eighty-six he hadn't been entirely sane. The firm had been going down the drain, and just when salvation seemed at hand in the form of Tony's new invention, he'd announced he was leaving and taking his patent with him. It must have been that final straw that had brought on his breakdown, frantic as he was with worry about the business, about being able to care for his family, and the shame of losing his home and removing Daphne from her private school.

Tony. Somehow, the terrible thing was connected with Tony, who had drowned on a fishing trip while Barry lay in hospital. And although it had, of course, been a terrible tragedy, there was no denying that his death had saved the firm. The longed-for patent had dropped into their laps, business had slowly recovered, and Ferris Engineering, of which he was chairman, was now the most prosperous firm in the area, as well as the most generous. At Dean's instigation they had set up various funds to assist young people

191

in the early stages of their careers, and as often as not employed them when they attained their qualifications.

That Saturday while Dean sat brooding in his car, Barry and Vivien's daughter and her husband called in on their way home.

'Did you see that thing in the paper, about the murders?' Daphne asked as they sat over a cup of tea.

Vivien raised an eyebrow. 'What murders?'

'That young couple in Penthwaite, ages ago.'

Barry's hand unaccountably shook, and he hastily put down his cup. 'When, exactly?' he asked.

'It was the summer you had your stroke, Dad. It was in all the papers, but since you were out of it, you probably never heard about it. They were holidaymakers, and someone bashed them both over the head and killed them. They never caught him.'

Barry gripped the arms of his chair as his brain fumbled after a memory and immediately shied away from it.

'So why drag it up again now?' Daphne's husband, Rob, was asking.

She shrugged. 'God knows, but someone's offering a reward for information. They'll be lucky, after all this time.'

'It's taken them long enough to get round to it,' Rob commented. 'Talk about cold cases – this one must be in the deep freeze!'

'It was a bad summer all round,' Vivien said reflectively, 'what with the firm being on the brink, then Tony drowning and Dad's stroke. I can understand the family wanting to get to the bottom of it, perhaps making one last attempt before a parent died.'

'Maybe,' Rob conceded. 'But in my opinion, they haven't a hope in hell.'

The equilibrium Kirsty established that afternoon at the club was, alas, soon shattered. That night she was woken by the continuous ringing of the doorbell, and struggled up through clinging layers of sleep to heart-thumping panic. Could it possibly be Angie? The snip was down, so she wouldn't be able to use her key. But even if she and Simon had quarrelled again, she wouldn't come back at this time of night.

Pushing the hair from her eyes she slipped out of bed, crossed to the window and, holding the curtain to one side, looked down into the garden far below. The street lights were out – a council economy, which meant it was after midnight, and still the ringing continued, echoing insistently round the listening house. Then, from one heart-beat to the next, it stopped, and the silence was almost as deafening. Immobile, she stood waiting, and after a full minute a shadowy form, indeter-minate in shape, emerged from the outline of the porch beneath her, slipped quickly down the path and out of the gate.

He'd gone, whoever he was. Clinging to the banister for support, she tiptoed down to the first floor and peered down the stairway to the hall. Her eyes had adapted to the darkness, and if he'd pushed anything through the letterbox, she'd be able to detect it. But there was nothing to detect. At least she'd not gratified him by putting on a light; he'd no way of knowing that he'd succeeded in waking her. Only a modicum of comfort, but it was all she had.

Shivering, she crept back to bed.

Fourteen

Kirsty, Kirsty! Why couldn't he get her out of his head? Why was he so strongly attracted to her, when, as part-owner of a successful business and brimming with self-confidence, she embodied everything that, over the last few decades, he'd come to loathe in women?

Where were the sweet, docile girls of his youth, who'd looked up to men? Gone, all gone! They'd joined the police, become army officers, vicars, doctors – all rightly men's jobs – flaunting their authority with infuriating complacency. He'd fantasized endlessly about pricking their self-esteem, taking them down a peg or two, but it was only recently that he'd dared turn fantasy into fact.

Surprisingly, the first few encounters were never reported – didn't want to lose face, he supposed – and this encouraged him to go further. He chose his victims with care – women who'd been fêted in the press for some achievement, pictured with a self-satisfied smile – and half the excitement had been tracking them down. Where was that superiority when they were flat on their backs beneath him, like that stupid little cow from the train who'd spent the whole journey on her mobile, ensuring everyone knew how important she was? Not so self-sufficient, was she, when she was crying and begging him not to hurt her?

The policewoman was a mistake – he accepted that, but she shouldn't have preached at him. The balaclava had, as always, been in his briefcase – too dangerous to leave lying around – so, on a whim really, he'd followed her, intending to teach her a lesson like the others. When she'd turned into that alley he'd made his move, but it had gone wrong from the first. The silly bitch had struggled and fought, yelling and shouting, and when she'd managed to claw off the balaclava, he'd pressed it over her mouth and, desperate to silence her, had gone on pressing.

He'd been stunned when she suddenly went limp, had tried in increasing panic to shake a response out of her, even if she had seen his face. And when finally he'd accepted she was dead, he'd vomited for long, agonizing minutes before stumbling away in the knowledge that he'd have the whole bloody police force after him. He'd been jittery for weeks, but as time passed he started to relive with growing excitement the moment the life went out of her. That, surely, had been the ultimate put-down, the unequivocal victory. Perhaps, once the heat had died down, he'd risk experiencing it again.

In the meantime, there was Kirsty. He'd sent the emails to unsettle her, make her uneasy, but she'd ignored both them and his gifts and she should be punished for that – punished above all for getting under his skin and coming between him and his sleep. It would need careful planning, but when the time was right he would make his move.

*   *   *

196

Summer gradually slid into autumn. Leaves turned colour, the days shortened. Adam settled into college life, where his astringent comments delivered in his Canadian accent had, to his surprise, made him popular with his pupils. In his spare time he searched the Web for information, but nothing new had come to light and there'd been no response to his press appeal. Eventually he decided to put it on hold until his visit to the Lakes, when he'd be able to deal with people more directly.

At Gateaux to Die For business increased after the summer lull with a spate of birthdays and anniversaries that, in addition to their regular orders, kept Kirsty and Angie busy. Though she and Adam had spoken on the phone they'd not met again, but Kirsty knew she must tell her aunt and uncle of their forthcoming trip, and when, during a Sunday lunch in late September, Janice enquired if she'd seen him recently, she took the opportunity.

'I haven't, no, but we've decided to go up to the Lakes together at half term.'

Roy laid down his knife with a clatter. 'You've *what*?'

Kirsty said steadily, 'We want to see for ourselves where everything happened, and Adam's found out a few things that—'

'*No!*' Janice was staring at her with horrified eyes. 'No, no, no! I won't hear of it!'

'You can't really stop us, Auntie,' Kirsty said gently.

'Roy, say something! This is just the kind of thing we've been dreading, ever since we heard Adam was coming over!'

197

Roy drew a breath. 'What exactly are you proposing to do up there?'

'Go the village and speak to the people who were there at the time.' She paused. 'I didn't tell you before because I didn't want to upset you, but Graham Yates gave Adam a recording of a programme on cold cases that was shown a few years ago. Mum and Dad's murder was one of those they looked at.'

Janice put a hand over her mouth. Roy said, 'And since we didn't hear anything, I presume nothing new came to light.'

'There are one or two things Adam wants to follow up,' Kirsty replied.

'Such as?'

She hesitated. 'I think it's better if we wait till I get back, then hopefully I'll have more to tell you.'

'*If* you get back!' Janice said in a high, cracked voice. 'If you start poking your nose in and those . . . those monsters are still around, they'll have no compunction in trying to silence you as well.'

Kirsty laid a repentant hand on hers. 'Auntie, every anniversary you promise Mum you'll find her killers. We want that too, and there's just a chance we might succeed. At least let us try.'

'But I didn't mean like that – not *personally*!' Janice's eyes were full of tears.

'We'll be on our guard, which Mum and Dad presumably weren't.'

Janice turned desperately to her husband. 'Roy, talk her out of it! Please!'

'I can't, love, not if she and Adam are set on it, but I'm sure they can take care of themselves.'

'*Oh!*' With a cry of distress and frustration, Janice pushed back her chair and hurried from the room.

Kirsty met her uncle's reproachful eyes. 'I'm sorry,' she said, 'but we're still going.'

It was the week before half term.

'Got any plans for next week?' Nick asked as he and Adam walked across the garden to Staff House.

'Yes, actually. I'm going up to the Lakes with Kirsty.'

Nick looked at him in surprise. 'Well, this *is* a *rapprochement*! I hadn't realized you'd made so much progress!'

Oh, what the hell? Adam thought; no point in beating about the bush. He dug his hands deeper into his pockets. 'Actually, we're going to try to discover who murdered our parents.'

His companion came to an abrupt halt. '*What* did you say?'

'That was at the root of the family split. They were killed when we were all up there on holiday, and a rather unseemly row followed about which members of the family should adopt us. One side was prepared to take us both, the other wanted only Kirsty. My side left almost immediately for Canada, and there you have it.'

'Slow down, slow down!' Nick protested. 'They were *murdered*? Kirsty said they died in a car crash.'

'That's what we were told. We only learned the truth this summer, which,' Adam added with a wry smile, 'might account for her seeming "complicated".'

'God, I wish I'd known! I could have made allowances – I thought she was just being difficult. But – *murdered*? What happened, exactly?'

Briefly Adam outlined such facts as there were.

'And no one was ever caught?'

'Nope. I've done some digging online and found a few points that bear investigation. I'm hoping a fresh look might produce results.'

'Mightn't it be a bit risky?' Nick said hesitantly.

Adam gave a short laugh. 'You sound like my relatives!' They'd reached the house and he pushed the door open, glancing at his friend's thoughtful face. 'Well, you did ask what I was doing next week! Sorry if the answer was more than you bargained for!'

On the Wednesday evening he phoned Kirsty. 'Ready to go?' he asked.

'Just about.'

'We finish at lunchtime on Friday. If we set off about two we should be there soon after seven. I've booked us into the George at Hawkston for the week.'

'It's about a five-hour drive, then?'

'Yep, just under three hundred miles, nearly all of it motorway. The traffic could be busy with the start of half term, but at least we'd be on our way.' He paused. 'Not getting cold feet?'

'Far from it – I'm raring to go!'

'Good. How did the relatives react to the news?'

200

'As you'd expect.'

'Well, they'll be only too grateful if we manage to crack it.'

'Do you really think we can?'

'Let's just say we've two pairs of fresh eyes and some ideas to follow up. I certainly reckon we're in with a chance.'

She felt a little thrill, composed equally of apprehension and excitement. 'Then let's go for it!' she said.

As Adam had foreseen, traffic was heavy, particularly around the junction with the M6, but once they passed the turn-off for Blackpool it lessened noticeably. He had switched the sat nav to mute, but Kirsty kept checking the progress of their car icon as it progressed steadily north towards their destination.

'I suppose we're retracing the route they'd have taken,' she commented at one point.

'The roads will be better now, even if busier, but yes, basically I suppose we are.'

'I wonder what they were thinking about as they passed this spot.'

'Probably trying to shut up a couple of screaming kids! By this stage we'd have been bored out of our minds.'

She laughed. 'You could be right.'

By the time they reached Hawkston they were more than thankful the journey was at an end. Tired, stiff and hungry, Adam turned into the hotel car park and drew into a vacant space.

'It's nearly eight o'clock,' he said. 'I suggest we go to our rooms for a quick wash, then straight down to dinner. I don't know about you but I'm starving. Then, over the meal, we can decide on our plan of action.'

The George was an old-fashioned hotel, with uneven flooring and low ceilings, but the rooms had all the equipment the modern guest required, wi-fi included. The bed, when Kirsty tested it, was deep and comfortable, and she had to resist the impulse to kick off her shoes and lie down.

Minutes later Adam, whose room was next to hers, tapped at her door, and they went down to the dining room. It was almost full, but the maître d' found them a small table tucked into a corner.

'If you're residents, sir, I suggest you book a table each evening. We'll be very busy during the coming week.'

Adam thanked him and passed Kirsty the menu. It offered a wide choice of interesting dishes and she looked forward to working her way through it during the next few days. When they'd made their selection and wine had been ordered, Adam leant forward purposefully. 'Now, we must plan our campaign – I brought my tablet down so I can make notes as we go along. Time's limited and we can't afford to waste a minute.'

'Have you thought of a cover story?' Kirsty asked. 'I mean, how do we explain our interest – is it for another article or TV programme, or do we admit who we are? No one's likely to remember Mum and Dad's name, but even if they did ours are both different, so unless we own up no one would make a connection.'

'I think we should go for the sympathy vote,' Adam decided. 'Two orphaned kids would have aroused a lot of sympathy at the time, and people are more likely to open up to us if they know who we are.'

'The downside is that if the killers are still around, they'll also know.'

'So what? They won't see us as any more of a threat than anyone else.'

Kirsty nodded. 'I suppose not. So, where do we start?'

'I want to look into the drowning of this Tony Vine, who, remember, was last seen on the day of the murders. He lived here in Hawkston, so we need to find out if his widow is still around and prepared to talk to us, so we can, as they say, eliminate him from our enquiries.'

'You think he might be important?'

'All we know is that he "disappeared" that Sunday – went out in the morning and was never seen again. But he might not have drowned straight away; it's just as conceivable that he killed Mark and Emma, fled to the lake, still wound up and, not concentrating on what he was doing, fell overboard.'

'An interesting theory; what did he do with the camera?'

'Dumped it in the lake? OK, it's pretty far-fetched, but he might at least have spoken to them – they often went there – and he could have mentioned them to his wife.'

'So how do we find her?'

'We could start with the phone book. At her age, she's likely still to have a landline.'

The arrival of their first course put an end to the discussion, and for the next hour or so they gave their attention to their meal, which was as enjoyable as the menu had promised. Having chosen the option of coffee in the lounge, they borrowed a phone directory en route, but disappointment awaited them: no Vines were listed.

'So either she's more "with it" than you gave her credit for and only has a mobile, or she's moved away.'

Adam slammed the directory on the table. 'Which means tracking her down will take more time and effort, dammit.'

'What about the firm her husband worked for? They might still be paying her a pension.'

He brightened. 'Clever girl! Provided they're still in existence, they could be our best bet.'

'Can you remember their name?'

Adam flicked through his tablet. 'Here it is: Ferris Engineering. Look it up while we still have the phone book.'

Kirsty did so. 'Well, they certainly still exist; they even have a boxed advertisement. Glendale Industrial Estate, Hawkston, and a phone number. Do you want it?'

'Yeah, read it out, would you?'

She did so, and he entered it on his tablet. 'They won't be there over the weekend, and on reflection it's doubtful if they'd give out information about employees or their relations. We might have to approach it obliquely. That being so, there's nothing to keep us in town tomorrow, so we'll head straight out to Penthwaite and see what transpires. I had another look at the video

204

before I left, to try to familiarize myself with the layout.' He looked at his watch. 'It's nearly eleven and all that driving is catching up with me. I suggest we call it a day and start fresh tomorrow. Breakfast at eight fifteen? We've another busy day ahead.'

As Kirsty prepared for bed, she realized with surprise that in nine solid hours of Adam's company, he hadn't once annoyed her. Progress indeed.

It was a forty-minute drive to the village, and once they'd left the outskirts of Hawkston they were into the countryside – fields of grazing cows, small wooded areas, hills all around. It was from the summit of one such hill that, like their parents before them, they had their first view of Penthwaite.

'I'll drive straight to the cottage,' Adam said brusquely as they began their descent, and Kirsty wondered if his emotions mirrored hers. 'There's probably nowhere to park in the centre so we'll leave the car there and walk back.'

Her heart was pounding as they entered the village. The main street was crowded with people strolling along in the autumn sunshine and children were playing on the green. Her hands clenched as they passed the post office-cum-general store which she knew their parents had frequented and which, they'd decided, would be their first port of call. It was all familiar from the video, but she was picturing herself being wheeled along here in her pushchair by parents she couldn't remember.

Then Adam was turning off the main street into a narrow lane. A few yards ahead on their right were the gates of a cottage, then the green expanse of a field, then three more, while across the lane a man was digging in his allotment.

'That explains something that puzzled me,' Adam said. 'I couldn't understand how Mark could lie on that drive all night with no one noticing him, but now it's clear enough.'

He drove a little farther and parked adjacent to the field.

'Do you think anyone's staying there?' Kirsty asked from a dry mouth.

He shrugged. 'It's half term, but not peak holiday season. It looked pretty shut up as we passed. Let's walk back and take a closer look.'

As they approached the cottage on foot, Kirsty instinctively reached for Adam's hand. He glanced at her but did not withdraw it, and when they reached the gateway they could see the curtains were all drawn. Adam pushed the gate open, and as they stepped inside they both came to a halt, visions of their father's death crowding into their heads.

Adam cleared his throat. 'We'll ring the bell, and if anyone answers, apologize and say we've got the wrong address.'

But no one came to the door. With the curtains drawn they were unable to see inside, and the garage, new since their last stay, blocked the route to the back of the house.

'All in all, a pretty useless exercise,' Adam commented.

'If we walk further up the main road, we

206

might be able to see into the back garden,' Kirsty suggested.

'We can give it a try.'

But again they were thwarted; the fields that lay behind the cottage were fenced off and they were unable to gain access.

'We learned more from the video,' Adam said, 'but at least we've *been* here and . . . paid our respects, which is more than anyone else has.'

In silence they walked back towards the village and turned into the shop. There were several people waiting to be served and only one woman behind the counter. They waited their turn, idly spinning the stand of postcards until the last person had left.

'Can I help you?' the assistant asked brightly.

'I hope so,' Adam said pleasantly. 'We're looking into a murder that took place here some years ago.'

The woman's expression changed. 'Was it you put that ad in t'paper?'

'It was, yes.'

'Well, all I can say is we've spent years trying to put it behind us. It was horrible, them ghouls coming from far and near, poking and prying and wanting to see where it happened – not at all the kind of publicity we needed. Any road, I weren't working here then so I can't help you.'

Kirsty said quietly, 'Perhaps we should explain that it was our parents who were murdered.'

The woman's eyes widened and a hand went to her mouth. 'Those little kiddies . . .?'

Adam smiled crookedly. 'We've grown a bit since!'

'Oh, I'm that sorry – I didn't know!'

'That's all right.' He paused. 'I believe a Mrs Birchall was postmistress at the time?'

'Me auntie, aye. Upset her dreadfully. She'd grown right fond of the . . . of you.'

'Is she still . . . around?'

'Aye; I took over when she retired, like – I'm Joan, by the way – but she still lives in t'village. I'm sure she'd be pleased to see you. Shall I give her a ring and see if she's in?'

'That would be wonderful!' Kirsty said warmly.

Joan disappeared into the back room and they could hear her excited voice as she spoke on the phone. Then she reappeared, smiling. 'Auntie will be delighted to see you. Go straight round if you like – she says to tell you coffee's on.'

She came round the end of the counter and walked with them to the door. 'Cross over t'road and take first turning on your left – Hollybush Lane. It's third house down on t'right, but she'll be looking out for you.'

They thanked her, waited for a tractor to lumber past and crossed over towards the green. Joan stood looking after them till a customer approached and she had to return to her work.

'That's a stroke of luck,' Adam said. 'Mrs B was the head of our list of priorities. Let's hope we'll do better with her than we did with Mrs Vine.'

As her niece had predicted, the ex-postmistress was standing at the open door of her house and came hurrying down the path, clasping their hands in hers, her eyes full of tears. She was a small, plump woman in her seventies, with a wrinkled face and short grey hair.

'I can't believe I'm seeing you again!' she said tremulously, her eyes raking their faces. She nodded at Adam. 'Aye, I recognize them big grey eyes!' And to Kirsty, 'But where have all yon curls gone?'

Kirsty smiled. 'I lost them when I was six and began to grow my hair.'

'Well, well, come in and tell me what I can do for you. I saw your advert, but I thought it were some nosy parker wanting to butt in again.'

They were shown into the front room, where a tray had been set out with coffee cups and a plate of biscuits.

'So you've come back after all this time – a kind of pilgrimage, like.'

'We'd have come sooner,' Adam said levelly, 'if we'd known what happened. Believe it or not, we've only just been told. Up till then, we believed our parents had been killed in a car crash.'

'Well, now, fancy that!' Mrs Birchall exclaimed, pouring the coffee. 'Still, I suppose it were kindly meant.'

'When we were children, yes. Not afterwards.'

She glanced at his set face. 'I wish I could say they caught 'em, but of course they never. Not so much as a hint as to who might have done it, or why.'

'It would be lovely,' Kirsty said quietly, 'if you could tell us everything you remember about our parents. We're trying to build up a picture of the week they spent here.'

'Well, I reckon I saw 'em more 'n most, since

209

they was allus coming in t'shop. Your dad was a great one for taking pictures. He'd wander round t'village with that camera of his hanging round his neck and your mum pushing the pram alongside.' She flashed them a quick glance. 'Some say it might have been camera as caused all t'trouble.'

Kirsty nodded. 'Can you think of anything . . . controversial . . . he might have photographed?'

'What could have been controversial, in a little village like yon? They went t'fête, that I do know. I saw 'em coming away about teatime, the little boy – you, sir – carrying a Donald Duck nearly as big as you were. And you, dearie, had that teddy of yours. I never saw you without it!'

Kirsty smiled. 'I still have it,' she admitted.

Adam turned to her in surprise. 'Kirsty, you haven't!'

She flushed. 'I know it sounds silly, but it's my only physical link with my parents. My aunt told me it was a first birthday present.'

'And that,' Mrs Birchall said sadly, 'were the last time I saw you. I couldn't believe my ears when I heard what had happened.' She reached for a handkerchief and wiped her eyes.

There was a brief uncomfortable silence. To break it, Adam said tentatively, 'I believe someone drowned in the lake that summer?'

Mrs Birchall sniffed and replaced her handkerchief. 'Yes, indeed, poor Mr Vine from Hawkston. Terrible it were, and weeks before they found him.'

'We'd have liked to speak to his widow, but she's not in the phone book.'

'Not as Mrs Vine she's not. She's Mrs Dean Ferris now.'

'Ferris as in the firm that employed her husband?' Adam asked quickly.

'Right enough. My sister's boy worked there and it caused quite a stir, I can tell you, them marrying within a year of Mr Vine's death; but she were a scatty little thing, Jack said, and like as not would have been lost on her own.'

'So she's still in Hawkston?' Adam tried to keep the excitement out of his voice.

'She is, aye.' Mrs Birchall frowned. 'Though I don't see what she has to do wi' your mum and dad.'

Adam and Kirsty exchanged a glance, but she deserved an explanation.

'The last time she saw her husband was on the day our parents were killed,' Adam told her.

'Get away!' Mrs Birchall stared at them.

'I read the newspaper archives, and that was the date she gave.'

'Well, I'll be blowed! With him being found all those weeks later, I never realized.' She paused. 'But I still don't see how there could be a connection.'

'Nor do we, but it could be worth looking into.'

'Well, I never!' Mrs Birchall seemed stunned by the idea.

'Do you remember anything our parents spoke to you about?' Adam prompted.

She shook her head. 'After it happened I went over everything they'd said, in case it might give a clue, like, but there were nowt of importance.

211

They said as they'd been t'church and were surprised to find it open, but vicar insists on that. Says a church door should never be locked. They were interested in old family monuments and asked if same families were still here. And they was allus going off having picnics, to the lake and suchlike, where the gentleman could take his pictures.' She gave a small, embarrassed smile. 'I never knew their name. It were in t'paper later, but I've gone and forgot it.'

'Franklyn,' Kirsty supplied. 'Mark and Emma Franklyn.'

'That's right – I remember now. Like t'President.'

'Did you see them that last day?' Adam asked.

'No, shop were shut, it being Sunday. Papers went out first thing, that's all. I don't hold with folks buying groceries and such on t'Lord's day when they've all week to do it. Some say it lost me business, but that's as maybe. I have my principles.'

It seemed they'd exhausted all she could tell them, and shortly afterwards they left.

'I suggest we have a bar lunch at that pub we passed,' Adam said as they walked back to the main road. 'The Wheatsheaf, wasn't it? And afterwards we can drive out to this lake everyone talks about. Though what it can tell us after all this time, God knows.'

'You seem rather deflated,' Kirsty remarked minutes later, as they settled themselves at a table in the bar.

He shrugged. 'I suppose I've been counting on this visit to open a few windows, but so far we've not learned much.'

'Adam, we've been here under twenty-four hours!'

He smiled reluctantly. 'You're right, we'll keep digging. And Mrs Vine-That-Was is definitely on the list. We should be able to find her now.'

So they drove out to Lake Belvedere, parked alongside a string of other cars, and did a circuit of the lake, which took most of the afternoon. It was a lovely setting, surrounded as it was by heather-covered hills. A skein of geese flew overhead, honking loudly, and brightly coloured mallards swam on the still water.

'I wish I had a camera myself,' Adam commented.

'It all looks so peaceful,' Kirsty said. 'It's horrible to think of Tony Vine dying here.'

They drove back to Hawkston in reflective mood, thinking back over the day and the people they'd met.

'Tomorrow,' Adam said, as they were approaching Hawkston, 'we can try to track down the barman where we had lunch that last day. He just might have overheard them discussing plans for the afternoon or know if there was anything special on that day, something they might have gone to see. And we can write up everything we've learned so far, which,' he added with a wry smile, 'shouldn't take long. Then, on Monday morning, we'll call on the Merry Widow.'

'Call on her?'

He nodded. 'We can't really give a good reason for wanting to see her, but if we just arrive on her doorstep she's not likely to turn us away.'

213

'She might not be in,' Kirsty pointed out.
'If she isn't we'll keep trying till we catch her. OK with that?'
'You're the boss,' Kirsty said.

Fifteen

Sunday was what Adam considered a wasted day. They located the pub mentioned in the video and enquired if a barman by the name of Antonio Bellini still worked there, only to learn that he'd returned to Italy two years previously. Nor, not unnaturally, could anyone they spoke to, either in the pub or the surrounding shops, recall any special event in Hawkston that Sunday twenty-six years ago.

'It was always a long shot,' Adam said philosophically. 'He'd have told that reporter all he knew – it was his *quart d'heure* of fame, after all. Not many people can say they served lunch to someone who was murdered later that day.'

They spent the afternoon visiting the museum and art gallery, both of which, unbound by Mrs Birchall's principles, were open on Sundays, and walked round the ruins of the Norman castle. By the time they returned to the hotel, they felt they had at least learned something of the history of the area, history that stretched back beyond the twelfth century.

With a break from concentrating on their research, they also learned a little more about each other and their lives during the long years they'd been apart. Kirsty asked after her cousins, and gathered from Adam's replies that he'd not

215

enjoyed a particularly close relationship with either of them.

'They resented me,' he said simply, and one look at his face convinced Kirsty it would be unwise to dispute the statement.

That evening they again borrowed the hotel phone book, and were confronted with a list of several Ferrises in the Residential section. 'So which do you suppose is her husband?' Adam asked rhetorically. 'BW, DW, HB or JL?'

'We could look on their website,' Kirsty suggested. 'That will probably show the directors, and possibly even their CVs.'

'Brilliant!' Adam switched on his tablet. 'Ferris Engineering, isn't it? And hey presto, here we go.'

Kirsty looked over his shoulder. The chairman was given as Barry William Ferris, and a little further delving revealed that he had married one Vivien Kendal in 1974. The Vice Chairman, Dean William Ferris, on the other hand, had married 1) Lucinda Parsons in 1976, divorced 1985, and 2) Marilyn Vine in 1987.

'Bingo!' Adam exclaimed. 'The other two are probably offspring. So – what's Mrs Dean Ferris's address?'

The house, standing well back from the road, was a handsome building of grey stone standing in an immaculate front garden still colourful with dahlias. On rising ground to the west of the town, it had magnificent views of the mountains that surrounded it on three sides.

As they walked up the path, Kirsty worried that

they hadn't found the right approach to gain Mrs Ferris's cooperation. How would she herself react, she wondered, if two total strangers arrived on her step with such an outlandish story? There was nothing, as far as she could see, to stop her closing the door in their faces.

Marilyn Ferris opened the door herself, a small, pretty woman whose fair hair was expertly cut and whose blue woollen dress, Kirsty surmised, bore a designer label. She looked from one of them to the other with a questioning smile.

'Mrs Ferris?' It had been agreed that Adam should open the proceedings.

'Yes?'

'My name is Adam Carstairs and this is my sister, Kirsty Marriott. We'd be very grateful if you could give us a few minutes of your time.'

She hesitated, as well she might. 'Are you Jehovah's Witnesses?' she asked uncertainly. 'Because—'

'No, no, nothing like that. Actually, we'd like to talk to you about . . . your first husband.'

She gave a little gasp and took a step back. '*Tony?*'

'Yes; it's just possible that he met our parents.'

She gazed at them blankly. 'I don't understand,' she said. From upstairs the sound of a vacuum cleaner reached them.

'I promise we're not confidence tricksters or anything,' Kirsty said quickly. 'The point is that our parents were murdered in Penthwaite in nineteen eighty-six, and we're trying to trace anyone who might have come into contact with them.'

'But . . . Tony's dead!'

'We know,' Adam said gently, 'and we appreciate that it might be painful to talk about him, but we'd be so grateful if you'd just let us explain.'

The vacuum cleaner hummed its way over the floor above, a reminder that at least she wasn't alone in the house.

'Well, I suppose . . .' A little reluctantly she stood to one side, and they went past her into the hall and through the door she indicated, finding themselves in a large sitting room whose picture window took full advantage of its mountain view.

She hadn't invited them to sit, and the three of them remained standing.

Adam began his prepared speech. 'I don't know whether you read about it at the time, but our family was holidaying in Penthwaite and both our parents were killed at their cottage, for no apparent reason. Their killers have never been caught.'

Marilyn's eyes widened. 'They were your parents? I'm so sorry. There was an ad in the paper, but . . .'

'I believe I'm right that you last saw your husband on Sunday the twenty-fourth of June that year?'

She drew in her breath, then nodded.

'It was the same day as the murders,' Adam said.

Marilyn's hand went to her throat. 'I'm not sure what you're implying.'

'That while of course it could have been coincidence, our parents often went to Lake Belvedere and might possibly have met him there.'

218

'It's possible, but I don't see that it's significant.'

'They died on the same day,' Kirsty repeated. 'Our father's camera was stolen, and the only explanation we can think of for their deaths is that they might have seen – and photographed – something they shouldn't have.'

Marilyn's eyes widened. 'And you think Tony might have seen it too?'

They both stared at her. Incredibly, that possibility hadn't occurred to them.

'He might,' Kirsty said after a moment.

'You're not suggesting he was murdered too?' Her voice had risen and she was gazing at them in horror.

'God, no!' Adam said quickly. But were they? Was it remotely possible that he had been?

Marilyn Vine made a sudden movement with her hand, as though dismissing the idea. 'You'd better sit down,' she said. 'I'll ask Heidi to bring us some coffee.'

She went out of the room and they heard her calling upstairs. Neither of them said a word until she came back and seated herself opposite them.

'I did hear about the murders, of course,' she admitted then, 'but I was out of my mind with worry about Tony, and I'm afraid everything else pretty well washed over me.'

'Tell us about him,' Adam invited.

'He was kind and funny and clever. I still miss him.'

'If it wouldn't upset you too much, could you tell us about his last few days? Was there anything different about him? Had he any worries, for instance? Money, work?'

'If you're suggesting he might have committed suicide, you can forget it,' Marilyn said firmly. 'But yes, he had worries. Who hasn't? There was some problem at work – he didn't say what, and to be honest I wasn't that interested, but Ferrises were going through a bad patch – almost on the brink of bankruptcy, though I didn't learn that until later.'

There was a tap on the door and a woman wearing an apron came in with three mugs of coffee on a tray, gave them all a hesitant smile and left the room.

'And it wasn't only Tony who was stressed out,' Marilyn added, handing them each a mug. 'My brother-in-law had a stroke, that same day, as it happens, and was in hospital for weeks. Parts of his memory never came back.'

'So three momentous things happened the same day,' Adam summarized, frowning. 'Your husband disappeared, your brother-in-law had a stroke, and our parents were murdered. That's quite a tally for one day.'

Kirsty said, 'Could you go through it, that Sunday, if it's not too upsetting? Was it a sudden decision, to go fishing?'

'He brought me breakfast in bed, and told me then. I wasn't best pleased: as you say, it was Sunday and I wanted him to spend it with me. But I knew he needed to be alone when he'd problems to sort out, and fishing always seemed to calm him. And he said we'd go out for dinner that evening, to make up for it.'

'So how did you fill the day?'

Marilyn smiled self-deprecatingly. 'In my usual

mindless way. I couldn't top up my tan – one of my favourite occupations – because it rained off and on all day, so I did my nails and watched TV.'

'You stayed home alone? No one called or phoned or anything?'

She shook her head.

'What time were you expecting him back?'

'He hadn't put a time on it, but—' She broke off. 'Wait a minute! Someone *did* phone! My God, I've never given it a thought from that moment to this!'

Adam leaned forward. 'Who was it?'

'Someone for Tony,' Marilyn said slowly. 'I don't think he gave a name, just asked to speak to him, and I said he wasn't in. And then he asked, as you just did, when I was expecting him back. That's what rang a bell.'

Kirsty's heart had started to hammer. 'And what did you tell him?'

Marilyn's hand shook suddenly and she put down her mug. 'I said I wasn't sure – *because he'd gone fishing*! Oh, *God*! You don't think . . .?'

Adam tried to keep his voice level. 'The caller didn't leave a message?'

She was still chasing her own, suddenly frightening thoughts, but after a moment she shook herself. 'Sorry. What did you say?'

'Did he leave a message?'

'No, I don't think so. God, why can't I *remember*?' Her hands gripped the sides of her head. 'Something about trying again later, I think.'

'But he didn't? Try again later?'

She shook her head.

'Then it couldn't have been anything important,'

Adam said firmly, anxious to dispel any suspicion she could have contributed to her husband's death. He cast around for a change of a subject, and his glance fell on a photograph on a side table, a smiling couple outside a church, the bride – Marilyn – in a suit, clutching the arm of a tall, dark man.

'That's your second husband?'

'Dean, yes. It was taken after our Blessing.' She paused. 'People were shocked when we married so quickly, but I don't think I could have survived those months without his help. And it was a very quiet wedding – not at all like my first.' She smiled ruefully. 'I still have photos of that, too, upstairs in a drawer. It didn't seem fair on Dean to leave them out, especially since he's not too happy about my keeping Tony's anniversary and insisting on dinner at the George. That's where we should have gone, that evening.'

'We're staying there,' Adam said.

Kirsty glanced at the photograph. Dean Ferris's face was a strong one, firm chin, challenging dark eyes, thick black hair springing back from his forehead. She wondered if Marilyn's description of Tony – kind, funny and clever – also applied to him, and somehow doubted it.

She said, 'We've taken up quite enough of your time, Mrs Ferris. I hope it hasn't been too upsetting for you.'

Marilyn shrugged. 'I'm afraid it's not shed any light on your parents' deaths.'

'It was always an outside chance,' Adam said, 'but if anything should occur to you later, perhaps you could call me.' He stood up and handed her a

222

card. 'Thanks for the coffee, and for going through everything with us. It was very good of you.'

'It brings it all back,' Marilyn said sadly. 'How long are you up here for?'

'Just till Friday. It's beginning to look like a wasted journey.'

'At least you tried,' she said.

'That might well be our epitaph,' Adam remarked, when they were back in the car. '*At least they tried.*'

'Oh, come on!' Kirsty protested. 'It's still only Monday!'

'Actually, something she said made me wonder: when I was going through the *Gazette* archives there was an article about a local firm in difficulties. I skipped it at the time, but I'd like to check back and see if by any chance it was Ferrises.'

'Does it matter? We know they were.'

'True, and since I only researched those few months, there'd be nothing on how and when they began to climb out of it.'

'Again, does it matter?'

'It might; after all, they're part of our research now, with the Vine/Ferris tie-up.'

'A very nebulous part, I'd have thought.'

Back at the hotel, he took out his tablet and checked through the notes he'd made prior to their visit.

'Yes, here it is – and it *was* Ferrises.' They read the article together and it made dismal reading – falling sales figures, lost contracts, trouble in the work force.

223

'They must have had an enormous stroke of luck,' Adam commented, 'to be able to turn things round after being that low.' He looked up, staring unseeingly across the room. 'I wonder . . .'

'What?'

He grinned, his face suddenly boyish. 'A sudden inspiration! If we're to find out how they did it, an oblique approach is called for. But it will be a strictly men-only exercise.'

'What exactly are you planning?' Kirsty asked suspiciously.

'A wooden horse strategy, tomorrow evening sometime.'

'Why can't I come?'

'Because you'd stick out like a sore thumb.' He raised a hand as she would have questioned him further. 'You'll have a blow-by-blow account in due course.'

And with that, she had to be content.

Marilyn stood just inside the front door till she heard their car drive away. Then she went up to her bedroom, opened a drawer in her tallboy and took out the topmost of a stack of photograph albums – not their wedding one, but that containing the last snaps she had of Tony. She sat back on her heels and slowly turned the pages, tears trickling down her face as she revisited happy days now long past. It was he who usually took the photos so there weren't many of him, and she lingered over the few she had – posing in a paper hat in front of the turkey that last Christmas; leaning against the rail on a boat trip on Loch Lomond; falling asleep in the garden over the Sunday papers.

Seven years they'd had together, that was all. She'd already been married to Dean over three times as long.

She started as the cleaner's voice reached her from downstairs. 'I go now, Mrs Ferris.'

'Thank you, Heidi. Your money's on the hall table.'

'I have it. I see you Wednesday.'

'Yes.'

The front door closed. She was alone – and she didn't want to be. She replaced the album with an affectionate pat and, going to the bedroom extension, called her sister-in-law's mobile.

'Viv, I know it's short notice, but are you free for lunch? I'm . . . in need of company.'

'Are you all right, Marilyn? You sound odd.'

'I've had a rather unsettling experience and I'd like to tell you about it.'

'How intriguing! I can spare an hour if we meet near my office. The Bistro at twelve thirty?'

'Perfect. Thanks. See you there.'

'How very strange,' Vivien commented when Marilyn had related her visitors' story. 'And how rotten for you, to have it all brought back again. Daphne said there'd been an ad in the *Gazette* asking for information. I suppose they must have put it in.'

'Do *you* remember those people being murdered?'

'I can't say I do. But at the time, remember, I was distracted too, with Barry being in hospital. I didn't hear the news or see a paper for weeks.'

Marilyn sipped her spritzer. 'It *is* extraordinary, though, that everything should have happened on the same day – Tony drowning, Barry's stroke, their parents' murders, and no explanation for any of it. I could never get my head around Tony falling overboard; a cousin of his had drowned as a child, and he'd always been obsessively careful around boats.'

'These things happen, and tragic though they were, they were three quite separate events. You're surely not wondering if there's a link?'

Marilyn sighed. 'I don't see how there can be. It's just strange, that's all.' She smiled at her sister-in-law. 'Sorry to have dragged you into this, but I had to talk to someone and Dean's in Germany all week negotiating a contract.'

'That's OK. Not sure I've been any help, though.'

'You were a sounding board, which was what I needed. Now I'll try to put it out of my mind.'

But if Marilyn succeeded in forgetting the episode, Vivien did not. Nor did she hurry back to her office, but went to sit in the municipal gardens, endlessly replaying the story she'd heard – a story that had resurrected half-formed, unacknowledged suspicions she'd been ignoring for more than twenty years.

All on the same day. It had never struck her as starkly as that, but she still couldn't see the relevance of that couple's murder. Where in the name of heaven did they fit in? There *couldn't* be a connection – of course there couldn't. And yet . . . She'd never got to the bottom of where Barry and Dean had been that afternoon, why they hadn't, as usual, returned home after their game of golf. Where, exactly, had Barry suffered his stroke? That had never been clear, and had some specific trauma instigated it, rather than a build-up of stress over the business? At the fête the previous day, she remembered suddenly, there'd been that curious atmosphere between the brothers, and Dean's uncharacteristic snapping at Pauline.

That had been the first instance of his unusual behaviour, but he'd acted even more oddly in the days that followed, paranoid about being at Barry's bedside when he emerged from his coma. Why? Brotherly love, or fear of what he might say as he came round?

She shook herself, but this time the doubts wouldn't go away. It seemed that while, all those years ago, these questions had been worrying her, Marilyn in turn had found it difficult to accept that Tony drowned accidentally. Could she be right? And if so, what other explanation could there be? She'd a horrible, creeping fear that everything came back to Tony. There was no denying it had been his invention that miraculously turned the fortunes of the firm, just when it seemed there'd been no option but bankruptcy. But Tony was a staff member; surely it would have come to them anyway, under the terms of his contract? His death couldn't profit anyone.

And to add to all that there were Barry's nightmares, which had grown more rather than less frequent over the years. Sometimes she wondered if that hidden part of his memory was using them to force itself to his attention, a fear that had rocketed when, last week, she'd returned home unexpectedly from a shopping trip to find him with his head on the kitchen table, sobbing uncontrollably.

Over to her left, the town hall clock gave its whirring cough and launched into its full peal, followed by two sonorous chimes. Two o'clock! She'd an appointment in fifteen minutes! Once more burying what could not be faced, Vivien hurried back to the office.

That afternoon, Adam and Kirsty drove out to the Glendale Industrial Estate to see for themselves the factory that had suddenly assumed importance in their investigation. But a high wall surrounded the site, and all they could glimpse through the tall iron gates was a multi-storey office block and a few sheds.

'What were you saying about a wasted journey?' Kirsty murmured, but Adam, who'd been surveying the surrounding area, shook his head.

'No, I've seen all that I need to.'

She turned to look at him in surprise. 'Is this by any chance reconnaissance for your wooden horse?'

'It is indeed.'

'Don't tell me you're planning a raid?'

He laughed. 'Hardly! Patience, little sister. All will be revealed.'

'I hope it's not going to take the whole evening, this plot of yours?'

'Hell, no. I'll be back in time for dinner.'

'Well, I suppose that's something,' she said.

At five thirty, when the iron gates opened and the work force began to stream through them, Adam

228

was back again, leaning against a bollard on the opposite pavement. The younger members, joking and pushing each other playfully, he ignored, biding his time, but he straightened when the older men appeared, walking more slowly, patting their pockets for a pipe or cigarettes. Two in particular fitted the profile he was looking for, both nearing retirement, deep in conversation – conversation that was surely destined not to end with a parting at the factory gates.

Unobtrusively he fell into step behind them, playing his hunch that they'd be making for the pub down the road and breathing a sigh of relief when they turned in its doorway. He followed them, thankful that, unwilling to abandon their discussion for more general chat, they'd taken their glasses to the only vacant table. Having acquired a glass of his own, Adam walked over.

'Mind if I join you?' he asked. 'This is the only free seat, and I've been on my feet all day.'

They nodded a little reluctantly and continued talking in low voices – something about the new Works Manager and the changes he was introducing.

'Sorry to butt in,' Adam said, 'but you work at Ferrises, don't you?'

They turned to him, annoyed at being interrupted but prepared to be civil to a stranger. 'Aye, that's right.'

'No worries about *your* jobs, then! I hear the firm's going from strength to strength.'

The bald man weighed him up. 'Yank, are you?'

'British, actually, but I grew up in Canada.'

'So what brings you to our neck o'woods?'

229

asked the other. 'Industrial estates don't usually figure on tourist maps.'

'I'm interested in the architecture,' Adam improvised smoothly. 'Not that I could see much, over that high wall of yours! It must be a great place to work, though, with all that job security. Family owned, isn't it?'

'Aye.'

The words 'blood' and 'stone' came into Adam's mind. Seeing their glasses were empty, he stood. 'Let me get you a refill. Same again?'

They hesitated, glanced at each other, then nodded, and he shouldered his way to the bar. Somehow he must get them to open up; perhaps this round would loosen their tongues.

'Name's Adam,' he volunteered, putting their drinks down on the table.

The bald man extended a hand. 'Joe,' he offered. 'And this 'ere's Bill.'

Adam nodded at each in turn and took a long draught of beer for much-needed Dutch courage. 'Another reason I'm interested in Ferrises,' he began conversationally, 'is that my family comes from these parts, and my dad used to know someone who worked there. Guy called Tony Vine. Is he still around?'

He hadn't the proverbial pin to hand, but was willing to bet that its dropping would have resounded like a gun shot. Innocently, he looked from one startled face to the other.

'Be in his late fifties by now, I guess,' he added into the growing silence. 'Do you know him?'

Joe cleared his throat. 'We knew Mr Vine, aye.'

'Knew?'

'He died, mate. Years ago.'

'Oh, I'm sorry.'

He waited expectantly, and sure enough Bill added in explanation, 'Drowned, like. In one o'local lakes.'

'Dad will be sorry to hear that. They lost touch when we emigrated in the eighties.'

Joe took a drink and wiped the back of his hand across his mouth. ''T'were in eighties it happened,' he said. 'Missing for weeks afore he were found. Firm were in a bad way then, and there were some as thought he'd done hisself in.'

'That's too bad. Quite a bright guy, I gather?'

'Aye, bright enough. It's thanks to him as firm pulled itself back from t'brink.'

Geronoimo! 'How was that, then?'

'Invented a new machine, didn't he?' Bill said. 'Leastways, modified an existing one that turned production on its head. Too bad he didn't live long enough to reap benefits.'

'So it wasn't in use when he died?'

'No. Rumour has it governor found it in his garden shed. Any road, patent was applied for and we never looked back.'

Adam caught a quick warning frown from Joe, and pounced. 'In his shed? You mean he wasn't working on it at the factory?'

'Seems not.' They were avoiding each other's eyes.

'But surely he'd have had everything to hand there?'

Bill shrugged. Apparently they'd said as much as they were prepared to, but they'd given him plenty to think about.

231

He finished his drink. 'I'm sure he'd have been glad to know he helped save the firm. Thanks for letting me join you; I won't impose any longer. Good to meet you both.'

'Ta for t'drinks,' Joe said.

'You're welcome.' And with a vague smile at them both, Adam made his way out of the pub.

'So it was more a question of the horse's mouth than the wooden horse,' Kirsty commented.

She and Adam were sitting over dinner at the George.

'Yes, but you do see what it means?'

'No, what?'

'That Vine didn't want the owners to know what he was up. That's the only explanation for his developing it at home.'

'But why?'

'I'm not well-versed in business contracts, but it seems likely that anything invented by one of its employees during working hours would legally be owned by the firm.'

'So?'

'So he worked on it in his own time because he wanted to hang on to the ownership.'

'Why would he want to do that?'

'God, Kirsty, *I* don't know! I'm just thinking aloud. I can't help feeling it's significant, though.'

'But he died, so the firm got it anyway.'

'Exactly.'

'Well, that's hard luck on him, but I can't see how it affects us.'

'Nor can I at the moment.' He topped up their wine glasses. 'I tell you one thing, though; I wish to hell we'd known about this before we saw Mrs Ferris. We'd have had a much better idea of what to ask her.'

'I doubt if it would have been much help; she seemed pretty vague about his work.'

'She might at least have known why he spent half the night working in the garden shed.'

They were silent for a while, busy with their own thoughts. Then Kirsty said, 'We have three days left. What else can we do?'

'Go to the police,' Adam replied promptly.

She looked startled. 'Really? You think they'll see us?'

'I'm damn sure they will. I'll phone in the morning and make an appointment. It'll be interesting to say the least to hear their take on the affair, and I also want to check if they knew Vine disappeared the same day.'

'There's probably no connection,' Kirsty pointed out.

'Nevertheless, they should be made aware of it if they're not already. And our turning up will show we're not giving up on this, cold case or not. With luck, it might give them a nudge.'

Detective Inspector Fleming was in his thirties, tall and slim, with keen blue eyes. He came to greet them with outstretched hand. 'Miss Marriott and Mr Carstairs? I believe you'd like to discuss one of our less successful investigations.' He ushered them into an interview room. 'The Penthwaite murders of 'eighty-six?'

'That's right,' Adam confirmed smoothly. 'The murder of our parents.'

The detective looked startled. 'Oh? I'm sorry – the names aren't the same and I didn't . . .'

'We were adopted by different sides of the family.' How many times had he said that in the last few weeks?

'I see.' Fleming put a folder on the table. 'Well, I've dug out the files and familiarized myself with the enquiry.' He looked up suddenly. 'God, were you the children in the house?'

They nodded.

'A lucky escape, by all accounts.' He shuffled through some papers. 'I have transcripts here of all the interviews conducted at the time – we weren't digitalized then – including the original phone call reporting discovery of the bodies, statements from people in the village and house-to-house enquiries. There are also details of extensive searches for the missing camera – charity shops, pawn brokers, car boot sales, you name it – conducted over a wide radius. As to the scene of crime, SOCO spent several days going over it, but apart from the shoe prints very few traces were found.'

'Traces?' Kirsty broke in.

'Of the perpetrators. Hairs, fibres and so on.'

Adam's face lit up. 'You have their DNA?'

Fleming shook his head. 'Unfortunately that facility wasn't available at the time.'

'But if you had a suspect now,' he persisted, 'you could extract DNA from these fibres and compare them?'

'Yes, indeed. A number of old cases have been solved by that means.'

'Where were these traces?'

'All in the main downstairs room. It had been raining the previous day and as I said there were two sets of muddy shoe prints, neither of which were Mr Franklyn's. All the males in the village had their footwear examined, but no match was found.'

Kirsty glanced at Adam, expecting him to bring up the subject of Vine, but he was still weighing the possibility of a DNA match. She said, 'A man was reported missing at the same time. Is that mentioned in the file?'

Fleming looked surprised. 'A missing person? Connected with this case?'

'That's what we're wondering. He disappeared that Sunday after fishing on Lake Belvedere, but his body wasn't recovered for some weeks, so its significance mightn't have been picked up.'

'A different team would have dealt with mispers,' Fleming replied, 'but "significance?" I can't see that it's relevant.'

'We feel everything unusual that happened that day is worth examining,' Adam said.

Fleming frowned. 'Who was this man?'

'Tony Vine,' Kirsty supplied. 'He worked for Ferris Engineering, and he'd just invented a machine that made their fortune for them.'

'And according to his wife,' Adam added, 'who, incidentally, is now Mrs Dean Ferris, there was a mysterious phone call that day, and she inadvertently let slip where he was.'

Fleming's frown deepened. 'What kind of phone call?'

'Someone asking for her husband, wanting to know when he was due back.' He held up a hand.

'All right, it doesn't sound suspicious in itself, but the caller refused to give a name, said he'd phone back but never did.'

'In my experience,' Fleming said drily, 'that frequently happens. However, I'll look into it, though if, as you say, his body was later found and there were no suspicious circumstances, the case would have been closed. And I still fail to see any link with your parents' deaths.'

'The lake's not far from Penthwaite,' Adam said. 'You must at least admit it's a coincidence. How often do two murders and a disappearance take place on the same day in such a small area?'

'As I say, we'll look into it,' Fleming answered smoothly, collecting his papers and returning them to the folder. 'Thank you for bringing it to our attention, and please accept our sympathy on the loss of your parents. It's extremely unfortunate that no one has so far been apprehended.'

There was little else they could do. Furthermore, the weather had turned wet and windy, not conducive to trudging round covering ground, both physical and metaphorical, that they'd already been over.

By Friday morning they were more than ready to pack their bags and set off for home. The change in the weather made motorway driving both tiring and depressing as spray from passing lorries repeatedly spattered their windscreen, added to which both were aware of anticlimax. They'd travelled to the Lakes hopeful of finding some hitherto unrecognized clue to their parents' murders, but that had not happened and, despite odd flashes of hope, they'd achieved nothing.

Nonetheless, Adam realized to his surprise that despite the disappointment, he'd felt happier during this last week than he could ever remember being. Was it, he wondered in a rare moment of self-analysis, because he'd spent it in the company of someone who, despite their long separation, was closer to him than anyone else on earth?

He felt a burst of affection for this newly found sister, and when he dropped her off outside her house, surprised them both by bending to kiss her cheek.

'Thanks for coming with me,' he said gruffly.

Sixteen

That same evening Dean Ferris returned from his trip to Germany to be greeted by his wife's story of her unexpected visitors and icy fear, kept at bay during his work trip, once again enveloped him.

He strode to the cabinet and poured himself a whisky. 'How the hell did they track you down?' he demanded roughly, downing his drink and pouring himself another.

'I've no idea. But as I say, they were wondering if Tony might have met their parents.'

He spun to face her, making her jump. *'But how did they know he was your husband?* Your name's Ferris now, remember!'

She shrugged. 'They didn't say, just that he disappeared on the same day – and I don't know how they knew that, either. It *is* odd, though, isn't it, two terrible things happening that Sunday – three, if you include Barry's stroke.' She glanced at him but he was staring into his glass, a closed look on his face. 'They think they were killed because they photographed something,' she went on. 'Their camera was stolen, you see. And if whatever it was happened at the lake, where they often went, it's possible Tony saw it too.'

Dean looked up, a pulse beating in his temple. 'You can scotch that idea,' he said thickly. 'Tony fell overboard, knocking himself out in the process – that was the official verdict. He didn't see *anything!*'

'Yes, dear, I know, but—'

'No buts.' He emptied his second glass. 'It must have been these people who put in the ad,' he said more calmly.

'I suppose so. I didn't ask them.' She hesitated. 'I don't know why you're so angry, dear; they're only trying to discover who killed their parents. You can't blame them for that.'

He drew a steadying breath. 'I'm not blaming them; I'm just appalled at the risk you took. I thought you'd more sense than to let complete strangers into the house.'

'They were a nice young couple—'

'That's a trick of the trade,' he interrupted. 'Promise me you'll never do that again.'

'All right, dear, I promise. But I wasn't alone – Heidi was here, and they could hear her Hoovering.'

'A lot of help she'd have been,' Dean retorted and, leaving her gazing after him in bewilderment, slammed out of the room.

Within an hour of Kirsty returning home, Janice was on the phone.

'Well?' she demanded. 'How did it go?'

Kirsty glanced at Angie and rolled her eyes. 'It was an interesting experience, but we didn't really learn anything.'

'What did I tell you? Well, at least you weren't murdered in your beds.'

'That *was* a relief!' Kirsty conceded, and after a moment Janice gave an embarrassed laugh.

239

'Sorry, darling, but I really was worried about you digging it all up again.'

'I know you were.'

'So what did you do up there?'

'We went to Penthwaite and spoke to the woman who was working in the shop at the time. She remembered us – it was quite weird.'

'Did you go to . . . the cottage?'

'Yes, but it's closed up for the winter, so we couldn't look inside.'

'Would you have wanted to?' There was a shudder in her voice.

'I don't know, Auntie. As Adam said, we were there to pay our respects.'

There was a brief silence. 'How did you get on with Adam?'

'Fine. He was . . . fine. We spoke to the police, too, and they told us what they'd done at the time. It sounded very thorough.'

'Not thorough enough, since they didn't catch anyone. Well, you've done what you set out to do. Now I hope you can put it all behind you.'

During the week Kirsty had been away the Christmas orders had begun to come in, and she and Angie settled down to a steadily increasing workload.

'A couple of weddings, as well as all the Christmas cakes, Yule logs and so on,' Angie said, checking her list. 'Who'd want to get married in November, of all months?'

'It's Auntie Jan's birthday, too,' Kirsty said. 'It's been a difficult year for her; I'd like to do something special.'

240

'Well, even if nothing came of your trip,' Angie commented, 'at least you're on better terms with Adam.'

'True, though it might take Auntie and Uncle time to come round. They still blame him for, as they see it, stirring things up again.'

'Have you given up hope of any further progress?' Angie asked curiously.

'More or less, but I doubt if Adam has; he still has a bee in his bonnet about the man who drowned.' She took down a large mixing bowl, her mind turning to more immediate matters. 'I did tell you, didn't I, that I'm having my hair cut in the lunch hour? It shouldn't take long, and I'll have a sandwich when I get back.'

'Fine by me. I'll just be having a snack too – I want to get this gâteau in the freezer.'

It was a cold, misty day and dead leaves squelched under her feet as she cut across the park on her way home. It seemed a long time since she'd sat there reading in the sunshine – and a long time since Alicia Penn's attack. There'd been no more since the policewoman's murder – nor, unfortunately, any news of an arrest. Perhaps the killer, fearful of discovery, had moved to pastures new.

She pulled her scarf more closely about her neck, momentarily regretting the trim that had exposed it. At least the kitchen would be warm and welcoming. At the thought of it she quickened her steps, emerged from the park on to East Crescent and hurried to the corner of her road. But as she reached it a car that had been coming down the hill braked and drew into the kerb beside her, its window lowering electronically.

'Kirsty! Just the one I want to see!' Matt Armstrong was leaning towards her across the passenger seat.

'Hello, Matt.'

'Can I have a quick word?' A car came up behind him, overtaking with an irritable toot. 'Look, could you get in for a minute? I can't stop here.'

'Matt, I'm hungry – I'm going home for lunch!'

'Only a minute, please. I'll drive round the park and deposit you straight back here.'

She sighed. 'OK.'

She slid inside, pulling the door shut and reaching for the seat belt.

'You say you've not eaten? Nor have I. I've a better idea, then; we'll find somewhere for a bite of lunch.'

'Sorry, I can't. Angie's expecting me back and work's piling up.'

'You have to eat,' he said.

'Really, I—'

'Our anniversary's coming up soon, and I'd welcome some suggestions for a cake.'

'I'm sorry, we don't do private commissions. You'd have to order it through one of our customers.'

'Nevertheless, if we discuss it, I'll have a better idea of what to order.'

'Look, it's kind of you to suggest lunch, but I really haven't time. Could you just . . .?'

It was too late. Instead of circling the park to take her home, he'd turned up the road by the

242

college that led past his own house and out of town.

'Matt!'

He gave a low laugh. 'An hour max. I'm willing to bet that's the minimum lunch break under some Act or other.'

She subsided into an annoyed silence. As the road climbed, the low cloud enveloped them and he switched on his headlamps. 'We could all do with cheering up in this weather,' he remarked, 'and life seems brighter with some hot food inside you.'

She'd come this way with Nick, Kirsty was thinking, on that rainy evening back in the summer. Nick. Adam hadn't mentioned him again, and she'd not liked to ask after him. He'd probably found himself – how had he described her? – a less *complicated* girlfriend.

The houses on both sides fell away to be replaced by fenced fields. From one of them, an invisible cow lowed as they passed.

'How does that poem go?' Matt asked lightly. '*No sky, no earthly view, No distance looking blue*, de-dum-de-dum-de-dum de-dee— *November*!'

'I was thinking much the same myself.'

'Have you read that book of mine that you bought at the library?' he asked suddenly.

Taken by surprise, she'd no time to prevaricate. 'Not yet, I'm afraid. I don't seem to get much time for reading.'

She leaned forward, peering through the windscreen. 'Wasn't that a pub we just passed?'

'Was it? Damn, I must have misjudged the distance in the mist. Never mind, there'll be another soon.'

She held down her growing impatience. 'I'd like to go home now, please. I really haven't time for this.'

He shook his head. 'The road's too narrow to turn here, and even if we could, a car might loom suddenly out of the mist and bump into us mid-manoeuvre. But don't give up – I know there's another pub along here.'

His voice had an odd note and she glanced at him uneasily. His hands were clenched on the steering wheel and sweat coursed down his face. It wasn't *that* warm in the car; what was wrong with him? From one moment to the next, disquiet slid into panic. Something wasn't right. What was she *thinking* of, driving blindly down deserted country roads with this man?

'Just stop here, will you?' she said quickly. 'The pub's not far behind; I'll walk back and phone for a taxi.'

He gave a short laugh and the hairs rose on the back of her neck. 'I can't just abandon you in the middle of nowhere! Chrissie would never forgive me.'

The middle of nowhere! Oh, God, she wished Adam was here! Or Nick. Or *anyone.*

'I want to get out!' she insisted, her voice rising. Then added in a flash of inspiration, 'I think I'm going to be sick!'

He stretched his arm out, pressing her back in her seat. 'Take deep breaths; you'll be all right.'

'Please stop the car!'

'Kirsty, I explained—'

Twisting free, she pressed down the door handle and the heavy door swung open. Beside her, Matt swore and started to brake. Fumbling for the seat belt release, she hurled herself sideways as they skidded to a halt, landing on her hands and knees on the wet verge.

'Kirsty! What the hell are you doing?'

She could hear him fumbling with his own seat belt and, bent double, she'd started to run when out of the mist a gate materialized just beside her. Regardless of possible bulls, she scrambled over it and ducked down behind the hedge, her heart hammering. What she was afraid of, she couldn't at that moment have said; it was a pure atavistic reaction to the smell of his sweat.

'Kirsty! For God's sake, come back! Where are you?'

She heard him run past her, his feet ringing on the surface of the road. 'Kirsty! Of course I'll take you home if you're that desperate! God, what are you thinking of?'

Again, instinct took over and without conscious thought she threw herself back over the gate and, reaching the car, scrambled into the driver's seat and locked the door. The key was in the ignition and she turned it with shaking fingers. There was a shout from down the road and, ignoring the risk of oncoming traffic, she turned in a wide sweep, mounting the opposite verge and bumping back on to the road. His figure loomed up ahead of her, arm raised but, pressing the accelerator to the floor, she hurtled past him down the invisible road.

Thankfully, as she reached the outskirts of town the mist lifted and, her heart still racing, she slowed down, guiding the unfamiliar car round the park and down the road where, less than an hour ago, she'd been sitting having her hair cut. A hundred yards farther on was the familiar outline of the police station, and she swerved into it and came to a halt.

Climbing out of the car on unsteady legs, she pushed her way into the building and over to the desk in the foyer.

'Can I help you, madam?'

She stared blankly at the man in front of her and, trying to marshal her tumbling thoughts, said the first thing that came into her head. 'I've been detained against my will. By Matthew Armstrong.'

The sergeant straightened, frowning. 'You . . .? Just a minute.' He glanced down at a scrawled note in front of him. 'Mr Armstrong, did you say?'

She nodded dumbly, starting to shiver with reaction.

'A Mr Armstrong's just rung in, madam, to report the theft of his car. By a Miss Kirsty Marriott. Would that by any chance be you?'

Seventeen

'I'm mortified, Angie! I overreacted big time!'

It was three hours later and Kirsty, still shivery, was ensconced in their sitting room wrapped in a duvet.

Angie handed her a mug of tea. 'Drink this; it'll help to warm you.'

'I mean, OK, he did insist I have lunch with him when I'd said no, but to be fair he couldn't just stop the car suddenly on my whim, not in that mist. And he didn't do anything *wrong*, try to make a pass or anything. All he did was push me back in my seat when he thought – rightly, as it happened – that I was becoming hysterical.' She shook her head despairingly. 'And what did *I* do? Leapt out of the car then proceeded to hijack it, leaving him stranded, and to add insult to injury, reported him to the police for abduction! And now he's heaping coals of fire by not even pressing charges – just glad, I was told, to get his car back undamaged! I've made a complete fool of myself, and if he wanted to he could make me a laughing stock, which could rub off on the business.'

'Why would he advertise the fact that you were frightened of him?' Angie sipped her tea, both hands round the mug. 'What I don't understand, though, is what made you flip? I mean, it's not as though he was a stranger – you *know* Matt

– but there must have been *something*, because you're the least hysterical person I know.'

'That's just it – I've no idea. Something to do with his sweat, perhaps. How pathetic is that? And what's even worse is that the police won't drop it. They insisted on examining me and taking my clothes for analysis, even though I told them he hadn't tried anything. By then I'd come to my senses and was trying to withdraw my complaint, but once the allegation had been made everything swung into motion and there was no stopping it. God, Angie, how can I ever face him or Chrissie again?'

Angie regarded her thoughtfully. 'You're still shaken, though, aren't you? Why won't you let me call your aunt?'

'Because she'd immediately assume I'd been raped. I've got the mother of all headaches, but otherwise I'm fine.'

'Then why not take a couple of paracetamol and lie down for a while? It's a good two hours till dinner.'

Kirsty smiled wanly. 'I never did get lunch, sandwich or otherwise!'

'I can make toast if you like?'

She shook her head. 'The tea's helping, but the thought of food doesn't appeal at the moment. I *will* lie down for a bit, though, if you don't mind. To shift the headache if nothing else.'

Her headache would have intensified had she known how diligently the police were following up her allegation, rescinded or not. While their colleague's murder remained unsolved, hairs or fibres relating to any kind of suspicious behaviour were being analysed for comparison with those retrieved from the scene, and time was of the essence.

The expense of speeding up their examination was therefore sanctioned, and an officer despatched to take them over to the lab in person and await the results.

When Kirsty had gone upstairs Angie returned to the kitchen to tidy up, still unsatisfied with her explanation – or rather lack of one. Why, suddenly, had she lost her nerve like that? It was so totally out of character. She'd have felt much happier if the Marriotts were told about it, but that seemed to be out of the question.

Then, midway through wiping the surfaces, a solution occurred to her. Adam! The two of them were on better terms now – perhaps he could get to the bottom of it.

Hurrying into the office she clicked on the college website for their phone number, reckoning classes should have finished for the day. Minutes later she was asking to speak to him, giving her name as Angela Thomas. Which, no doubt, would set him wondering!

She was kept on hold for several minutes while they tried to locate him, then there was a click and a voice said in her ear, 'Adam Carstairs.'

Stupidly, she was surprised by his Canadian accent. 'Oh, hi,' she said hesitantly. 'You don't know me, but I'm Kirsty's flatmate and business partner.'

'Ah, *Angie*! But . . . is she OK?'

'Yes. At least – well, yes.'

'Now you're worrying me.'

'I'm sorry. She's OK, but she had an unpleasant experience today, and—'

'Not another of those damned emails?'

So she'd told him about them. 'No, not that. Look – I know it's a bit of a cheek, but could you possibly come round?'

There was a pause, then: 'Why isn't she calling me herself?'

'She's having a rest.' Angie paused. 'Please. I'm a bit worried about her and she won't let me phone her aunt.'

He gave a short laugh. 'Understandable. OK, if you think I can help I'll be round in fifteen minutes.'

'Thanks so much, Adam,' Angie said gratefully.

He was as good as his word, and she breathed a sigh of relief as she answered the door, sizing him up as she did so. Of medium height, he bore only a passing resemblance to Kirsty, but the eyes that returned her scrutiny were the same grey as hers.

She smiled. 'Sorry, do come in. The sitting room's upstairs.'

'I know.' He followed her up and into the room he remembered. Though it was dark outside the view from its windows was still spectacular, a panorama of the brightly lit town. Adam glanced briefly at it, then turned to face her.

'So – what's the story?'

Angie indicated a chair, sitting opposite him as he seated himself, and launched straight into her account. He listened intently, his eyes never leaving her face until she came to the end.

'So nothing untoward actually happened?'

'No. But she was really frightened, Adam – that's the only explanation for her jumping out – and it's just not like her.'

'Do you know this man?'

'Yes, as I said, he's the husband of a friend. Well, they're both friends really, though we know Chrissie better. We've even had dinner at their house. He's an author,' she added inconsequentially.

Adam thought for a minute, then shook his head. 'He must have said or done *something* to alarm her. I mean, one minute she's happy to get in his car — or at least, agrees to do so – and the next she's in full flight.'

'I know. It doesn't make sense.'

'Might the emails have worried her more than she let on, and her imagination suddenly ignited?'

'It's possible, though she seemed to shrug them off.'

'What's your opinion of them?'

'They were a bit creepy, to be honest. We told the police – not that there's much they can do without knowing who's behind them – but there haven't been any for some weeks now, thank goodness.'

'You think the sender knows her personally?'

Angie shivered. 'He certainly knows where she lives because he delivered the nettle bouquet himself.' There was a long pause, then she added tentatively, 'I hope you don't mind my calling you, but I needed to talk it over with someone and you seemed the obvious person.'

He nodded, getting to his feet. 'I'd better go and have a word with her.'

Angie rose hastily. 'I'll ask her to come down . . .'

But he was already halfway to the door. 'Which is her room?'

She hesitated. 'On the next floor, the door on the left, but I really think . . .'

'Don't worry, I'll knock first!' he said over his shoulder, and started up the stairs.

Angie looked after him anxiously. How would Kirsty react to his suddenly appearing in her room? And would she blame her for contacting him?

Kirsty heard the tap on the door and stretched sleepily.

'Is it dinner time?' she called, expecting Angie's head round the door.

'Not yet.' Unbelievably, it was Adam's voice. Was she still dreaming? She struggled into a sitting position, pulling up the duvet to cover herself.

'May I come in?'

She was definitely awake and it was definitely Adam. But . . .?

'Yes,' she answered doubtfully, pushing the pillow behind her for support.

He opened the door and switched on the light. She looked incredibly young, he thought, with her hair ruffled and her eyes blinking in the sudden brightness.

'Angie told you,' she said.

'Yes.' He came in and sat on the end of the bed. 'And now I'd like *you* to tell me.'

'But you already—'

'Starting much earlier. How well do you know this man?'

'He's the husband of a friend.'

'I know that, but how well do you know *him*? Or rather, how well did you, before today's episode?'

'I've met him several times,' she said slowly, 'but always in a crowd.'

'Did you like him?'

'He was . . . all right.'

'What didn't you like?'

'Well, he has rather a high opinion of himself. He's a writer, and—'

'Yes, Angie said. But you never felt . . . apprehensive in any way?'

'Not in the slightest.'

'Even today, when you got into his car?'

'No; I was just annoyed at being waylaid. I was hungry and wanted my lunch.'

'But he invited you to join him, and despite your saying thanks but no thanks, drove out of town?

'Yes.'

'So were you nervous then?'

'No, I was still annoyed, especially when we passed a pub and he said he hadn't noticed it.'

'You didn't believe him?'

She hesitated. 'I'm not sure.'

'But you started to wonder where he was taking you?'

'Perhaps. I . . . don't know, really.'

'Well, did his manner change in some way? Did he try to touch you or anything?'

'Not then, no.' She frowned, thinking back. 'His voice was a bit . . . trembly and he was really gripping the steering wheel.' She gave a little shiver. 'And he was sweating, when it wasn't hot in the car.'

'He was sweating,' Adam repeated thoughtfully.

'I suddenly felt I had to get out but he refused to stop, though to be fair the road was narrow and the mist was obscuring visibility. In fact, that might have been part of it; I felt somehow locked with him in . . . in an invisible world, if that doesn't sound too fanciful.'

'You said he hadn't touched you *then*. Does that mean he did later?'

'Only to hold me back when I struggled to open the door.' She shook her head helplessly. 'There was no reason for me to take off like that. Honestly, Adam, I don't know what got into me. I feel a complete fool.'

He looked at her for a moment longer. 'Well, no harm's done, and it seems he's not going to land you with a criminal record for stealing his car.'

'I'll have to write and apologize,' she said miserably.

It seemed he'd get no further. Adam straightened and his glance fell on the soft toy on the chair. 'So that's the famous teddy you were never seen without!'

Kirsty smiled, wrenching her thoughts from the day's trauma. 'Yes, that's Bear.'

He bent forward and picked it up. 'He looks rather the worse for wear.'

'So would you if you'd spent years being dragged around by your ear!'

Adam smiled, pulling gently at the tuft of fur. 'Yes, it looks as though a repair job was carried

254

out at some stage. See the different-coloured thread?' He turned the toy over in his hands. 'In fact, he seems to have had an internal op at the same time. Same colour thread, anyway.'

'Perhaps his squeak needed replacing.'

His expression suddenly changed. 'Hang on. When we were in Penthwaite you said this was your only link with Mum and Dad.'

She looked at him questioningly. 'Yes?'

'Well, just suppose . . .' He started prodding at the worn fabric. 'I don't know if it's the squeak, but there's certainly something hard in here.' He looked up. 'Have you any scissors?'

'Oh, look, you're not going to—?'

'*Scissors*, Kirsty!'

'In my manicure set. Top drawer in the dressing table.'

He moved swiftly to retrieve them then, returning to the bed, carefully slit the stitches in the bear's middle while Kirsty watched in bewilderment.

'I don't know what you think—' She broke off as he slid his fingers into the hole he'd created and began feeling around.

'God, Kirsty!' Adam's voice was shaking.

'What? What is it?'

Carefully, so as not to tear the fabric, he withdrew his bunched fingers and held out his hand. In his palm lay a small black cylinder and, as she stared at it unbelievingly, he pulled off the cap and tipped out a rolled-up film.

She swallowed convulsively. 'You don't think . . .?'

'Oh,' he said softly, 'but I do!'

'You mean it wasn't in the camera after all? It's . . . been there all the time?'

He nodded.

Unable to take in the enormity of their find, she shook her head helplessly. 'But why didn't they take it straight to the police?'

'God knows. And they couldn't have felt there was any urgency about hiding it, or why would she have gone on to mend the ear at the same time?'

'Unless she'd been sewing the ear on, and that's what gave them the idea of a hiding place?'

'Well, we'll never know, but it was a damn good one. Who'd think of looking for it in a child's toy?'

Kirsty stared, fascinated, at the shiny brown roll. 'And that holds the answer to who killed them?'

'With luck, yes. Otherwise, why should they have *been* killed?'

'I – can't take this in!'

Adam fumbled in his pocket and drew out his mobile.

'Who are you phoning?'

'Graham Yates. He's a photographer, isn't he? With luck, he'll be able to develop it for us.'

'After all this time?'

'God knows. We can only hope.'

She held her breath as he clicked on Graham's number, but it switched almost at once to the answering service. Adam swore and ended the call.

'I'll try again later; it's not a message to entrust to voicemail. Too bad I don't know his mobile number.'

256

Instinctively Kirsty reached out to him and he took her hand, gripping it tightly.

'We've done it, sis,' he said. 'I really think we've done it!'

Marilyn Ferris lay rigidly in bed, staring up at the ceiling and listening to her husband's rhythmic snores. During the hours of daylight she could dismiss the thoughts that swam into her head as being outlandish, absurd. But in the dark they returned in force, refusing to be ignored. She drew a deep breath. Very well; she would face them once and for all and prove to herself how nebulous they were.

Her first hint of unease had come when she read out the ad in the personal column and Dean had reacted so strangely, snatching the paper out of her hands and hurrying out of the house with it. He hadn't brought it back, either. It puzzled her at the time, but he'd shrugged it off and the incident had slipped from her mind.

More alarming was the visit of those young people with their horror story. Their questions had reminded her of that phone call, the day Tony disappeared. True, it mightn't have been important, but now *everything* that day acquired significance. Who, when she came to think of it, would have phoned Tony on a Sunday, of all days? And why hadn't he rung back as he'd said?

Even more unsettling was the fact that Dean had again behaved oddly when she'd told him of the visit, and for some reason had since avoided all her attempts to return to the subject.

Another thing – which again was not the norm

257

but for which perhaps she should be grateful –
was that although Dean had been agitated and
on edge since returning from Germany, he'd also
been exceptionally caring, bringing her flowers
and chocolates and taking her out to dinner.
They'd even made love a couple of times, an
increasingly rare event these days.

She moved restlessly. Taken separately, these
instances could easily be discounted, but linked
together they assumed worrying proportions. Yet
again she thought back to Adam Carstairs and
his sister, mentally replaying their conversation.
First came bewilderment that they should know
when she last saw Tony, then shock on learning
it was the day their parents were murdered. How
had Adam later summarized it? *'Your husband
disappeared, your brother-in-law had a stroke
and our parents were murdered. That's quite a
tally for one day.'*

Their parents, it seemed, had often gone to the
lake, and although they'd been killed at their
cottage, it was possible that what they'd seen had
taken place there. Adam had even wondered if
Tony might also have seen it. Or . . .

A new and terrible thought came into her head,
squeezing her heart in an iron grip as she froze,
letting it sink into her consciousness. *Suppose
the terrible thing they'd witnessed had been
happening to Tony?*

To Adam and Kirsty's frustration, Graham Yates
continued to be elusive. On the Saturday, having
still been unable to raise him and clinging to the
unlikely possibility of his phone being out of

order – a possibility denied by British Telecom – they drove out to his home, to find no car in the drive and the outer door firmly shut. A man was working in the next-door garden and Adam called over to him.

'Excuse me, could you tell me if the Yates are away?'

The man looked up. 'Know them, do you?'

'Yes, as a matter of fact he's my godfather. My name is Adam Carstairs.'

'Ah. Well, you can't be too careful these days. Yes, Sue's mother has moved into a care home and they've gone over to help her settle in.'

'Wonderful!' Adam muttered under his breath. He raised his voice. 'Have you any idea when they'll be back?'

'Monday, I believe. Want me to give them a message?'

'No, it's OK, thanks, I'll contact him then.'

'Bloody infuriating!' Adam raged as Kirsty pulled her car door shut.

'It is,' she agreed, 'but having waited twenty-six years, I suppose we can last another two days.'

He nodded grudgingly. 'It's just that having got so close, I'm now obsessed with the fear that the culprits will somehow get wind of us and manage to escape.'

'If they're still in that area they'll know we've been asking around,' Kirsty pointed out. 'In which case, it might already be too late.'

'Proper little ray of sunshine, aren't you?' He glanced as her as he started the engine. 'By the way, I told Nick the whole story.'

259

He saw her quick frown, but all she said was, 'Oh? Why?'

'Chiefly because he asked what I was doing over half term.'

'And what was his reaction?'

Adam flicked her another glance. 'He was more concerned about you than anything.'

She spun to face him. '*Me?*'

'I told him you'd only just learned the truth, and he regretted having snapped at you.'

She didn't speak, and Adam continued, 'In fact, he's asked after you once or twice. I shouldn't be surprised if he contacts you again.' Still no response. 'Would you like to see him?'

'That's for you to wonder and him to find out,' Kirsty said tartly, and he wisely let the subject drop.

On Monday morning there was another bombshell, in the form of an excited phone call from Lois.

'Kirsty, you're never going to believe this! Matt Armstrong's been taken in for questioning in connection with that murder! Chrissie's beside herself!'

Kirsty's legs gave way and she sat down abruptly, coldness washing over her.

'Kirsty? Are you there?'

'I'm here. But . . . I don't understand . . .'

'Nor does anyone, but I have to warn you – she's got it into her head that it's your fault! Don't ask me why, she was quite hysterical – going on about you stealing his car of all things, and him being kind enough to let you off. "And this is how she repays him!" she said. Sounds quite bizarre to me!' She paused. 'Can you make sense of it?'

'It was all a mistake,' Kirsty said out of a dry mouth. But was it? Oh, God, was it? Or was her blind instinct for self-preservation totally justified?

Lois was rattling on. 'Her mother came and collected her and bore her off to Brighton or wherever, so now we'll only have press reports to go on.' She paused again. '*Did* something happen between you and Matt?'

Kirsty closed her eyes. 'It's a tremendous shock,' she said with difficulty, 'but thanks for letting me know. I'll be in touch.' And she switched off her phone, her heart thundering.

'What's a tremendous shock?' Angie enquired, coming into the room. 'Kirsty? Kirsty, what's happened?' She hurried over, taking hold of her friend's arm.

Kirsty looked up at her blindly. 'Matt has been taken in for questioning about the murder,' she said.

Angie gasped, her eyes widening. 'You're not serious? *Matt?* My *God*! Just think, if you hadn't made a run for it, he might have killed you too!'

Eighteen

Matt's arrest was reported on the lunchtime news, though he featured only as 'a local man helping police with their enquiries'. Relatively few, Kirsty hoped, would be able to put a name to him, and she prayed Lois wouldn't repeat Chrissie's allegations.

Adam hadn't been reassuring. 'But let's face it, she's right, isn't she?' he'd said, after his initial shock. 'Following on your adventure, the obvious explanation is that they matched fibres and such from your clothes with those the killer left on his victim.'

She was stunned at the thought. 'God, do you think so?'

'Seems logical. You did well to run, my girl!'

She shuddered. 'It just doesn't seem possible – not someone we know! And he hasn't been charged or anything. They could still release him.'

'Time will tell. In the meantime, Graham should be home this evening. With luck, I can take the film round.'

'I want to be there when he develops it,' Kirsty said quickly.

'I'll call him first and let you know the score.'

'Something horrible's just occurred to me,' Angie said when Kirsty rejoined her in the kitchen. 'The police thought the attacker and the murderer

262

were the same man, didn't they? Which means it must have been Matt who raped Alicia, his own sister-in-law!'

'That's *sick*!' Kirsty exclaimed.

'And one more thing for poor Chrissie to face,' Angie added soberly.

It was late that evening before Graham Yates answered his phone.

'Adam!' he exclaimed. 'Good to hear from you! How . . .?'

'Graham, the most amazing thing has happened!' Adam broke in, unable to contain himself any longer. 'Kirsty and I have found a film that we're pretty sure is the one Mark took that last day.'

'Hey, slow down! You've *what*? Where? How?'

'I'll explain when I see you. Will you be able to develop it?'

'Depends what condition it's in,' Graham said. 'Whether it's been stored in a cool dry place and so on.'

Adam sent up a quick prayer that Bear hadn't been hugged too enthusiastically or seen the inside of a washing machine. 'It looks OK from the outside.'

'Well, I'd certainly be fascinated to have a look at it. I—'

'When can I bring it round?'

Graham gave a short laugh. 'Yesterday, for preference?'

'Sorry, it's just—'

'Of course, I understand. How about tomorrow?'

'That would be perfect. Will you be able to tell at once if it's salvageable?'

'Probably, but bear in mind that it's God knows how old, so the image will have regressed and base fog increased. It'll need special treatment – I'll have to change my processing routine, for instance – but it can probably be done.'

'Have you the right equipment?' Anxiety was strident in Adam's voice.

'The equipment, yes. Not so sure about the paper; it'll have to be higher grade than usual, but if I haven't any I could no doubt get hold of some.'

'Obviously we'd reimburse you for any expense.'

'Adam, your father was my best friend. If I can do anything to help nail his murderers, believe me I'll do it, if it takes my last penny.'

Thank you,' Adam said gruffly. 'Tomorrow evening, then? And I think Kirsty would like to come.'

'It'll be great to see her at last. Eight o'clock-ish?'

'We'll be there,' Adam said.

They didn't speak as they drove out to the Yates's house the next evening. Both were tense, turning over in their minds the possible answers now lying within their grasp. But suppose Bear *had* been through the washing machine? Suppose the film had been damaged beyond repair? They'd be back to square one again.

Sue greeted them at the door. 'Hello, Adam. And Kirsty – how lovely to see you after all this time! Come in, Graham's expecting you.'

He came into the hall to meet them and, taking hold of Kirsty's hands, kissed her on both cheeks. 'I've waited a long time for this!' he said. 'I'd hoped to watch you growing up, but your aunt had other ideas. No doubt she had her reasons.'

'Thanks so much for agreeing to help us,' Kirsty said.

'Well, come in and let the dog see the rabbit.'

They all went into the sitting room and Adam produced the canister from his pocket. His hand was shaking as he passed it over.

'Where did you find it?' Graham asked curiously as he tipped out the film.

They related the story and he shook his head incredulously. 'It was pretty quick thinking on Mark and Emma's part. What an ingenious hiding place.'

'A bit too ingenious,' Adam remarked feelingly. 'It was sheer luck that we found it at all.'

'But they'd have been expecting to retrieve it themselves as soon as they got home,' Sue reminded them.

Noting their suddenly sober faces, Graham said briskly, 'Well now, what part of the film do you think might be incriminating?'

Adam cleared his throat. 'If, as we think, he'd only just seen this . . . incident, they'd be at the end – always supposing he finished the film. Why, won't you be developing all of it?'

'Of course, but first I suggest we do a test run, which would mean cutting eight or nine inches off the beginning. The danger is that this would have to be done in the dark and I might inadvertently cut through a negative, but if it's unlikely to be a crucial one it might be worth risking. Several inches would be taken up by the tongue so we'd only get two or three images, but it would help me judge the increase in base fog and assess from that how much to increase the development time to achieve a reasonable image.' He looked from one to the other. 'Prepared to risk it?'

They both nodded at once.

'At least we'd know then what we're looking at.'

'Could you do it now?' Kirsty asked.

'Yes, it'd only take about forty minutes.'

'Just time for coffee and a chat!' Sue said.

'Then I'll leave you in the capable hands of my wife. I'm as curious as you to find out what we have here.'

They were the longest forty minutes of their lives, and in fact it was closer to an hour before Graham rejoined them.

'Unfortunately it wasn't as straightforward as I'd hoped,' he began. 'The test process shows that due to age and storage the negs are likely to have a higher level of fog than I anticipated, which means I'll have to increase development and then use a ferricyanide reducer to cut the base density.'

Adam grimaced. 'I'm afraid that's a bit technical for me. Does that mean they're retrievable, or not?'

'Oh yes; the results won't be perfect but they should be good enough for your purposes.'

'Can we see them?' Kirsty asked eagerly.

'Of course. They're not quite dry, so take care only to hold them by the perforated edge. If you lift them to the light and look through this magnifier, you should be able to make out the subject matter.'

There were, as Graham had said, only two images,

both seemingly taken at the fête Mrs Birchall had mentioned. It was just possible to make out an infant Kirsty nursing what appeared to be a baby rabbit and, on the other, Adam eating an ice cream.

'You'll be able to develop the whole film, then?' Adam asked anxiously.

Graham nodded. 'It'll be a fairly lengthy process, but we should achieve the end product sometime tomorrow. I'll let you know as soon as I have something.'

All through his classes that Wednesday Adam was longing to sneak a glance at his mobile which, of necessity, was on silent; but each time a lesson ended and he checked, it remained stubbornly uncommunicative. Suppose after all the film proved useless? It didn't bear thinking about, but whatever the outcome, Graham had promised to let them know.

Fortuitously it was as he reached the staff room at the end of the afternoon that his mobile finally rang. He snatched it up and retreated to a corner, turning his back on the others in the room. 'Graham?'

'We have lift-off,' Graham said crisply.

'It worked? You could . . .?'

'It did and I could.'

'So what have we got?'

'Come over and see for yourself.'

'Give me half an hour,' Adam said.

Kirsty, forewarned by his call, was at her gate when he drew up.

'Did he say what was on it?' she demanded as she slid into the car.

'No, but it must be significant – he said we have lift-off.'

'So the answer was in Bear all this time.'

'It would seem so.'

There was an air of suppressed excitement about Graham as he admitted them.

'Well, I reckon we've got 'em red-handed,' he said with satisfaction. 'Mark used a long-focus zoom so the faces should be identifiable. All we have to do now is track down who they belong to.'

He lifted a pile of prints from the table and sifted through them. Kirsty moved closer, leaning in to look as Graham handed over the first he'd selected. 'This is the start of the action,' he said.

The scene appeared to have been taken from a hill above Lake Belvedere, showing the lake bathed in watery sunshine. A boat bobbed at its edge, and on the bank three men stood facing each other, one with his back to the camera.

Adam's eyes narrowed suddenly. 'Is that a fishing line? There, propped against that rock? God, Kirsty! One of them must be Tony Vine!'

Graham flashed him a look of enquiry, but they were already passing to the next print, in which a man was gesticulating. By the scene after that he'd closed in to confront one of the others, his stance aggressive.

'Now look at this,' Graham said grimly.

They flicked through the remaining prints in shocked silence as the grim sequence played out – the punch, Vine on the ground, the raised rock, the actual blow, the third man belatedly hanging on to the attacker's arm. But the shot of that third man kneeling beside him, his face raised, provoked an instantaneous and horrified reaction.

'God, I *recognize* him!' Adam exclaimed.

And Kirsty: 'The photo at Mrs Ferris's! Adam, it's her second husband! Oh, that poor woman!'

'You're not saying you *know* that man?' Graham demanded in amazement.

'Not personally, thank God.' Adam's voice was shaking. 'But we can tell you his name. It's Dean Ferris.'

'Then we've got him!' Triumph rang in Graham's voice.

'He wasn't the killer,' Kirsty pointed out, but he dismissed the mitigation.

'Believe me, he's no innocent. See what happens next.' And he handed over the final two prints: the inert body being heaved into the boat and the two men rowing out into the lake.

'Murder most foul,' he summarized. 'Now, tell me how the hell you've managed to identify two of the three men.'

Sue, who'd been hovering quietly in the background, came in with a tea trolley. 'I thought you'd be in need of something after all that,' she said. 'Sit down and relax for a while, and you can go through the rest of the photos. They brought back so many memories to Graham and me, seeing you as we knew you all those years ago. There aren't any of Mark, unfortunately, him being the photographer – it's the same in our family – but there are one or two of Emma, bless her.'

So, still shaken and disbelieving, they looked at the remainder of the prints, nearly all of which had been taken at the fête, while the hot tea served to diminish their shock, as Sue had intended. And they explained about Tony Vine's disappearance on the crucial day and their visit to his widow, now Mrs Dean Ferris.

'So what's the next step?' Graham asked.

'We take the film to DI Fleming,' Adam replied promptly.

'Will it be enough to nail them?' Kirsty asked.

'Enough to bring them in for questioning, that's for sure,' Graham pronounced. 'Any idea who the third man was?'

'No, but he and Ferris must be close, if not before this happened then certainly after, though it's possible he could have died in the interim.'

'It's Mrs Ferris who I feel sorry for,' Kirsty commented. 'Imagine discovering you're married to someone who saw your first husband murdered and helped to tip him in the lake! You're right, Graham, he's almost equally to blame. Even if he didn't strike the blow, he helped dispose of the body and kept quiet all these years. For that matter he might have been the one who killed Mum and Dad.'

'They must have spotted Mark when they were out on the lake,' Graham surmised. 'Though how the hell they knew who he was or how to find him, God knows. I doubt if *we* ever shall.'

'But why kill Mum too?' Kirsty demanded, a catch in her voice. 'What had she ever done to them?'

They stayed talking it over for another half

hour, then Adam got to his feet. 'I must get back – there's a staff meeting at eight. We can't thank you enough, Graham, for producing these for us.'

'To say you're welcome is an understatement. I'll be waiting with bated breath for the next instalment.'

'How soon can we go back?' Kirsty asked, as they drove away from the house. 'Will we have to wait for the weekend? I can manage anytime, but—'

'It can't be tomorrow, unfortunately,' Adam said. 'I have wall-to-wall classes, but Friday's free. We could make an early start then.'

'Couldn't we fly up, rather than face that long drive again?'

He shook his head. 'The nearest airport's miles from Hawkston; it would mean all the hassle of arranging for a hire car and still having to drive fifty-odd miles. Not worth it.'

'I'll book rooms at the George, then. Will you phone Fleming in advance?'

'No. I'd rather see his face when we hand him the prints. If the other man's local, he's sure to know him.'

'Friday it is, then,' she said.

They set off at nine. It was a dark, dreary morning and the traffic was unexpectedly heavy.

'I'd hoped with it's not being half term the roads might be quieter,' Adam said. 'Not that we can do much about it.'

The miles slid past with frustrating slowness and it was increasingly difficult to control their

271

impatience. In need of hot food and a brief respite, they made an unscheduled stop for lunch and felt the better for it, especially since as they drove north again the weather began to improve. The mist cleared and a thin, wintry sun shone from a colourless sky. A good omen, perhaps.

'Suppose Fleming isn't on duty?' Kirsty asked at one point.

'Suppose no such thing,' Adam returned shortly.

'You're still not going to ring and check?'

'No; I want to take him by surprise, see his reaction.'

It was a quarter to four when they drove into the car park at the George Hotel and, tired and stiff, went in to register and leave their overnight bags.

'A quick freshen-up, then full speed ahead for the police station,' Adam instructed, leaving her at the door to her room.

'Aye, aye, sir!'

As she brushed her hair, Kirsty glanced at her reflection in the mirror. What would have happened before she looked at it again? An impatient tap cut short her musings and she hurried to rejoin her brother.

'Sorry, sir, DI Fleming's not in his office.'

'Do you know where he is?' Adam asked shortly.

''Fraid not, sir.'

'Well, please could you find him? We need to see him urgently.'

'Perhaps DS Black could help? He—'

'Sorry, no; it must be the DI. He knows the background to this.'

'I'll see if I can trace him, sir. If you'd care to take a seat?'

Unwillingly, Adam and Kirsty seated themselves on the hard chairs in the foyer. It was some minutes before they were called back to the desk.

'I'm afraid DI Fleming's out of the building, sir.'

Adam swore softly. 'But he is coming back?'

'He's expected, yes, sir, but not before five o'clock at the earliest.'

'We'll wait.'

'Very good, sir. I'll order some tea for you.'

'This wouldn't have happened if you'd made an appointment,' Kirsty complained.

'It's not long to wait – only an hour or so.'

'Five at the earliest, he said. It could be six or even seven.'

'Then we'll send out for soup and sandwiches,' Adam replied, poker-faced, and with a shrug she resignedly picked up a magazine and started to flick through the pages.

DI Fleming came striding through the door at five minutes to six, stopping short on seeing them sitting there. Adam and Kirsty rose as one, and after a momentary hesitation he came towards them.

'Miss Marriott, Mr Carstairs! This is a surprise! I thought you'd gone home long since!'

'Oh, we had, Mr Fleming, but we have some important new evidence for you.'

'Evidence?'

'Concerning the death of Tony Vine and in all likelihood our parents' as well.'

Fleming shook his head in bewilderment. 'We discussed all this, and I thought I explained—'

'Please, Inspector. We've something of vital importance to show you.'

He glanced impatiently at his watch. 'Very well, you'd better come in here.' He opened the nearest door and ushered them into a small room containing four chairs and a table.

'Now, what have you got?'

Adam laid the last ten prints of the film on the table. 'If you remember, we mentioned a man who'd gone missing the day of our parents' murder, and you said you'd look into it. Perhaps you'd like to run through these. They were taken by our father shortly before his death.'

Fleming threw him a startled glance, then picked up the prints and they watched his face change as he went through them.

'Where did you get these?' he asked in a strangled voice.

'My father had removed the film, so although the killers took the camera, they never got their hands on it. Either he or my mother hid it in one of my sister's toys. We found it quite by chance last week and a friend of his was able to develop it.'

The detective was still staring unbelievingly at the prints, going from one to another and back again.

'We're pretty sure Tony Vine, the missing man, is the one being killed, and we recognized Dean Ferris as one of the others.' He paused. 'Do you know the third man?'

'His brother Barry,' Fleming said dully, almost

to himself. Then, 'But . . . this is unbelievable! Can you vouch for the authenticity of the film?'

'I'd say it's beyond question, but if you need verification you could contact Graham Yates, who developed it for us. And you did say you still had samples taken from the cottage; all you'd have to do is compare them with the Ferrises' DNA.'

'Thank you, Mr Carstairs, I don't think I need you to tell me my job,' Fleming said stiffly, adding in a more conciliatory tone, 'but I do understand you need to clear this up, and I assure you we'll set wheels in motion straight away.'

'We have to leave on Sunday, but here's my card. You will keep us informed?'

Fleming nodded briskly. 'You'll be updated with progress under the Victims' Charter, when, for instance, someone is arrested or charged or appears in court.' He sat back in his chair, shaking his head. 'I have to say you seem to have stumbled on something quite extraordinary, but I must stress that it is now in the hands of the police. You may be sure it will be thoroughly followed up.'

He stood, holding out his hand to each in turn. 'Thank you very much for bringing this to our attention.'

Nineteen

Flashback: June, 1986

It wasn't their best game of golf, as the Ferris brothers were only too aware; nor did the weather conditions help. There was a persistent drizzle that every now and then intensified into a heavy shower, making it more a feat of endurance than an enjoyable pastime. In addition, their anxiety about the proposed meeting with Tony made it an effort to respond to the usual joking comments of their competitors.

To add to their frustration, the bar lunch was considerably lengthened by their being joined by another group of friends from whom it was difficult to break away, and it was consequently well after three thirty before they could escape. Barry made straight for the pay phone in a corridor behind the bar.

'Hello?' It was Marilyn's voice.

Instinctively, he deepened his voice slightly. 'Could I speak to Tony Vine, please?'

'I'm sorry, he isn't in.'

Barry hesitated. Dean nudged him, and he continued, 'What time are you expecting him back?'

'I don't know exactly; he's gone fishing. But he won't be very late, because we're going out for dinner.' A pause. 'May I give him a message?'

'I – no, it's not important.'

'May I ask who's calling?'

So she hadn't recognized his voice. Barry said quickly, 'He won't remember my name. We met at a conference, and as I'm in the area I thought we might have a drink together . . .'

'Well, I'm sorry, but if you'd like to call back tomorrow?'

'Yes, I'll do that. Sorry to have troubled you.' And he quickly put the phone down.

'Why all the cloak and dagger?' Dean enquired.

Barry shrugged. 'Didn't want to go into why I was phoning on a Sunday. She said he's out fishing.'

'He'll be at Lake Belvedere,' Dean said. 'That's where he always goes.' An idea struck him. 'We could corner him there.'

'God, Dean, do you know how big that lake is? How the hell would we find him?'

'It's worth a try. Otherwise it'll have to be at work tomorrow, which could be awkward.' He checked his watch. 'We'd better get a move on, though, if we're going out there; it's nearly an hour's drive, and he could have packed up and left by the time we get there.'

Barry came to a decision. 'Right, let's give it a go.'

They barely spoke on the drive, each busy with his own thoughts. At least the weather had improved, and a weak sun was glinting on the wet roads. By the time they drew into the parking place it was almost four thirty. Only one other car stood in the normally busy space, and to their

277

relief they recognized it as Tony's. At least he was still here.

In fact, as they rounded the corner of the hill bordering the lake, they saw him almost at once a few hundred yards away, a solitary figure motionless on the bank, rod in hand. Quickening their footsteps, they hurried through the wet grass, and only when they were within feet of him did he become aware of them.

'Good God!' he exclaimed. 'What the hell brings you here?'

'We wanted a word, Tony,' Barry said placatingly. 'We got off on the wrong foot on Friday, and we need to get things sorted before tomorrow morning.'

Tony turned his attention back to his line. 'As far as I'm concerned, they *are* sorted.'

'Look,' Dean began, 'you've every right to be annoyed with us putting a spoke in your wheel. It's just that we were so worried about finances—'

'Point is,' Tony said expressionlessly, 'you *never* listened to me. I'm supposed to be Development Manager – how the hell can I do my job when every time I suggest a new angle or any kind of innovation, you slap me down? It's been going on for years and frankly I've had enough of it. Now that I have my own prototype, it's time to branch out by myself.'

'But you'd have to start from scratch,' Barry argued. 'We've got the set-up all ready for you – all you'd have to do is install the machine and off we'd go. And if it's as successful as you claim, perhaps you could adapt it for use in other departments.'

Tony gave a grim smile. 'If you'd spoken like that a year ago,' he said, 'things would be very different now.'

'What are your terms for staying?' Barry demanded urgently. 'A partnership? You've got it. Salary increase? Definitely, once we're out of the wood. Name your price. Sole responsibility for—'

'Sorry, you're wasting your breath. My mind's made up.'

Barry bit back his irritation. 'At least let's talk it over. So far, we know nothing about this machine except that it dramatically cuts production time. We only have your word for it; give us a demonstration, and we can discuss the best means of—'

'Of what? Taking over control of it, and shunting me sideways?'

'Of course not!' Barry ran a frustrated hand through his hair. 'God, what do you think we are – a couple of crooks?'

Lifting his line out of the water, Tony propped the rod against an adjacent rock before turning to face them. 'Look, boys, I'm sorry it's come to this. I don't want to leave with any bad feelings, so let's end our association on a friendly note. I'll work out my month's notice and then I hope we can part with a handshake.'

Barry had begun pacing back and forth. 'You don't seem to realize that you're arbitrarily consigning us to the scrap heap!' He paused, trying to control his breathing. 'We're on our uppers, as you well know, and you have it in your power to save us. If we have to beg, OK, we're begging. Postpone going for a year. Keep control of your patent, if that's what you want, but put it to use at Ferrises. Then, once it's established and we've built one of our own under licence, you can go down south or wherever and start up yourself. That's not asking too much, surely?'

Tony turned towards his rod. 'You'll have to excuse me, it's time I was breaking down my tackle. We're eating at the George this evening, and I'm in need of a long, hot shower.'

Barry caught hold of his arm and spun him round, his face infused with rage.

'Haven't you heard a word I just said?'

Tony stiffened. 'Didn't *you* hear what *I* said?'

'Be reasonable, man! This year or next – it's surely immaterial to you, but the difference between life and death for us!'

'I'm sorry, but as I said this has all come too late. Now, please let go of my arm. I have to pack up.'

Barry's hands dropped to his sides. His breath was coming in ragged gasps and for a timeless moment the two men stood face-to-face. Then, with a smothered exclamation, Barry balled his fist and lashed out, catching Tony on the chin and sending him crashing to the ground.

'Barry!' Dean stared at him, appalled, but Barry, all control gone, had bent to pick up a rock and, before his brother realized his intent, brought it down forcibly on Tony's head. Then, impelled by his own momentum, he began to rain blow after blow on the man beneath him, whose struggles abruptly ceased. Frozen with horror, Dean

280

watched unbelievingly for another heartbeat before leaping forward, seizing his brother's arm and holding it, suspended, inches above the injured man.

'My *God*, Barry, what are you doing?' he gasped. 'You could have killed him!'

Barry wiped a hand across his mouth, his shoulders heaving. Releasing his arm, Dean dropped to his knees, feeling increasingly frantically for a pulse. And found none. White-faced, he stared up at his brother and slowly shook his head. 'You *have* killed him!' he whispered.

The next few minutes were a blur as they acted instinctively and in silence. Somehow they succeeded in half-carrying, half-dragging Tony's body to his boat, still bobbing alongside, and tipped him inside. It wasn't until they'd scrambled in after him and started rowing that Barry glanced up, and froze.

'What is it?' Dean demanded hoarsely. Trembling from shock, he was concentrating on rowing and preventing himself from vomiting.

'There's someone up there – on that ledge!' Barry swallowed convulsively. 'God Almighty, could he have seen what happened?'

Dean followed his pointing finger. 'You're imagining things,' he said through chattering teeth. 'There's no one there.'

'But there was! It was a flash of light that caught my eye – could have been reflection from a pair of binoculars, or a camera.' Barry's voice rose. 'God, Dean, what should we do? Go after him?'

'Get real – if there *was* anyone, we've no idea who he was. Come to that, he wouldn't know who we are, either. Just keep your head and let's concentrate on ditching Tony, then we can get the hell out.'

In the middle of the lake they paused to look around them. There was no sign of a living soul, only the surrounding hills to bear witness to their act. Without a word they heaved Tony and the rock that had killed him over the side, watched numbly as the waters closed over him, and started back again.

'I know who he was!' Barry said suddenly.

'Who?'

'The bloke on the ledge; his sweatshirt stood out like a sore thumb against the stone. It looked familiar, but I couldn't place it.'

'So who was he?'

'The father whose kid tried to pinch the ball at the fête. Someone said they're the family who are renting the Barlow cottage – where Viv and I stayed a few years back, remember? When she was on her rural history kick?'

'Well, he still won't know who *we* are, even if he saw anything. He might just have arrived.'

'But we have to make sure,' Barry insisted agitatedly. 'He saw me close up at the fête – if it *was* binoculars, he'd have no difficulty recognizing me.'

'Bloody hell! What can we do?'

'Call round there with some excuse – a lost dog or something – and see if he reacts.' They scrambled ashore, where Tony's rod was propped against the rock, its iridescent fly gleaming in silent accusation.

'Put the rod and line in the boat,' Dean directed, shaking, 'and we'll shove it off.' Odd, he thought fleetingly, how he seemed to have taken charge, but Barry was unravelling fast. 'Leave the oars in the rests,' he added. 'With luck, it'll look as though he fell overboard.'

'He did,' Barry said grimly, but he followed his brother's instructions without question. Then, after a swift look round to make sure no one was about, they hurried back to their car.

As she'd intended, Emma had put the children to bed earlier than usual, and within minutes both were sound asleep. There was no meal to prepare – after a substantial lunch in Hawkston, she and Mark had decided on a snack supper – so she settled down to write the postcards she'd bought, first to her parents, then to Mark's, filling the available space on each with her small, neat writing as she detailed their doings of the past week. Then, as she picked up the card destined for Lynne and Harry, it occurred to her that while Kirsty was asleep it would be a good time to extract her beloved Bear and do the necessary repair.

Having managed to retrieve the toy without disturbing her daughter, she returned downstairs with it and her sewing kit, and quickly and neatly secured the ear. She was snipping the thread when she heard the screeching of tyres outside, and the next minute the door burst open and Mark half-fell into the room. She came to her feet, staring at him in alarm.

'Mark! For God's sake, what's wrong?'

White-faced and dishevelled, he drew a shuddering breath. 'I've just seen someone being murdered!' he said.

Jerkily, repetitively, he recounted what he'd seen from his vantage point on the ledge.

'I was using the zoom lens,' he ended. 'It was like having a ringside seat.' He shivered convulsively.

Emma's wide, frightened eyes dropped to the camera still round his neck. 'And you actually *recorded* it all?'

He nodded and, divesting himself of the camera, opened it with fumbling fingers, extracted the film and replaced the camera in the bag.

'Then take it to the police! Straight away!'

'God!' he exclaimed. 'Why the hell isn't there a bloody phone? I'll have to go down to the village.'

'Don't waste time phoning!' Emma urged. 'Take it straight to the police station in Hawkston – it's evidence!'

He hesitated. 'It's late now; there won't be anyone there.'

'Then phone from the village and leave a message, and we'll all go down in the morning.'

Mark had started shaking. 'I got a pretty good look at the killer – you'll never believe it, Emma! It was the man who handed out the prizes yesterday – I'm sure of it!'

'It can't have been! He's quite well known, they said. But the police won't have to take your word for it if you show them the film.'

He sighed, resigning himself to the loss of some of his best shots. 'Well, as you said, we'll take it in the morning. In the meantime . . .' he looked feverishly round the room, 'we need to put it somewhere safe, in case anyone comes looking for it.'

Emma frowned. 'Who would come looking? The police aren't likely—' She broke off, her eyes going wide with horror. 'You don't mean those men? They didn't *see* you, did they?'

Mark hesitated. 'No. No – I'm sure not.'

Ironically it was those last few words, intended as confirmation, that gave rise to doubt. 'Mark! They didn't, did they?'

'It's just that I was crouching behind a gorse bush, but in the excitement I must have stood up, and only realized I had when the film finished. But by that time,' he added quickly, 'they were already out on the water. It's just a safety precaution, but where can we put it where no one would think of looking?'

Emma looked wildly round the room, then her eyes fell on the toy and the pair of scissors lying beside it. 'Inside Bear?' she suggested doubtfully.

'Excellent! Well done! Cut him open and slip it inside. It'll be safe there till the morning.'

Quickly, Emma cut a hole in the middle of the soft, furry body, slipped the film in, buried it among the kapok stuffing and sewed it up again. 'Now go and make your phone call and get back as quickly as you can. I shan't be happy till we're both safely inside with the door locked.'

'God!' Mark said wretchedly. 'Why did I go the lake this afternoon? Why didn't—?'

'Go!' Emma commanded. And he went.

Picking up the teddy bear, she patted his stomach in apology and carried him back to her daughter's cot, placing him within reach of the sleeping child. It was as she was turning away that, to her surprise, she heard the front door open. Mark should have been well on his way by now.

She went to the head of the stairs. 'Mark?' she called softly.

There was no reply.

Twenty

Dean sat in the car drumming his fingers on the steering wheel, his mind a maelstrom of panic and horror. He was still having difficulty taking in what had happened. Had Barry *really* killed Tony, and had he, Dean, helped him to dispose of the body? Or was it some ghastly, ongoing nightmare? If so, he fervently wished he could wake up. And where *was* Barry, for God's sake?

They'd agreed that only he should go to the cottage, in the guise of a man worried about his missing dog. To this end, they'd parked the car out of sight and Barry had got out, saying over his shoulder, 'Shan't be long.' But – Dean checked his watch – that was ten minutes ago, for Pete's sake. What was he *doing*? God! he thought suddenly. Suppose he'd lost his head again, as he'd done at the lake? But no, that just couldn't happen. Barry was no killer; what had happened there had been an aberration, a temporary loss of control brought on by sudden, ungovernable anger. All the same, it shouldn't be taking him this long.

Increasingly uneasy, he got out of the car and stood for a moment looking about him. It was quiet at this end of the village, no casual passers-by were likely to come along. The rain had moved away and the sky was a freshly washed blue, with innocent white clouds scudding across it. They had no place in this living nightmare.

He glanced down the lane and, seeing the cottage gates, started to walk towards them. There was no sign of Barry but a car stood in the drive, so presumably if the man who'd been on the ledge was indeed staying here, he must have returned from his outing.

Dean hesitated, then, making up his mind, turned into the gateway, and as he did so stubbed his toe on a small white rock that had been edging the path and become dislodged. Kicking it aside, he looked up and his random thoughts skidded to a halt as he stiffened in disbelief, his heart leaping into his throat.

Lying alongside the car was a still form – an eerie, impossible replica of Tony on the banks of the lake. *No!* his brain screamed. Stumbling, he ran into the drive and over to the body. A young man in a garish sweatshirt, as Barry had described, lay with unseeing eyes staring up at him, a bloody gash on the side of his head.

Vomit rose in Dean's throat, but he couldn't afford the luxury of expelling it. He turned in dread to the open door of the cottage, from which no sound was emerging. Encased in fear, Dean went slowly forward, pushed the door open farther, and came to a halt on the threshold. Barry was standing motionless at the foot of a steep staircase, his back to the door, a rock – the twin of the one he'd tripped over – in one hand and a brown canvas bag in the other. He *must* be dreaming! Dean thought in terror. This *couldn't* be happening again! But as he went slowly forward, he saw what Barry's body had been screening from him – the body of a young woman lying splayed on the floor.

Incapable of speech, Dean touched his brother's arm. Barry turned, but there was something odd about him – something that added to the horror of the scene. One side of his face seemed to have slipped, making it appear uneven, and his eyes had a blank, bewildered look.

'Barry!' Fear for his brother momentarily eclipsed the horror. 'Baz, what happened? Are you all right?'

Ridiculous question. Barry continued to stare mindlessly as Dean took his arm and shook it. 'Barry, don't do this to me! For God's sake, what's wrong with you?'

His brother made an attempt to speak but no sound came, and finally the truth exploded in Dean's head. A stroke! He'd had a stroke! He must get him to hospital immediately!

Averting his eyes from the young woman and the gash in her head, Dean coaxed his brother, still clutching both bag and rock, out of the cottage, pulling the door to behind them and, bypassing the second body – or was it the third? he thought hysterically – managed to help him into the car.

He remembered little of the drive, his mind having closed down on everything except the need to drive quickly and safely to Hawkston Hospital. Once his brother had been wheeled off on a trolley, Dean, still on autopilot, phoned Vivien. She arrived within fifteen minutes, but

Barry was still undergoing tests and they were unable to see him.

'What *happened*, Dean?' she demanded, white-faced. 'You were playing golf, weren't you? I expected him home some time ago.'

He was ready for her questions, having used the time it took her to get there to concoct a story of sorts. 'That's right; we had lunch in the bar as usual and some of the gang joined us, so we were late getting away.'

'But where did you go? Why not come straight home?'

'There are problems at work – you know that, Viv. We thought a walk in the country might help to clear our heads.'

True, as far as it went.

'And then?'

Now for the improvisation. 'We'd gone some way when Barry tripped over a rabbit hole and lost his footing. I helped him up, but he seemed – disorientated, somehow. We decided to go straight back to the car, but it was further away than I'd realized and he seemed to be getting worse.'

She laid a sympathetic hand on his arm. 'It must have been awful for you.'

'A nightmare,' he said inadequately. 'I hope to God he's all right, Viv. I know time is vital in these cases and it must have been a good forty minutes before I got him here.'

'We can only hope and pray,' she said.

It was, in fact, days before they learned the extent of the damage the stroke had caused. In the meantime, to add to Dean's troubles, Tony's unaccountable absence was a topic for much speculation at work, and Marilyn, increasingly frantic, kept phoning to say the police wouldn't take his disappearance seriously. It wasn't until his boat was found floating some way down the lake that they began seriously to search for him and Dean braced himself daily for news of his discovery. None came.

Meanwhile, the papers and news bulletins were full of the double murder in the holiday cottage at Penthwaite. The victims were named as Mark and Emma Franklyn from down south somewhere, and apparently there'd been two children in the house at the time, thankfully unharmed. Police were puzzled by the seeming lack of motive, since money and jewellery had been left untouched and there was no sign of anything else having been taken. *Except the canvas bag*, Dean thought. He'd examined it at the first possible opportunity and found it full of what looked like expensive photographic equipment including a camera – no doubt the reason Barry had taken it. But when Dean fearfully opened it, there was no film inside. *Had* that young man been taking photos of them, or was that all in Barry's fevered imagination? The absence of film seemed to indicate the latter. At any rate, the bag was now buried under a pile of old clothes and blankets in his loft. God knows what he was going to do with it.

He could also, he thought ungratefully, have done without Pauline's clinging sympathy. She'd appointed herself his carer during his anxiety about his brother, and insisted on spending every night with him, 'so he wouldn't be alone'. But he *wanted* to be alone, dammit! After the non-stop play-acting at work and with Vivien, he needed space to himself.

It was as he was lying awake one night that a sudden thought struck him and he sat up abruptly. In all the horror of the killings and Barry's illness, he'd totally overlooked the cause of it all – Tony's patent application. Suppose Marilyn had come across it? He must try to get hold of it as soon as possible.

Beside him, Pauline murmured sleepily, 'All right, sweetie-pie?'

Dean drew a measured breath. 'All right,' he confirmed, and lay down again.

The following evening he called on Marilyn straight from work, and was filled with guilt at her appearance. Gone was all her bubbly good humour, her sense of fun. She looked wan and tearful, and on opening the door to him, burst into tears and half fell into his arms. He held her closely, patting her back and aware of an inappropriate shaft of desire. Truth to tell, he'd always fancied Marilyn, with her blonde hair and big blue eyes.

Dismissing the thought, he led her gently back into the house. 'I hate to disturb you at a time like this,' he said, 'but I think Tony brought some papers back from the office, and we really need to have them.'

She wiped her eyes on a scrap of lace hand-kerchief. 'I'm sure he did,' she said with a sniff. 'He spent a lot of time working in the evenings.'

'You . . . haven't seen them lying around?'

She shook her head. 'They're probably in his desk in the dining room.'

As, indeed, they were, and Dean drew a deep breath of thankfulness. The patent application lay ready for posting, along with the specification of the miracle machine and various other papers relating to its invention. Marilyn, who had gone to make coffee, called from the kitchen, 'Any luck?'

'Yes – yes, thanks, I've found them.'

'Good.' She came back with two mugs and handed him one. 'What do you think has happened to him, Dean?' Her eyes filled again. 'We were supposed to be going out for dinner. I sat here in my new dress and waited and waited and he never came.'

His heart ached for her. 'I'm so very sorry, Marilyn.'

She put a hand to her mouth. 'Oh, how awful of me – I should have asked. How's Barry?'

'Not rallying as quickly as we'd hoped.'

'Isn't it dreadful to think he was taken ill at just about the time that Tony—'

She broke off, and Dean repressed a shudder. 'I know,' he said inadequately. 'Black Sunday.'

'It was indeed. I – I don't know what to do.' Her hands were twisting in her lap. 'Tony always took care of everything, but until he's . . .' Her breath caught on a sob. 'Until we have some definite news one way or the other, the bank won't give me any money.'

He cursed himself for not anticipating this. 'Don't worry, Marilyn, that's easily fixed: I'll arrange for his salary to be paid to you, and if there's anything else I can help with, you only have to ask.'

'Oh, thank you!' she breathed. 'That's so kind, especially when you have troubles of your own.'

'I mean it – anything you need.' Indeed, he felt belatedly responsible for her, ashamed that her plight hadn't occurred to him before. The least he could do now was take care of her until everything was sorted out.

Dean had been dreading his first meeting with Barry. Vivien met him in the doorway of the ward. 'It's good news,' she said in an undertone. 'He's got his speech back, and the use of his arm, thank God. The main damage was to his memory. Parts of it have been wiped clean, the doctors say. It might come back, or it might not – they just don't know. I'll leave you with him for a while – I'm in need of a coffee.'

Tentatively Dean approached the still figure in the bed. 'Barry?'

Barry turned his head and his face lit up. 'Dean! Good to see you!'

'How are you?'

'Getting there, they tell me. But what happened, exactly? Can you fill me in?'

Dean looked at him uncertainly. 'Well, it was a stroke—'

'I know *that*, lad! But where was I when it happened?'

A cold hand closed over Dean's heart. 'You don't remember?'

'The last thing I remember is drinks in the bar at the club. Weren't we going to drive out somewhere?'

'Oh, God,' Dean said tonelessly.

'Well? Were we?'

'We were going to see Tony,' Dean said fearfully.

'Oh, yes, Tony! What's all this about him going missing? It was in one of the papers.'

Dean felt behind him for a chair and lowered himself carefully on to it. Was this an act? Could Barry really have forgotten the nightmare into which he'd plunged them both and in which he, Dean, was still embroiled? And if so, would he be left to carry the guilt alone for the rest of his life?

'You remember about Tony's patent application?' he prompted desperately.

'God, yes.' Barry grimaced. 'It sounds callous, but if he doesn't turn up, it'll come to us after all, won't it?'

'I suppose it will,' said Dean aridly.

Twenty-One

The phone rang out in the hall. Marilyn half rose, but Dean waved her down and went irritably to answer it. 'Yes?'

'Dean – thank God!' It was Vivien's voice. 'I have to speak to you. Did Marilyn tell you about the visitors she had while you were in Germany?'

'She did,' he admitted cautiously. *Vivien?* She couldn't possibly know the truth – could she?

'Can you come straight round – by yourself?'

'Vivien, I've only just got back from—'

'I know; I was watching for your car.'

The coldness intensified. God, his whole world was collapsing about him. 'Well, I suppose I—'

'Tell her Barry's had a fall or something. Half an hour?'

Useless to protest any further. The inevitable was finally catching up with him. 'I'll be there,' he said.

Vivien was waiting at her open front door and, as soon as he was within reach, caught hold of his arm and pulled him inside.

'It's Barry,' she said in a low voice. 'He's completely gone to pieces.'

Dean stared at her, his mind spinning. 'I know he's not been at work, but his secretary said he had flu. I meant to phone but I've been so—'

'It's been coming on for weeks – you must have noticed,' Vivien broke in, 'but it was when I told him about Marilyn's visitors that he just simply . . . folded, and he's not said a single word since. I wanted to phone you at once, but he became very distressed, shaking his head violently, and I was afraid if I did it would make things worse. I called the doctor, but after examining him he said there's no sign of another stroke and prescribed a sedative, which he's refused point-blank to take. In the end I couldn't take any more and phoned you anyway.'

Dean closed his eyes on a wave of nausea. 'And it was when you mentioned those people that he really lost it?'

'Yes, when I told him they'd asked about Tony.' Vivien's face was white in the dim hallway. 'God, Dean, I've been imagining all kinds of horrors. Perhaps now you're here he'll speak to you.'

'Where is he?'

'In the kitchen. He sits there for hours on end, sometimes staring into space, sometimes with tears streaming down his face, and when I try to comfort him he just shakes me off. I've been out of my mind with worry.'

Dean moved slowly down the hall and stood in the doorway, scarcely able to believe the man at the table was his brother. Barry had aged in the week he'd been away. His flesh hung loosely on him, his eyes were sunken, he was unshaven and his hair was uncombed.

Vivien went past him into the room. 'Dean's here, darling,' she said. Barry raised his head and stared with dull eyes at the figure in the doorway.

Reluctantly Dean moved forward. 'Hello, Baz. Not feeling too good?'

Barry reached up suddenly and grabbed his arm, the tightness of his grip making his brother flinch.

'It didn't happen, did it, Dean?' he demanded urgently, his voice cracking. 'I'm hallucinating, aren't I? Tell me it's just a nightmare!'

'Your memory's come back.' It wasn't a question.

Barry dropped his arm and covered his face with both hands. 'Oh, God, God, God!' he said rapidly through his fingers.

Vivien dropped to her knees beside him, reaching out for him. He'd begun rocking backwards and forwards and she had trouble holding on to him.

'Tell me,' she said.

He shook his head violently, dry sobs racking his body.

She looked up at Dean. 'Then for the love of God, *you* tell me! Anything has to be better than this.' She paused. 'It was Tony, wasn't it? Marilyn says she couldn't believe he'd drowned.'

'Yes,' Dean confirmed flatly, 'it was Tony.'

'But what happened? I know you'd had your differences, but—'

'He was going to leave,' Dean said. 'And take his patent with him. He was quite adamant about it. We decided to make one last attempt to change his mind, and thought we'd have a better chance away from the office.'

Vivien closed her eyes briefly, dreading what would come next. 'But could he do that? Take the patent, I mean? If he'd developed the machine while he was at the firm—'

'Barry wouldn't sanction the expense.'

'Oh, yes, I remember now. But—'

'So he worked on it at night and weekends, in his own time. We'd have had no legitimate claim to it. God, Viv, we never meant to harm him, but we were stressed out of our minds about the firm and this would have saved our bacon.' He paused. '*Did* save our bacon.'

'So you *killed* him?'

Neither man spoke and, stumblingly, she worked out a terrible scenario. 'Then you heaved him into the boat . . . and rowed out with him . . . and . . . oh my God!'

She released Barry and sank back on her heels, staring unbelievingly at these men she'd been close to most of her life, yet had perhaps not known at all.

'Go on!' Barry instructed in that broken whisper. 'Tell her the rest.'

'The *rest*? God in heaven, you're not saying that young couple . . . *No!*' She put her hands over her ears.

Dean recited the bare facts like an automaton. 'He was on a ledge, snapping us. The light glinted on his camera, so Barry went after him.'

She searched desperately for reasons not to believe him. 'But how could you know who he was, or where to find him?'

'It was his sweatshirt – he'd worn it the day before, at the fête. Someone said he was staying at the Barlow cottage.'

There was a long silence, then, speaking almost

to herself, Vivien said softly, 'I can *just about* understand, in the state you were in, that you temporarily lost control and lashed out at Tony, but to be callous enough to row out and dump his body . . .'

They waited, motionless, for her to continue.

'And then to go after that young man – who might have been simply snapping the view – and kill him too, *and his wife*!' She drew a shuddering breath. 'I don't know how they died, and I don't want to. But – oh, God, whatever state of mind you were in, that was *premeditated*!'

Another long silence, the only sound in the still room that of their breathing. Then Vivien said dully, 'And that was what brought on the stroke?'

'Yes,' Dean replied with remembered bitterness. 'Leaving me to pick up the pieces.'

'That's right,' Vivien agreed, in a new, hard voice. 'You got off pretty lightly, didn't you, Barry? You inherited the patent, the firm prospered and you've lived happily ever after, without even the memory of what you did to haunt you. Until now. Well . . .' She rose to her feet. 'Now we have to tell the police.'

The two men gazed at her incredulously, identical expressions on their faces.

'We can't do that!'' Barry exclaimed.

'What difference would it make now?' blustered Dean.

'So you continue to get away with it? No! Those young people deserve to know the truth. And so,' she added after a beat, 'does Marilyn.'

Dean reached out blindly, fumbled for a chair

and sank on to it. *'Are you out of your mind?'* he demanded in a shaking voice.

'Do you think I could live with either of you, knowing what I know now? As for Marilyn . . .'

Dean leant forward urgently. 'Think for a moment, Viv. What possible good could it do? It would destroy her, and as for the two who started all this, they never knew their parents. OK, they're curious about what happened to them, but that's all. It's not as though they remember them personally. And to be strictly accurate,' he added in belated self-defence, *'I* didn't kill anybody!'

'"Accessory after the fact", isn't that the expression? God help me, I accept that Barry committed the murders, but he was incapable of anything further. It was you who tidied things up after him. And a damn good job you made of it!' she ended bitterly.

Into another silence the clock in the hall chimed eight times.

'I must get back,' Dean said. 'She'll be wondering what's keeping me.' But he made no move to rise.

Barry reached pleadingly for his wife's hand, but she moved away.

'I'll give you both till tomorrow evening to get your act together and turn yourselves in,' she said. 'If you haven't done so by then, God help me I'll report you myself.'

Marilyn's night-time imaginings no longer disappeared with the coming of daylight. Increasingly over the last two weeks she'd been haunted by the possibility that the young couple's murder

301

was somehow related to Tony, though she couldn't for the life of her see how. Even if by some fluke they *had* witnessed his accident or whatever it was, why should that have led to their deaths?

Nor could she tie in the change in Dean's behaviour, though in her unsettled state she could have exaggerated that, and the half-formed fear, originating with Adam's comment, that the day's third disaster – Barry's stroke – might also have a connection, was out of the question; after their golf game he and Dean had gone walking on the moors, which was where he'd been taken ill. They'd been nowhere near the lake.

In an attempt to dismiss her doubts she took the morning paper into the drawing room and had just sat down when Vivien phoned. 'Will you be home all morning?' she asked, her voice unusually grave.

Marilyn felt a prick of apprehension. 'Yes?'

'All right if I pop round in about half an hour?'

'Aren't you working?'

'From home today. Allegedly.'

Marilyn waited for an explanation, but none was forthcoming. 'I'll have coffee ready,' she said.

One glance at her sister-in-law's strained face, the shadows under her eyes and her general air of distraction resurrected Marilyn's dormant fears. This, she knew at once, was to do with Tony.

Heart hammering, she stood aside for her to enter and led the way into the drawing room, where a coffee pot awaited them. Vivien seated herself and Marilyn poured the coffee with surprisingly steady hands.

'Well?' she said, passing her a cup.

'I've come to ask for your help,' Vivien said in a low voice, 'though God knows I've no right to.'

Thoughts, fears and suspicions, buried for years, collided to form a composite whole. In direct contradiction to previous conclusions, Marilyn said with certainty, 'Barry was there, wasn't he? At the lake?'

Vivien's eyes widened and she hastily set down her cup. 'Has Dean . . .?' But he couldn't have, or her question would have been superfluous. She drew a deep breath. 'Marilyn, I'm so very sorry. Yes, Barry was there – but so was Dean.'

Marilyn lowered herself carefully into a chair, holding her mind in abeyance. 'What happened?'

Vivien leaned forward. 'You must believe me, I knew nothing about this when we had lunch, but it was what you told me that brought it all to a head.'

'*What happened?*'

'We didn't see much of each other in those days, did we?' Vivien went on steadily as though she hadn't spoken. 'But you must have been aware we were in desperate straits financially. The firm was going under fast and Barry was under an enormous strain, not sleeping, drinking too much, working all hours. If you remember, we had to sell our home, move into that awful little house and send Daphne to the local comp. Only a miracle could save us, and lo, a miracle materialized in Tony's inspired idea for a revolutionary machine. He argued that it would save us thousands and lead to the firm growing bigger and more prosperous than ever.'

303

'Go on,' Marilyn said aridly, her coffee untouched on the table beside her.

Vivien's eyes dropped to her knotted hands. 'But Barry wouldn't finance it. He daren't risk the capital outlay on what he feared might prove to be only a pipe dream.'

She glanced at Marilyn, but her face was expressionless. 'So, as you must know, Tony did all the work on it at home and, as you also know, the machine was all he'd claimed for it. But he resented Barry's lack of faith in him and decided to retain ownership of his invention instead of passing it to the firm – which, since he'd worked on it in his own time, he was entitled to do. On top of that, he gave in his notice.'

Marilyn's head jerked up. 'I never knew that!'

'He didn't tell you he was leaving Ferrises?' Vivien stared at her unbelievingly.

'No, I'm sure he didn't. I'd have remembered.'

'He'd come into some money from an aunt, apparently, and was going to use it to set up his own business in Surrey. Perhaps,' she added, 'he didn't want to worry you till it was all settled. After all, you weren't interested in the business, were you?' Despite herself, accusation had crept into Vivien's voice.

It was well deserved, Marilyn knew. Much as she'd loved Tony, it was true his work hadn't interested her, any more than Dean's had. Dean! Her breath caught. God! But Vivien was continuing.

'They tried desperately to persuade him to stay, offered him a partnership – which they should have done long before – but it was too late. He'd made up his mind and he wouldn't change it.'

'So they killed him,' Marilyn said flatly.

'They knew he'd gone fishing, and hoped that away from the distractions of the office they might talk him round, but it was no good. I don't know the details – only that Barry suddenly snapped, lashing out and knocking Tony to the ground. And when they realized he . . . wasn't breathing, they panicked and put him in the boat.'

'No!' Marilyn breathed, her hands to her mouth. 'Please, no!' Then, dragging her mind from the horrors of her husband's death, 'But that couple . . .?'

'The man had been on the hill taking photos. They were afraid he'd seen what happened so Barry went after him, and . . . of course his wife was there.' Vivien squeezed her eyes shut. 'That was what brought on his stroke,' she continued after a minute. 'Dean arrived later, you must believe that, and by the time he got there the couple were dead and Barry was completely out of it.'

'It was Barry who did all the killing?' Marilyn asked from a parched throat.

Vivien nodded, tears trickling unchecked down her face. 'When he came round he'd lost his memory – that was genuine, Marilyn – and it's only in the last month or two that it's started to come back. All these years it's been Dean who's borne the burden of it.'

'And married me out of guilt and pity.'

'No! You mustn't think that! He's always been crazy about you. He still is!'

Marilyn put the thought aside to re-examine later. 'You said you wanted my help.'

Vivien dried her eyes. 'Yes. When I finally learned the truth I gave them till this evening to turn themselves in. We haven't spoken of it since, but I made it clear that if they didn't, I'd go to the police myself. And I'd . . . very much like you to come with me.'

'Of course,' Marilyn said matter-of-factly. 'They might go more willingly, though, if we all went together.' She caught Vivien's surprise. 'As to Dean, it's far too soon for any decisions, but I don't mind accompanying him and Barry to the police station. In fact, I feel I owe it to Tony.'

Empty-headed little Marilyn had more back-bone than she'd given her credit for, Vivien thought admiringly. 'I'll suggest it, certainly,' she said, 'but if they try to put it off for any reason, we'll go alone. Agreed?'

'Agreed,' Marilyn replied.

While Adam and Kirsty had been at the station darkness had fallen, but the police forecourt was brilliantly floodlit, and they were further illuminated by the headlamps of a car turning in at the gateway and parking in a vacant slot.

'Odd to think,' Adam commented as they started down the steps, 'that Dad will have solved his own murder, as well as Mum's and Tony Vine's.'

So he'd finally dispensed with 'Mark and Emma', Kirsty noted thankfully. 'Do you really think it's over?' she asked anxiously.

'Bar the shouting,' Adam replied with confidence. The four people from the car were walking towards them, and Adam suddenly gripped her

306

arm. 'My *God*, look who it is! The mountain is coming to Mohammed!'

Kirsty gasped as she recognized the man nearest to them as Dean Ferris. The other was obviously his brother, and her throat closed as, almost unbelievingly, she finally faced the men who'd killed her parents. Then Marilyn caught sight of them, gave an exclamation, and they came to a halt. After a swift, startled glance, the two men averted their eyes but Marilyn detached herself from the group and, as the others continued towards the building, came over to Adam and Kirsty.

'I want to thank you,' she said in a low voice. 'My husband and brother-in-law are about to make a statement, but it might never have happened if you'd not come asking questions. At very long last, Tony and your parents will finally receive justice, and I thank you for that from the bottom of my heart.'

Neither of them spoke, and after a moment she nodded in acknowledgement of their wordlessness and went to rejoin the others. Tightly gripping each other's hands, Adam and Kirsty watched them go slowly up the steps and into the police station.

Twenty-Two

So it was over. While the Lakeland murderers were finally being brought to justice, events had moved fast in Westbourne. The town was buzzing with the revelation that local author Matthew Armstrong had been charged both with the murder of PC Megan Taylor and the rapes that had taken place in Bellington and Lacy Park. DNA found at all three scenes matched that obtained from the suspect during another incident – thankfully unspecified.

Kirsty shook her head sadly. 'Poor Chrissie. How can she possibly come to terms with this?'

'Just as well she's with her family in Brighton,' Angie observed. 'I doubt if she'll ever come back; someone said their house is going on the market.'

'In the report I read, police had found what were referred to as "incriminating documents" in his study. You'd have thought he'd be more careful, wouldn't you, than write anything explicit in a diary or whatever? No doubt more details will emerge at the trial.' She shook her head again. 'I still have difficulty believing the whole thing; I keep thinking of him at the tennis club and the library and at his house. He seemed so – *ordinary.*'

Angie gave a short laugh. 'I doubt if he'd thank you for that!'

* * *

Unaware and uncaring that he was the subject of so much speculation, Matt in his custody cell had retreated into a world of his own in which nothing was quite as it seemed. His mind continually went back over the acts he had committed, relishing the reliving of them: the girl from the train, snooty Alicia and the policewoman. Well, he'd taught them a lesson all right; too bad he'd not had the chance to take more of them down a peg or two. And Kirsty. Ah, Kirsty!

It had been exciting, that time she'd been in the car, totally unaware of what he had planned for her. Of course, he should never have stopped when he saw her on the corner. It had been a risk, but suddenly catching sight of her had thrown him. Obviously there'd been nothing he could do then, but knowing what lay in store had been deliciously tantalizing. Pity it would have to go on hold for a while, but next time he'd make sure there was no way she could escape him.

In the book he was now writing he'd called the heroine Karen – as close as he dared go. It was strangely satisfying being able to manipulate her, in print if not in life. He wondered suddenly if he could request his computer and files, and finish the book while he was here? Jeffrey Archer had done it, hadn't he, not to mention Wilde! He'd ask the warder who brought in his meals.

Smiling to himself, Matt began to plan his next chapter.

'Kirsty?'

She stiffened, her heartbeat quickening. 'Yes?'

'It's Nick.' There was a brief pause. 'Look, I've

been aware for some time that I owe you an apology, but I didn't want to intrude when you and Adam had so much going on.'

'I'm sorry too, Nick. I could have been a lot more forthcoming.'

'Does that mean you forgive me?'

'There's nothing to forgive. Really.'

'Then can we start again?' He laughed. 'I seem to remember saying that before!'

'Perhaps we'll get it right this time.'

'I certainly hope so. How about Saturday? I gather from Adam that on Sunday you're lunching with the family.' A smile crept into his voice. 'Does that mean he's been welcomed back into the fold?'

'Very definitely! With our parents' murders solved at last, my aunt and uncle can't do enough for him, and the lines have been buzzing between here and Canada. It looks as though the long family rift is at last over.'

'Well, that's great news!'

It was indeed, Kirsty thought. The family was coming together, the murders were solved and her mystery stalker was unmasked and behind bars. And, perhaps best of all, over the last few months she and Adam had become as close as any other brother and sister. All at once the future looked much brighter – and maybe, just maybe, Nick would be a part of it.

'And to answer your question,' she said, 'I'd love to see you on Saturday.'